The Flooded Earth

The Flooded Earth

Mardi McConnochie

pajamapress

www.pajamapress.ca   info@pajamapress.ca

 Canada Council   Conseil des arts
for the Arts   du Canada
 ONTARIO ARTS COUNCIL
CONSEIL DES ARTS DE L'ONTARIO
an Ontario government agency
un organisme du gouvernement de l'Ontario
 Canada

The publisher gratefully acknowledges the support of the Canada Council for the Arts and the Ontario Arts Council for its publishing program. We acknowledge the financial support of the Government of Canada through the Canada Book Fund (CBF) for our publishing activities.

Library and Archives Canada Cataloguing in Publication
McConnochie, Mardi, 1971-
[Escape to the Moon Islands]
        The flooded Earth / Mardi McConnochie.

Originally published as Escape to the Moon Islands. Crow's Nest,
        New South Wales, Australia : Allen & Unwin, 2016
ISBN 978-1-77278-049-9 (hardcover)

        I. Title. II. Title: Escape to the Moon Islands

PZ7.M4784133Esc 2018   j823'.92   C2018-901766-X

Publisher Cataloging-in-Publication Data (U.S.)
Names: McConnochie, Mardi, 1971-, author.
Title: The Flooded Earth / Mardi McConnochie.
Description: Toronto, Ontario Canada : Pajama Press, 2018. | Originally published by Allen & Unwin Australia, 2016 as: Escape to Moon Islands: Quest of the Sunfish 1. | Summary: "Avid sailor Will lives with his mechanic father while his twin sister Annalie goes to a prestigious school run by the Admiralty, the naval power that brought stability and governance following worldwide flooding forty years before. When their father suddenly flees Admiralty searchers, the twins and Annalie's school friend Essie set out to find him on the family's sailboat. The children face pirate attacks, storms, and unfriendly shores, and rescue a marooned former slave. They also must cope with new questions about the intentions of the Admiralty, and about their own father's past"— Provided by publisher.
Identifiers: ISBN 978-1-77278-049-9 (hardcover)
Subjects: LCSH: Twins – Juvenile fiction. | Sailing ships – Juvenile fiction. | Survival at sea – Juvenile fiction. | Family secrets – Juvenile fiction. | BISAC: JUVENILE FICTION / Science fiction. | JUVENILE FICTION / Action & Adventure / Survival stories. | JUVENILE FICTION / Dystopian.
Classification: LCC PZ7.M336Fl |DDC [F] – dc23

Cover design by Rebecca Buchanan
Text design based on original by Midland Typesetters, Australia

Manufactured by Friesens
Printed in Canada

Pajama Press Inc.
181 Carlaw Ave., Suite 251, Toronto, Ontario Canada, M4M 2S1

Distributed in Canada by UTP Distribution
5201 Dufferin Street Toronto, Ontario Canada, M3H 5T8

Distributed in the U.S. by Ingram Publisher Services
1 Ingram Blvd. La Vergne, TN 37086, USA

For Annabelle and Lila

Spinner's flight

The last night Will and his father spent together was a very ordinary night—so ordinary you'd almost call it boring. Both of them were working—Spinner on a broken wind turbine, Will on the trucks of a skateboard—but the pace of the work was slow and relaxed. Songs from Spinner's distant youth played on the old reconditioned soundbox.

"C'mon," said Will, "we've listened to enough of your old-guy tracks. I want to put some *good* music on."

"You wouldn't know good music if it sat up and bit you," Spinner said amiably.

And it was then, just as Will was deciding whether to argue his case or just lunge for the controls, that there was an urgent beating on their front door.

"Who is it?" Spinner called. It was wiser not to open your door at night.

"Truman," came a voice. Truman was a pedicab rider who lived in the neighborhood.

Spinner unbolted the door and Truman fell into the room, gasping as if he'd just run the race of his life. "They're coming," he blurted.

1

"You've heard this?" Spinner asked sharply. "Or have you actually seen them?"

"With my own eyes," Truman said.

"How far behind are they?"

"Not far," Truman said. "You'd better get gone."

Spinner clapped Truman on the shoulder. "Thanks," he said, "and so should you. You don't want to be here when they arrive."

"Watch yourself," said Truman.

Spinner was usually slow-handed and easygoing, but now he was electric with energy. "Come on," he said to Will, hurrying into the living quarters at the back of the shop. "We don't have much time. Thank goodness your sister's away."

Will followed him, bewildered. "What's going on?"

"Trouble," Spinner said. "And the less you know the better. Collect up your things and go over to Janky's place."

Janky was Will's best friend. "Okay," Will said, "but where are you going?"

Spinner was busy pulling useful things from cubbyholes and stuffing them into a backpack. He didn't answer Will's question.

"Spinner?"

Spinner looked up at him, his face uncharacteristically tense. "Get your stuff. We don't have much time."

Will clattered upstairs to his little bedroom and grabbed some clothes at random, still not really understanding what was happening.

When he came down again, Spinner was counting the money in his cash box, a worried look on his face.

2

"Here," Spinner said, holding out some bills, "you'd better take this. I'm sorry it's not more."

Will took it, disturbed. "Are you going to tell me what's going on?"

"I can't," Spinner said. "I'm sorry Will. I knew this day was coming, but I hoped..." He trailed off. "Whatever happens, whatever you hear about me, stay with Janky and his mom. They'll keep you safe."

"But I want to come with you."

"I'm sorry, son. You can't. Not this time." Spinner looked at Will, his face filled with love and tenderness and anxiety and all the words there was no time to say. Then they both caught the sound of heavy vehicles in the distance, their engines roaring.

"I'll send word when I can," Spinner said. He hugged Will tightly. "Be careful. Be safe. Now go." His hard hand pushed Will in the back, propelling him toward the door.

Will looked back one last time and saw Spinner, the wiry old man, with his coif of silvery hair standing up like a parrot's crest, packing a few last essentials into a backpack. Spinner looked up at him and his dark eyes blazed. "Go!" he roared.

And Will pushed out the back door and into the night.

Spinner's secrets

Will arrived, breathless, on Janky's doorstep, and they let him in without question. Janky's house, like most of the houses in the area, had been flood damaged, but it was in better condition than most, and didn't have that moldy smell so many of them had.

"You can stay as long as you like," Janky's mom said, pulling spare sheets and blankets from a cupboard. "You can count on us."

She asked very few questions about what had happened, something Janky, for one, found weird.

"But what do you think's going on?" he asked as he made up a bed for Will on his bedroom floor.

"I don't know," Will said, still a little dazed by the suddenness of it all.

"Truman must have said who it was that was after your dad."

"Nope."

"So who do you think they were?"

"I don't know!" Will said irritably.

"Janky!" shouted Janky's mom from two rooms away. "Stop hassling him!"

Janky lowered his voice and continued. "Did you see what they were driving?"

"Nah," Will said. "But I heard them. Something powerful. I'd guess all-terrain vehicles."

Janky nodded eagerly. "So who drives those?"

"Admiralty."

"Brotherhoods."

"Why would the brotherhoods be after my dad?"

"I don't know," Janky said. "Maybe he had secrets."

"Spinner didn't have any secrets," Will snorted. "Not in our house. Those walls are like paper."

"He obviously had at least one secret," Janky said.

Will humphed. He couldn't argue with that.

"Hey, you can borrow my shell if you want," Janky said.

A shell was a small handheld communication device. You could use it to make calls (voice or vid) and send messages; you could join the links with it. Most shells had virtual keyboards that turned them into computers for study or work. Some of the newer models came with accessories like headpieces or sunglasses that connected wirelessly to the shell and displayed information directly in front of your eyes. This function was definitely kind of useful, but the real reason people liked them was because the sunglasses looked cool, and the headpieces were like jewelry— decorative, customizable, and ever-changing. Janky's shell was a very basic model—his mom wouldn't fork out for retinal-display sunglasses.

"What do I need your shell for?" Will asked.

"To let Annalie know what's happened."

Annalie was Will's twin sister, and she had been away at boarding school in Pallas for almost a term now. Will and Annalie were very different people—Annalie was bookish, Will the restless opposite of bookish—but in spite of this they had always made a good team, until high school separated them.

"No need to call her," Will said. "Not until I know more."

"The whole thing may have blown over by tomorrow anyway," Janky agreed.

"Maybe," Will said.

That night, while Janky snored beside him, he picked over his memories looking for clues about what might be going on, but came up empty.

The next morning Will was up early, hanging around while Janky's mom made breakfast, trying to find out what she knew about the situation.

"So my dad must have told you *something*," he said.

"Nope."

"But he must've made some kind of arrangement with you, right? Like, 'If anything should ever happen to me...for example if the Kang Brotherhood comes after me—'"

"The Kang Brotherhood?" Janky's mom looked at him incredulously.

"So, it wasn't the Kangs?" Will said, feeling like he was getting somewhere. "Was it the Three Knives?"

6

"Will," Janky's mom said, "I don't know what's going on with your dad. He's been good to me over the years, and if there's anything I can do to help you out, you know I will. But I don't have any secret information."

"Has he been in contact with you?"

Janky's mom looked concerned. "He hasn't contacted you?"

Will shook his head. "I don't have a shell."

Janky's mom put her hand on his shoulder reassuringly. "Whatever this is, I'm sure it'll blow over soon. Don't worry, Will. He'll be back."

Will nodded, not quite trusting himself to say anything. He grabbed a piece of toast and stuffed it into his mouth instead.

Janky's mom told them absolutely positively to stay away from the workshop that morning. "You two are going to school, and if I hear any different, you'll be in *big* trouble," she said sternly.

But of course that was never going to happen.

Will put on a borrowed Janky-smelling school shirt, but as soon as they were around the corner from Janky's house he announced he was going back to the workshop to look for clues.

"You coming?" he asked.

Janky squirmed. "You know I would," he said, "but I bet Mom calls the school to check up on us."

"So?"

"When she's mad," Janky said feelingly, "she's mean." He paused. "I can tell school you're sick?"

"Thanks, man," Will said.

7

He turned around and doubled back, hoping to avoid a chance encounter with Janky's mom, picking his way along the lumpy, bumpy streets of Lowtown.

Lowtown was one of the nicer parts of the huge slum where Will lived. It was called Lowtown because it was low-lying and water damaged, but it was not the worst area of the slum—that was Saltytown, where the water lapped at the houses and only the most desperate people lived. There were other parts too: the Eddy, the area surrounding the small unofficial port mostly used by smugglers and pirates; Firetown, which was where you went to get drunk; and Kang, Three Knives, and Korrupter—neighborhoods that took their names from the brotherhoods that controlled them. Lowtown was one of the safer parts of the slums, but it wasn't a comfortable place to live, work, or walk.

Forty years ago, the slums had been ordinary suburbs of Port Fine, a large and busy seaport. Then the cataclysmic rise in sea level known as the Flood permanently reshaped coastlines all around the world. Huge swathes of low-lying real estate were inundated, and much of Port Fine was damaged or destroyed. Once the ocean had settled into its new level, the emergency government decided which parts of the city of Port Fine should be saved, what should be rebuilt, and what could be ignored. The main port was rebuilt, its shipping lanes cleared, and the port reopened for business; the parts of the city on high ground were kept. They drew a line around the rest of the city, the parts on lower ground. Beyond this line, they did not rebuild. Whole sections of the city were written off, like a wrecked car that wasn't worth fixing. In these parts, no one made any attempt to repave the streets that had been potholed or washed away, run new electricity cables, fix the damaged water mains, or restore the flooded metro lines.

There was no compensation offered to the people whose homes had been beyond that arbitrary line. The Flood had made their homes worthless, but there was nothing they could do about it. The scale of the disaster was too vast. Some people got out and tried their luck elsewhere; many more stayed, ruined by the Flood, living among the wreckage as best they could, an underclass trapped by poverty. There were refugees, or "illegals," living in the slums too: people who'd escaped from other flood-ravaged countries and entered Dux illegally, hoping for a better life.

The Flood's effects were different in every country. Dux was geographically very large, and many of its major cities, including Pallas, the capital, along with much of its agriculture and industries, were inland, where the Flood didn't reach. Countries that were low-lying, or had lots of major coastal cities, or relied on crops that grew near the sea, were devastated by the Flood; afterwards, many economies simply collapsed. Forty years on, Dux was thriving again, and there were other countries where things still went on more or less as they always had; but many other countries could not get out of the cycle of poverty, famine, illness and violence. A steady stream of unhappy people left these places, looking for a better chance somewhere else—anywhere else.

Spinner, Will and Annalie were Duxan citizens, not illegals, but their reason for living in Lowtown had never been entirely clear to Will. Whenever he or Annalie asked why they couldn't move somewhere nicer, Spinner always said, "What do you want to move for? We live a good life here!" And it was true— they *had* led a good life. At least until now.

Will hopped over the potholes as he hurried to the workshop, hoping that when he got there he'd find Spinner brewing his first coffee of the day, ready to explain that the whole thing had been a silly mistake.

Because it *had* to be a mistake, Will thought furiously. Spinner wasn't the kind of guy to get in trouble with anyone. He ran his little workshop. He fixed things. He built new things, useful things. He found old stuff from the wreckage of the old prosperous world and made it work again. How could anyone have a problem with him?

Will came round the corner into his street. The front door of the workshop was ajar; his heart leaped hopefully. Spinner always left it that way when he was open for business. He walked to the door, hoping to see Spinner there waiting for him.

But as soon as he stepped inside he knew Spinner was not there, could not be there. Because something terrible had happened.

Trashed

The workshop was a large open space, lit from above by skylights that Spinner had found and installed himself. It had rows of shelves reaching all the way up to the roof, filled with a collection of components and parts, hardware and gadgets, mechanical objects of every vintage, neatly sorted and arranged. Behind these shelves was the counter, and behind that was the workshop proper, where Spinner worked on the things he invented or found and reconditioned or fixed for other people.

Now the workshop was in chaos. One of the shelving units had been tipped over. Broken bits of gears and housings were scattered on the ground. Gadgets lay smashed and ruined. The millions of drill bits and nails and nuts and screws Spinner had painstakingly collected and sorted over the years spread, glistening, across the floor.

Will walked cautiously through the mess, screws rolling under his feet, a feeling of helpless fury rising in his chest. Spinner's workspace had always been a miracle of order and calm: every tool had its designated hook or drawer. But now the pegboard where the tools hung was ripped off the wall; the workbench, built from heavy slabs of old wood, was knocked over; and the cupboards that had held larger tools—tools Spinner had painstakingly gathered over many years—were stripped bare.

The furniture was smashed. All the stock Spinner had kept to sell or barter was damaged or gone. For a few long moments, all Will could do was stare at the mess, struggling to take in the scale of this loss.

What happened here? he wondered. *Why would someone hate Spinner so much they'd want to tear the place apart?*

He walked to the door that separated the shop from the apartment at the back and discovered it had been kicked in.

Of course, they had been here, too. The apartment consisted of one comfortable room with a sofa and chairs at one end, a table and a little kitchen at the other, with three little bedrooms up a steep flight of stairs. The laundry and bathroom were out the back. The tall bookshelf that usually held Spinner's collection of books was also on the floor. Most of the books were gone, apart from a couple of childhood favorites that lay splayed about, their covers torn. Holes had been punched in the plasterboard walls, as if whoever had been here was looking for secret hiding places. Cupboards had been broken open and kitchen canisters emptied out. The floor was a mess of rice, flour, and sugar, crisscrossed with footprints.

Will hurried upstairs and checked the bedrooms. His own room was first: the cupboards hung open, his things littered the floor, and his mattress had been pulled off the bed and slashed open. *Nothing in there but lumps*, he thought defiantly. He glanced into Annalie's room next. Destruction there, too, although there had been less to tear down; she'd taken her favorite things away to school.

Then he went into Spinner's room.

It, too, had a slashed mattress, and the cupboard doors all hung open. But the thing he noticed immediately was that Spinner's clothes were gone. Not all of them—a few never-worn oddments still hung there. But his regular clothes had been taken.

This was the first hopeful sign. If Spinner's clothes were gone, perhaps he'd got away too.

Will walked slowly back downstairs, trying to make sense of all this. Perhaps the people who'd done this weren't being destructive for the hell of it. Maybe they were looking for something. But what?

He went into the kitchen, wondering if there was anything left to eat, and a loud squawk almost made him jump out of his skin. He looked up and saw Graham, Spinner's parrot, perched outside the window, flapping and tapping frantically to be let in.

He opened the window and Graham came rocketing in. He landed on Will's shoulder, rubbed his beak against Will's face and squawked deafeningly.

"Graham," Will said, "where's Spinner?"

According to family legend, Spinner had acquired Graham in the immediate aftermath of the Flood, when Spinner was still a young man. Graham had been part of a pre-Flood experiment that put

13

chips into parrots' brains in an attempt to boost communication between humans and animals. Of course, many parrots could talk, even without chips in their brains; but Graham's language skills were exceptional.

"Spinner gone!" Graham said.

"I know that, but where?" In his excitement, Graham was digging his claws into Will's shoulder. "Ow, Graham, you're hurting me. Why didn't he take you with him?"

"Graham got lost."

"Lost? What happened?"

"Cars come. Big black cars."

"I heard the cars. Do you know who was driving them? Were they in uniform? Were they Admiralty?"

"Uniform," Graham agreed, bobbing up and down. "Spinner and Graham ran to the Eddy."

"To the boat?"

"Boat, yes, but men were there."

"So you couldn't get to the boat?"

"Men already on the boat."

"So then what did you do?"

"Spinner and Graham go to noisy house."

"What kind of noisy house?"

Graham ruffled up his feathers, looking sulky. "Noisy. There was a cat."

"What happened, Graham?"

"There was a cat. It tried to eat Graham." Agitated, Graham flew up into the air and whirled in circles before settling down on a kitchen shelf, higher up the wall. "Graham got lost. Spinner got lost."

"But do you know where he was going? Did he tell you? Who did he go to see at the noisy house?"

Graham swung his head from side to side, making a distressed noise. "Graham want biscuit."

"You can't have a biscuit! I need to find Spinner, you stupid bird!"

Graham squawked angrily at him.

"All right, fine." Will stumped to the cupboard and got Graham a biscuit. "Now can you tell me anything else about what happened?"

But Graham had nothing more to add.

A visitor

"Hurry up girls! The sports fields are waiting!" The first-year girls were racing to get out of their school uniforms and into their sports uniforms. This was quite a process, as the uniform had many pieces to it: tie, blazer, shirt, skirt, lace-up boots, and when you took it all off you weren't allowed to just hang it on a peg or stuff it in a locker until you were ready to put it all back on again. Everything had to be hung or folded according to regulations, or you were in big trouble.

"Last five girls out of the change rooms will do an extra lap of the oval!" the sports teacher boomed.

"Really, though, is that an efficient use of everyone's time?" Annalie murmured to her friend Essie as she rolled her socks into the regulation donut shape. "Making the people who got ready first stand around even longer while they wait for the slow ones to do an extra lap of the oval?"

"They pretend they care about efficiency," Essie agreed, "but really they just like to torture us. Especially the unsporty ones."

"You there! Rehang that blazer! Call those shoes properly aligned? Do something about that hair! What?" This last demand was directed at an older student who had appeared with a message. The sports teacher frowned. "Annalie? Where are you? You're wanted at the office. You've got a visitor."

Essie raised her eyebrows at Annalie excitedly. "Who do you think it is?"

"I don't know," Annalie said. She couldn't think of anyone who'd come to see her except Spinner. "Maybe it's my dad."

"What are you waiting for?" snapped the sports teacher. "Office!"

Annalie slammed her locker shut and headed for the door, aware of the buzz of curiosity around her— *The weird girl had a visitor? How did that get her out of sport?*

The sports teacher was already shouting again. "Now! The rest of you have exactly one minute to be changed and ready! I'm counting!"

Could it really be Spinner, come to surprise her? A smile began to spread across Annalie's face as she hurried toward the front office. She hadn't seen him since the beginning of term—not face to face, anyway—and she missed him desperately.

At the front office they directed her to a small meeting room. She hurried to the door, fully expecting to see Spinner, her heart beating fast with pleasurable excitement, so when she walked in and saw another man entirely, her first thought was that she had walked into the wrong office.

"Annalie," the man said, "it's good to meet you at last."

He was tall and solid, with black hair above a high forehead and a long, lined, hollow face; big shouldered and barrel chested; no longer young; wearing a dark T-shirt and pants with a leather jacket. He looked at her with eyes that were set deep into dark sockets, but which had a lively brightness as they studied her. There was something disturbing about the intensity of his gaze.

He came toward her, holding out his hand. After a moment she realized she was supposed to shake it. "I'm Avery Beckett," he said. He had a very firm grip.

"Pleased to meet you, Mr. Beckett," Annalie said.

Beckett gestured to a pair of slightly uncomfortable-looking armchairs placed at a conversational angle, and they both sat.

"How are you settling in?" he asked.

"Okay, I guess," she said.

"This must be quite a change of pace for you. Has it been a difficult adjustment?"

She realized he knew something about her circumstances, and at once she found herself going on the defensive. "Not at all," Annalie said, rather stiffly. "I'm doing very well here."

Beckett seemed to notice her discomfort, and smiled, a wolfish smile that showed his canines. It wasn't entirely reassuring. "You must be wondering why I've come to see you. I'm a friend of your father's."

Annalie was surprised.

"We haven't seen each other for a long time. Since

before you were born, in fact." He paused, studying her face. "You look like him. But you have your mother's coloring."

"Did you know her?" Annalie had never known her mother, who died when she was a baby. Spinner had no pictures of her, and became reserved and unhappy whenever she was mentioned. When Annalie was little she'd been desperate to know more about her mother, but as she grew up she'd learned to keep her curiosity to herself.

"I knew her very well," said Beckett. "She was very intelligent. Truly a wonderful mind. And a beautiful girl, too."

Annalie felt as if he was trying to flatter her, and it made her uncomfortable.

"Actually, I was the one who introduced them. Your father and I were working together—the building we worked in is just down the hill from here. I brought your mother in to join our team, and that's how they met."

Annalie frowned. "That can't be right," she said. "My father never worked here."

"He certainly did," Beckett said, "for many years."

"Are you sure you've got the right person?"

Beckett's lips pulled back to reveal his teeth again. The effect of it really was disconcerting. "Your father's name is Ned Wallace, but he answers to Neddy or Spinner. Loves boats and fixing things. Has a big scar on his leg where he ripped it open trying to get inside a shipping container he found at sea and nearly drowned. Has a talking parrot called Graham."

Beckett smiled. "I remember when he got Graham. I warned him those birds can live a really long time."

"Sixty years in captivity," Annalie said. She studied Beckett, curious and unsettled. How could this man have known her father for so long, and yet she'd never met him? "I'm sorry, Dad never mentioned you."

"No," Beckett drawled. "I don't suppose he did." He paused. "The sad fact is, your father and I were good friends and colleagues once. But then he stole something from me, something very valuable. And I haven't seen him or spoken to him since."

Annalie felt a jolt run through her, as if she'd been jabbed with a cattle prod. "Spinner stole something?"

"I know—at first I didn't believe it either. But there's no doubt it was him."

"I don't believe you," Annalie said. "He's not that kind of person."

Beckett looked at her appraisingly. "You're very loyal, and that's an excellent quality. But you'll find as you get older that people have many different sides to them. Secret selves. Secret histories. Things they've done that they might wish they hadn't done, but can't undo."

Annalie looked at him with hostility, but said nothing.

"The thing is, Annalie, the item your father stole is very important, and we really need to get it back."

"Who's we?"

Beckett bared his teeth again, in what was clearly meant to be a reassuring smile. He reached into his pocket, took out a business card, and gave it to her. It had an Admiralty crest on it, and identified him as working for the Department of Scientific Inquiry & Special Projects.

"Your father stole top-secret research from my department," Beckett said, "and we're very anxious to get it back."

"Why are you asking me?" Annalie said.

"Your father's been living off the grid for some time now. But you know that, of course. Why else would you have been living where you did? He only popped back into view this year—when you came here." Beckett paused, letting that sink in for a moment. "Ever since Ned went missing I've been hoping I could track him down before my superiors did. We were close once. If I could just find him and talk to him myself, I might be able to convince him to return the item voluntarily. Then we might be able to do some sort of deal to reduce the severity of his sentence."

"What do you mean?" Annalie asked, a chilly feeling making her scalp tighten.

"He's stolen top-secret research from the Admiralty. That's treason. If he's found guilty, they're never going to let him out."

Annalie stared at Beckett, horrified.

"Earlier this week, they finally managed to work out where you've been living. They sent a team round to arrest your dad, but he wasn't there."

"Where was he?" Annalie asked.

"I was hoping you might be able to tell me that," Beckett said.

The revelations had been coming so rapidly that it took a moment for Annalie to realize that Spinner was actually missing. Fear and abandonment tingled inside her. Where had Spinner gone? And what about Will?

The big man was watching her intently, his upper lip lifting to show those teeth, as if subconsciously he wanted to eat her. "Spinner needs our help, Annalie. Will you help me?"

A thought came to her, very clearly: *I don't trust this man.*

Her mind started working quickly. "Where did they look for him?" she asked.

"At the workshop, and on the boat," Beckett said. "There was nobody there."

Damn, Annalie thought. *So he knows about the boat.* "That's very strange," she said.

"The good news is, there's still time for him to turn himself in. He can still do a deal. If I help him tell his story, I'm sure there are mitigating circumstances. Maybe he can even avoid jail time. But only if I can find him before they do." Beckett paused, trying to read her. "Do you have any idea where he might have gone?"

"Well…" Annalie began, thinking, *Do I say nothing? Make something up?* The truth was, she didn't know where Spinner was hiding. But she also had an urge to put this man off the scent. If she could send him off on a wild-goose chase, perhaps it would buy Spinner some time—wherever he was. She gave Beckett a good-girl smile. "You know Spinner. He's pretty secretive."

"Does he have any old friends? Someone he could rely on in a tight spot?"

"If I tell you, do you promise he won't go to jail?"

"I can't promise that," Beckett said. "What he did was very serious. But I promise I'll do absolutely everything in my power to help him cut a deal and get him back to his family as soon as possible."

"There is someone he might have gone to," Annalie said, improvising. "But he's hard to find."

Beckett's face brightened, and he flicked on his shell. "Go on," he said.

"Spinner had an old friend, an old smuggler friend," Annalie said, making her voice sound reluctant. "He used to work out of the Eddy, but then things got too hot for him and he had to get out."

"What was his name?"

"Lagoon. Like the body of water."

"What was his real name?"

"I don't know. Actually, I think his wife used to call him something else. Frid?"

"Fred?"

"No, Frid."

Annalie watched Beckett's fingers flying over the virtual keyboard.

"They moved to Grunland."

"Grunland? Are you sure?"

Grunland was a small island nation far to the east that had been marginal even before everything went wrong. Its low-lying coastline had seen it ravaged by the Flood, and its population had shrunk from small to minuscule.

"We went there once. Horrible trip. Such rough seas, I was sick as a dog."

23

"Do you remember where in Grunland?"

"I forget what it was called," Annalie said regretfully. "But I remember it was on a super dangerous strait with absolutely massive tides. There were all these little islands and a huge body of water passing through a little tiny gap. They had a house there, all by itself. It had a blue door."

Beckett's fingers added all these details.

"And when was this?"

"Two years ago? Three years ago? Wait, I was ten—or was I nine? I couldn't have been eight. Or maybe…I'm not sure. It was a couple of years ago."

"And do you know if they're still in contact?"

Annalie shrugged. "I guess they probably are, but I don't know."

"Any other details you can think of?"

"His wife's name was Sun," Annalie said. "Oh, and Lagoon had a great big tattoo of a sea monster. It went right around his arm and all the way down his back. It was amazing."

Beckett added these details to his list. "Thank you, Annalie," he said. "You've been very helpful. Now, if you think of anything else, let me know, any time, day or night. You've got my details."

Annalie fingered the card he'd given her.

Beckett flicked off his shell and stood. Annalie stood too. The man towered over her.

"You won't let anything bad happen to him, will you?" Annalie said, looking up at him pleadingly.

"I'll do my best," Beckett said, and bared his teeth at her one last time.

Triumph

From the moment she'd arrived at Triumph College, Annalie had been acutely aware that she did not fit in.

Girls like her didn't get into the Admiralty's colleges, and especially not Triumph, the most prestigious of them all. Girls like her, living out on the periphery of things, were lucky to get an education at all. There were schools where she came from, of course, run by charities or religious groups. But most kids from the slums never even thought of applying to take the entrance exams for the elite colleges. That's because most kids didn't have a dad like Spinner. He'd insisted that they let her take the exam, and he'd insisted, once she aced it, winning a full scholarship, that they let her in—the first-ever kid from Lowtown.

She hadn't wanted to go. She hadn't wanted to leave her friends and her home. Most of all, she hadn't wanted to leave Spinner.

"You've got brains, Annalie," he'd said. "You can do anything you want. There are so many wonderful things you could do with your life. But you've got to get a good education."

There was a high school at home, she'd argued, she could go there. "If it's good enough for Will, why isn't it good enough for me?"

Spinner looked embarrassed. "We both know Will's going to be out of school the second I stop forcing him to go. School just isn't his thing, no matter how much I'd like it to be. But it's different for you. Our high school won't do: no one from there goes to university. You won't get anywhere if you go there."

"What if I don't want to go to university?"

"I want you to have the chance," Spinner said. "Don't lock yourself out of the possibility of a decent future."

"You never went to university and we have a good life," Annalie protested.

"I'm happy with our life," Spinner said gently, "but there are certainly more comfortable lives to be had." He smiled. "You could do great things, Annalie. You can be anything you want to be. There's plenty of time to decide, but if you don't start by getting a good education, you've already made most of your choices before you've even begun."

Spinner had high hopes for her—medicine, science, something valuable to society—and the only way to enter those professions was through the Admiralty.

Forty years ago, before the Flood, the Admiralty was just Dux's navy—admittedly, the world's largest standing navy, but still under the control of the government. Then the Flood happened; the government collapsed—many governments did all around the world—and the Admiralty took control, "until the emergency passed". A number of other navy forces joined with Dux's Admiralty, forming a Federation of Allied Nations, ensuring that there was no corner of the oceans the Admiralty and its naval allies could not reach. Now, the Admiralty still led Dux's emergency government. There were elections, but the parties merely competed to see who would join a coalition with the Admiralty, and everyone knew who was *really* in charge. Emergency measures introduced to rebuild Dux after the Flood and never repealed meant that the Admiralty had a hand in almost everything, from government contracts all the way through to education. If you wanted to go to university, you had to pay for your education by spending the same number of years in the Admiralty. Three years of science meant three years in the Admiralty; six years of medicine meant six years as an Admiralty doctor. A portion of that had to be spent on active service, at sea. Even if you weren't academically inclined, the best way to get ahead in life was to sign up for a few years of naval service.

Even though many people—Annalie among them—thought this was horribly unfair, competition to get one of the very few places at university was so fierce that it was almost impossible for ordinary people to get in at all. If you didn't get into one of the top schools (either an Admiralty college or one of the other elite schools) you had very little chance of passing the entrance exams that would let you into university. Annalie was not at all sure she even *wanted* to go to university, but as Spinner said, it was better to have choices. The Admiralty colleges had a full scholarship program for underprivileged kids, and there was a lot of talk about seeking out the best and brightest minds wherever they were to be found. This made it sound like there ought to be a reasonable cross-section of society at Triumph.

The reality turned out to be rather different.

Annalie began to see what she'd signed up for on her very first day, when she and Spinner arrived at the school and saw the electric cars pulling up out front, disgorging girls in jewel-studded jeans, or long dresses covered in ruffles, or tiny skirts with decorative tights and coordinating high-heeled shoes; every one of them dragged two, three, four suitcases of luggage. At that moment, she understood what she had never really understood before: she was poor.

At home, Annalie had lived happily in a small handful of things—shorts in summer, long pants and a sweater in the winter, a cut-down old waterproof coat to keep the rain out, shoes rarely. She'd been astounded when the school uniform list had arrived—summer uniform, winter uniform, sports uniforms, all with matching hats and socks and shoes and regulation underwear. Luckily you could buy some of it second hand, but Annalie still couldn't quite believe anyone could ever need so many clothes. She'd traveled to school in her shorts and her old canvas sneakers with the toes poked through. But as she and Spinner walked through the school gates, they both realized they'd made a mistake.

"I'd forgotten what teenage girls are like," Spinner muttered, looking at them with dismay. Then he turned to Annalie with a fierce expression, and said, "Don't forget, you've got just as much right to be here as any of them. You aced that entrance exam. You're as good as any of them." He tapped her temple with a finger. "It's what you've got up here that really matters. Okay?"

"Okay," Annalie said, almost as disturbed by his anxiety as by the sight of all the girls in their finery.

While he was with her she'd managed to stay proud, even when people stared at her shabby shoes and Spinner's faded old pants. They were his better pants, but when she saw what the other dads wore, and noticed Spinner was a whole generation older than the rest of them, she understood how odd the two of them looked.

It wasn't until he'd gone and she was unpacking her things in her new dormitory that she truly began to see how things were going to be. The other girls—she had five roommates—had arrived with cases full of casual clothes in a rainbow of colors. They lined up fragrant bottles on top of their chests of drawers, and Annalie was embarrassed to realize she didn't know what these were for. Following the school's list, she had brought a toothbrush and toothpaste, a comb, soap, shampoo. Shop-bought toiletries had seemed like a luxury when she got them, but now she saw how pitiful they looked compared to what the other girls had.

And it wasn't that the other girls in her dorm teased her; they simply stared, and said nothing, and left her alone, as if she were a wild beast dropped inexplicably into their midst.

Girls who weren't living at such close quarters were less reserved. After she heard one girl whispering—audibly—about her clothes that first day, she changed into her school uniform and never took it off again.

At breakfast on her fourth day, someone came up to her and asked, "Is it true you never wash your hair?" There was a burst of giggling around her and Annalie didn't know what to say. At home, she had only washed her hair intermittently—it hadn't seemed all that necessary. She had noticed that her roommates all seemed to spend a lot of time each day washing and tending their hair, but it hadn't occurred to her that she might be expected to do so as well, and it *definitely* hadn't occurred to her that anyone might be watching her to see what she did. It horrified her to realize the other girls were scrutinizing her and finding fault with her behavior.

Before she'd come to school, she'd worried that perhaps she wouldn't be able to keep up with the school work—she'd never studied any foreign languages—but it turned out that the lessons were the easiest part of her day. It was dealing with the other girls that was hard.

If it wasn't for Essie, she wasn't sure she'd have made it through the first month.

Swamphead

Essie was one of the girls who shared Annalie's dormitory. Although they slept, dressed, ate, played sports and took all their classes together, Essie did not exchange a word with the girl from Lowtown until several weeks into the term.

One mid-week evening, Essie was in the junior common room, trying, and failing, to make sense of her maths homework when an outbreak of giggling snapped her back into the room. She knew at once it was not the nice kind of giggling, and a shiver like icy water went down her back.

She looked up, and saw Tiffany and her gang sashaying toward her. Tiffany was a pretty second-year girl with auburn hair and eyes as dead and cold as deep space, and Essie could only watch helplessly as she approached, leaving eddying swirls of curiosity in her wake. A few heads turned to see whatever drama was about to unfold; many more kept their heads down, afraid of attracting Tiffany's attention.

"Essie!" Tiffany said, sliding into the chair next to her. Tiffany's dark-haired friend, Sandra, followed her lead and slid into the chair on Essie's other side.

Lina, a hard-faced blonde, sat down opposite. "How are you doing?" Tiffany continued, her voice a sing-song of concern.

"Okay," Essie said.

"Okay? Really?" Tiffany cocked her head to one side then the other, pushing her face a little too close to Essie's. Essie tried to shrink herself inconspicuously away.

"I saw your daddy on my newsfeed again," Tiffany said, her voice as sweet as ant poison. "It must be so devastating for you."

"Devastating," agreed Sandra.

"So embarrassing," Lina said. "Having a crook for a dad."

"Lina!" scolded Tiffany. "You shouldn't say things like that to her. She *knows* what her daddy is. *Saying* it just makes it harder for her." Tiffany turned back to Essie with a smile. "I mean, imagine if *your* daddy had done all the stuff Essie's daddy's done. Taken bribes. Stolen money. Built shonky developments that fell down and killed people. Can you imagine how her family must feel, knowing they've got blood on their hands?"

Essie said nothing. Her face was burning.

Tiffany picked up Essie's shell and began playing with it. "I mean, imagine how you'd feel if everything you owned was bought with blood money. All your clothes. All your devices."

Essie stared longingly at her shell—it was still new, the latest model—wishing she were brave enough to ask for it back, afraid that asking might make things worse.

32

Tiffany switched it on and Essie gasped. Her messages and feeds popped up. Tiffany scrolled back and forth through them. "How can you bear joining the links when everything's all about what a vile scumbag your daddy is? It's all anybody's talking about. If I were you, I'd throw my shell in the bin. I seriously would."

Tiffany held the shell up over her head, her eyes locking challengingly with Essie's. The smile was gone now. There was just pure calculation—*How far will you let me take this? How far will I go?* Lina and Sandra hovered beside her, avid. There was no knowing, with Tiffany. You never could tell where the limits were—or if she had any.

"Please—" Essie breathed, reaching out hopelessly for the shell that was already beyond her reach, knowing she was falling into the trap, and she saw Tiffany's ugly pleasure. But before it could go any further, Essie's shell was whisked out of Tiffany's hand.

"I'll take that," said a small, firm voice.

Tiffany's head snapped round, outraged.

Annalie held Essie's shell. She was not tall for her age, with a head of thick brown hair and very dark eyes; right now they blazed with stern determination. Everyone knew that she had grown up in a shantytown, beyond the edges of the civilized world. It was rumored that she'd come to school in rags, that she was illegal, that she was in a gang. Essie wasn't sure who she should be more afraid of, Tiffany or Annalie.

"Oh look. It's the swamphead they let in," Sandra said.

Swamphead meant slum-dweller, someone dirty and dangerous and criminal. It was not at all the sort of term you'd usually use to someone's face.

Tiffany smiled with bright malice, and Essie felt her stomach turn over with anxiety. "The swamphead! I thought there was a smell in here!"

Everyone's eyes were on Annalie now. Essie felt a shrinking sense of sympathy—Annalie was possibly the only girl in the school who was more notorious than she was.

But Annalie didn't look afraid. She gave Tiffany a look that was almost scornful. "Come on, is that the best you can do?" she asked. "What are you, seven years old?"

Tiffany got up then, drawing herself up to her full elegant height to stare Annalie down. "What did you say?"

Annalie cocked an eyebrow. "Do you have a hearing problem?"

Tiffany's fine face molded into a sneer. "You don't belong here, swamphead," she said. "And neither does she," she added, tossing a look of death at Essie, as if to remind her she wasn't off the hook yet.

"Is that right?" Annalie said, unimpressed.

"Swampheads are scum," Tiffany said.

For a moment, Tiffany's words hung in the air, and Essie felt a little ripple of shock run through the room. Plenty of people had thought it; no one had quite dared to come out and say it.

Annalie's look turned cold. "You don't know anything about me," she said, slowly and deliberately. Essie noticed her small hands curl into fists.

The other girls began to twitter and murmur, shifting about; Tiffany eyed Annalie, her eyes darting a little as she tried to weigh up what was happening: should she push it further? Was it worth the risk? Did she dare to back down and risk the loss of face? Annalie was an unknown quantity, and in that moment, Tiffany was perhaps not quite brave enough to risk it. The moment of inaction stretched, and then Sandra helpfully said, "Leave it, Tiffany. She's not worth it."

Given permission to back down, Tiffany pulled her face into an arch sneer, as if she'd won the encounter. "I'll be watching you, swampy," she said. And the three of them walked out.

Essie felt the breath go out of her. She hadn't realized she'd been holding it. She felt a little dizzy.

"Here," Annalie said, holding her shell toward her.

"Thanks," Essie said, taking it, and then for a moment neither of them knew quite what to do. "Would you like to sit down?" she asked.

Annalie sat.

"You're brave to take her on," Essie said. "I just hope she's not going to come after you next."

"She's not so scary," Annalie said.

Essie looked at Annalie nervously, trying to get her measure. "I thought you were going to hit her," she said.

Annalie smiled and looked down at her hands. "That was the idea."

"Were you bluffing?" Essie was startled by the audacity of it. "Would you have actually done it though?"

"Hit her, you mean?" Annalie hesitated. "I don't know."

Not "no," Essie thought. For a moment she tried to imagine the life this girl had come from, picturing newsfeed footage of refugees in water-riddled slums, and action films featuring the violent brotherhoods who ran those slums. Neither of them seemed to have much to do with the twelve-year-old girl sitting beside her now.

"What was all that about, anyway?" Annalie asked.

Essie felt a blush seeping into her face again. "You know the Tower Corp scandal?"

Annalie shook her head.

"The building that fell down? It's been all over the feeds. They say my dad was responsible."

Essie's father, Everest Wan, was a property developer. As a young man, the Admiralty had posted him to the Department of Reconstruction, which was responsible for rebuilding the flood-damaged cities; much of the actual building work was done by private companies, and soon enough Everest Wan had started his own company, Tower Corp, and was hard at work putting up office towers and apartment buildings. It was more than just work to him; it was a mission to give people a place to call home.

The week Essie started at Triumph there was a horrible disaster. A newly completed tower building collapsed, killing and injuring hundreds of people. At first a storm was blamed for the disaster, but then it emerged that there had been problems with the construction—building materials stolen and substituted with cheaper ones, engineering reports faked, bribes solicited and paid. The company responsible? Tower Corp.

Essie went home the weekend after the news broke, and there were awful scenes. Her mother cried, her father cried, insisting he'd known nothing about the corruption, that he was as devastated and shocked as anyone by what had happened. Essie went back to school reassured that her father had done nothing wrong. But every day, more evidence came out about the company and the way they did business. None of it was good, and it became harder and harder for Essie to keep believing that her father really hadn't known what was going on. If he *didn't* know, then he was an idiot; but if he *did* know, he was something far worse. Neither thought was very comforting. Lately there had been talk of criminal charges. Her parents were worried they were going to lose everything.

Now it was Annalie's turn to look embarrassed. "I don't really keep up with all that stuff," she said awkwardly.

Of course, Essie thought. Annalie just didn't seem to *get* the links. She had a shell—it was a school requirement—but it was nothing like the shells the other girls had. It was old and out of date, although it had all the basic functions, like a virtual keyboard you could activate to type your schoolwork. But as for all the other stuff a shell could do—playing music, running newsfeeds, gaming, messaging, taking photos, getting information; in fact, anything you might need to do ever—Annalie didn't do any of it. Most kids their age walked around in a constant blur of information coming through their shell's virtual displays, but Annalie didn't even wear a headpiece. It was possible her shell was so old it wasn't compatible with headpieces. And although Essie thought it must be strange to be so cut off from what was going on in the world, it also meant that Annalie was possibly the only girl in the school who didn't give a damn who her father was.

"Why give *you* a hard time?" Annalie was saying. "You didn't make the building fall down, did you?"

Essie shook her head and laughed uncomfortably, feeling a little glow of gratitude toward her, and for a moment they both looked away awkwardly, unsure what to say next.

Essie fiddled with her shell and her maths homework popped up. It caught Annalie's eye. "Are you still working on that?"

Essie groaned. "Don't you just hate maths? It's so hard here!"

"Do you think so?" Annalie said, then stopped herself. "I could help you with it if you like."

"That'd be great," Essie said, "if you don't mind."

"What else am I going to do?" Annalie asked dryly, looking around the common room.

Essie glanced around too, and noticed for the first time that although some of the girls had formed into little knots and were talking and laughing together, most of them were sitting alone, their headpieces pulsing and glittering as their feeds poured each private, individual stream of news and pics and music into each private, individual head.

"Okay," Annalie said, angling the shell so they could both see it. "This is what you have to do."

Over the weeks that followed, Annalie and Essie became good friends. Annalie helped Essie with her math, and Essie helped Annalie with her languages (Essie had learned several at her primary school). It soon became clear to Essie—and to the rest of the class as well—that Annalie was dauntingly clever. But she also had surprising gaps in her knowledge. She had no real idea what a shell was for, beyond the basics; she had never searched the links; she had no newsfeeds of her own and couldn't really understand the point of them. Essie tried introducing her to some of her favorites—fashion, music, celebrities, cat vids—but Annalie confessed she found most of them either boring or baffling.

"I'd rather read a book," Annalie said.

"You're so weird," Essie sighed.

Spinner the thief

Annalie left the interview with Beckett, her head spinning. It was too late now to go back to sport, so she went to her dormitory and sank onto her bed. The other girls would be back soon, and she needed some precious time alone to try and make sense of what she'd just learned about her father.

Could any of it be true? Had Spinner really once been a scientist, working on top-secret projects for the Admiralty? Spinner was very smart—she could imagine him using his ingenuity and mechanical know-how to help create something important, maybe even top secret. But the Admiralty part? That was harder to imagine.

Spinner ran to his own schedule, did things his own way. He wasn't much of a one for rules. As long as things got done, he didn't much care how they got done. This, Annalie knew from her school, was not the Admiralty way. Triumph College was all about rules and regulations, systems and processes. Following the timetable. Meeting the deadlines. Everything perfect to the last detail. Everyone held to the same exacting standards. There was a right way and a wrong way to do everything, from making your bed to plaiting your hair and organizing your school supplies. There were locker inspections and desk inspections to make sure everything was in its place. Everyone kept explaining how important it was when you were at sea to pull your weight, to work together, to make the team stronger. Annalie didn't feel like she was part of a team. It felt more like being in prison.

If Beckett was telling the truth about her dad once working for the Admiralty, it did make her wonder what Spinner was thinking when he encouraged her to go to an Admiralty school. All this time she'd assumed he had no idea what he was letting her in for, and now it turned out he'd known exactly what it was like—he'd been a part of it himself. But he'd never let on, not for a single moment.

Spinner had never really been an Admiralty-hater, like a lot of the grown-ups she knew. It wasn't a good idea to criticize the Admiralty publicly, but you'd hear plenty of adults grumbling privately about living under the jackboot of a military dictatorship, because they didn't like the immigration laws, or customs controls, or they thought boat registration fees were too high.

Spinner wasn't political like that; if you tried to pin him down he'd say that the Admiralty did a lot of good things in a difficult situation, and if you *really* pressed him he might say that perhaps it was time to agree that the state of emergency had passed, and it was time to let the civilians do more of the work. But he wouldn't go any further than that.

How strange to think that Spinner had once been part of the Admiralty. She knew he'd never gone

41

through a school like Triumph—things were different when he was young, before the Flood. But had he served on an Admiralty ship, like she would have to one day? In a way it was easy to imagine Spinner, who loved the sea, as an able seaman on an Admiralty ship. It was harder to imagine him following all the rules and regulations that drove her so crazy.

And as for the part where he went off to work on a top-secret project and stole their research? That part was completely impossible to imagine.

Spinner was not a thief. She knew that for sure. Spinner was supremely honorable. He'd never steal something that didn't belong to him. Never.

But if he hadn't stolen the research, why had they been living off the grid? She understood now that that was exactly what they'd been doing. There was no question her father could have made a better living if he'd wanted to—made more money, lived in a more comfortable house in the official part of town, with indoor plumbing and a permanent power supply. But that would have made him visible. And he'd managed to stay hidden all this time—right up until the moment he sent her to school.

A cold feeling washed over her. What if it was her fault he'd been recognized after all this time? She could see now that he'd taken precautions; she was enrolled under her mother's surname, Go, not Wallace. "It doesn't mean anything, it's just what's on your birth certificate," Spinner had said casually, giving her some vague story about a mistake made at the registry office that he'd never quite got around to correcting. He'd done it to protect her—and himself. But somehow, in spite of his precautions, they'd found him, and now his past had come roaring back to catch up with all of them.

Where have you gone, Spinner? Annalie wondered, lonely and afraid. *And what am I supposed to do now?*

Then something surprising happened.

Her shell rang.

Will

Annalie's heart started to beat faster. She picked up her shell and checked the number. Her shell didn't recognize the caller.

"Hello?" she said, cautiously.

"Annalie? It's Will."

Relief flooded through her. She had never been so glad to hear her brother's gruff voice. "Will! What's happened? Are you okay?"

"Yeah I'm okay. But there's something I need to tell you. Spinner's done a runner."

So Beckett was telling the truth about that, at least: Spinner really was missing. "Tell me what happened."

Will filled her in on the events of the previous evening, then told her what he'd found when he went back to check the workshop.

"They messed the place up pretty good," he said.

"Did they find what they were looking for?" Annalie asked.

"What makes you think they were looking for something?"

"I know they were." And she told him about the visit she'd just had from Beckett.

44

"So what is it they think he stole?" Will asked.

"He said it was top-secret research. Whatever it is, it's important." Annalie hesitated, then said, "You don't think he did it, do you?"

"Spinner? No way."

"That's what I thought," Annalie said, relieved.

"Remember when we lifted that stuff out of Old Man Hang's garden and Spinner got so mad and made us give it back?" Annalie remembered it well. "He'd never steal anything. There's no way. I bet this Beckett guy's just trying to set him up."

"The only way to find out for sure is to find Spinner. Do you know where he's gone?"

"Nope. He wouldn't say."

"But did he say when he'd be back?"

"Nope. He just told me to stay at Janky's."

"Hey, Annalie!" She heard Janky's voice in the background.

"Hey, Janky," Annalie replied. "But he must have given you *some* idea—"

"If he had, I'd tell you," Will said, a little crossly.

They were both silent for a moment.

"Do you think he might have taken the boat somewhere?" Annalie asked. "Beckett said they'd checked the boat but he wasn't there."

"I haven't been down there yet," Will confessed. "I'll go there now and let you know what I find," Will said. "Talk to you later."

"Wait. Will—"

"What?"

"Be careful."

45

Will made a *pfft* sound. "I'm always careful," he said, and hung up.

Annalie rolled her eyes. "Yeah, right."

The *Sunfish*

S pinner's boat was called the *Sunfish*. It was a 39-foot-
long ketch with two masts and a hull painted bright
yellow. It was a sailing boat, with various enhance-
ments and modifications that Spinner had designed
and built himself, including an engine with a solar-
powered battery. The boat had been designed for
long-distance solo sailing, although Spinner didn't
often need to sail by himself; the twins had been
crewing for him since they were tiny.

Spinner's business was based in his workshop, but
the three of them spent a lot of time at sea, often going
on quite long voyages. They had all sorts of reasons
for taking the boat out: sometimes they took a load
of reconditioned machinery or spare parts to sell at a
regional market, or they made a delivery of something
Spinner had built. Sometimes they went looking for
things he needed—parts, components, the carcasses
of old machinery. At other times, it seemed, they just
went for fun, to see new places or old friends. Spinner
had a lot of friends in far-flung places, and getting to
them could be perilous, but Will loved the long sea
voyages—they were the best times of all.

School always made Will feel shut in and restless; he much preferred being at sea with Spinner. He loved the pleasure of those moments when his dad left the boat in his hands, loved the rhythms of the days at sea, the way the sun and the tides and the weather dictated the work, rather than something as random and silly as following a clock. At sea, you worked when you needed to work, and when you didn't need to, you did nothing at all. Sometimes the water was rough, sometimes it was hard work, and sometimes it felt like they might actually be going to drown; but Will always felt safe with Spinner on the boat. He had a feeling, although he would never actually admit this to anyone, that the *Sunfish* would always protect them, him and Spinner and Graham and Annalie. It was a special boat, and he loved it.

Spinner kept the *Sunfish* at a mooring in the Eddy. Will and Janky headed down there, stopping only for an after-school snack to refuel them for the trip.

The Eddy smelled, as usual, of saltwater and rotting seaweed. Something about the way the water flowed into the Eddy at high tide meant that there were always piles of rotting seaweed collecting there. It was low tide now, and they could see the large extended family known as the Kelpies hard at work collecting it up to sell on as fertilizer. The Kelpies had cornered the market in Eddy seaweed.

"You know how profitable that business is?" Janky remarked, looking enviously at the kids their age who were hard at work hauling and bundling the seaweed into reeking piles.

48

"So profitable they can afford to keep the Three Kings as muscle," Will said.

"I heard someone tried to steal their patch once and they caught them and staked them to the bottom of the Eddy to drown, and when the tide went out the bodies had been all chewed up by fish," Janky said with bloodthirsty enthusiasm. Everyone had heard this story, and Will had no idea whether it was true, but they loved repeating it to one another.

They walked along the busy promenade, following it out to where Spinner had a mooring, far up the west side of the quay. Will began to hurry as they drew closer, trying to pick out the familiar shape of the *Sunfish*'s masts from among all the other boats lying at anchor.

At last he reached the spot where the *Sunfish* was usually moored, and his heart sank. The boat was gone, and another was moored in its place. Anger boiled up inside him. Gone for less than a day, and already someone had stolen their mooring? It was too much. He thought he saw movement aboard the interloper's boat, and then a man came up from below decks, whistling. Will shouted at him, "Hey! Hey you!"

The man looked around to see who was calling him.

"Yeah you, buddy!" Will shouted.

Janky yanked on Will's arm. "You reckon this is a good time to be calling attention to yourself?"

Will realized he was right, and the two of them ran away and didn't stop until they were well out of sight of the boat owner.

"What do you think happened?" Janky asked. "Do you think your dad might have taken the boat himself?"

"Graham said the Admiralty were already here when they got here," Will said gloomily. "They must have impounded it."

"Or stolen it," Janky offered. "Or sunk it."

Will glared at him.

"But they probably impounded it," Janky said hastily. "If it was Admiralty, that's what they would've done."

"They keep them over at the shipyard in the new port, don't they?" Will said.

"That's where they put my uncle's boat when he got pulled in for smuggling."

"Did he get it back?"

Janky nodded. "Eventually. It took months though."

"Months?"

"They told him when he got it back that if they ever caught him again, they'd burn the boat."

"Did he stop?"

"Course not."

"And?"

"They burnt the boat."

They both walked along in silence for a little while.

"So now what?" Janky said.

"I need to get the boat back, don't I?"

"How?"

"Dunno yet."

"If they catch you, you'll get in *heaps* of trouble. Why don't you wait until your dad comes back?"

"What if he doesn't come back?" Will said.

"He will," Janky said, not sounding very convincing.

Will felt bristly inside, angry with himself for letting out the thought that Spinner might not come back, as if by saying it he had risked making it come true. "They wrecked the workshop and stole all our stuff. The boat's all we've got left. I have to get it back."

Janky walked beside him in silence, skepticism rising off him like a smell. "I just don't think it's the best idea," he said finally. "Your dad wouldn't want you to get in trouble, would he?"

"He wouldn't want them to burn our boat either," Will said. "Anyway, if they don't catch me, I won't get into trouble."

Janky just looked at him and shook his head.

Don't do anything stupid

"It's gone," Will reported. "We think the Admiralty's impounded it."

"Can they do that?" Annalie asked.

"They can do whatever they want."

They both knew this was true.

"Don't suppose you've heard from Spinner?" Annalie asked.

"Nope. You?"

"No. It's just so frustrating not knowing anything."

"Yeah, I know. I'm sure Graham knows where Spinner went, but the stupid bird couldn't tell me."

"What do you mean? Did Graham go with him?"

"Yeah, he was with him, but then he got lost and came home again."

"He was *with* him?" Annalie repeated, excitement rising. "But didn't you—"

"Of course I asked him," Will interrupted, already knowing what she was going to say, "but he didn't make any sense."

"You've got to ask him the right questions. Be patient with him."

"I *was* patient!" Will said impatiently.

Annalie let that go. "Maybe tomorrow you should ask around a bit. See if anybody else saw where he went. If we just had a couple of clues—"

"Yeah, totally, I might do that," Will said.

Annalie frowned, detecting something in his voice. "You *might* do that?"

"I mean, that's a good idea, yeah."

"You're up to something, aren't you?"

"No," Will said. "I'm not up to anything."

"Truly?"

"Spinner told me to stay put and keep my head down and that's what I'm going to do."

Annalie didn't believe him. But she was in Pallas, halfway across the country. What could she possibly do?

"Okay," she said, still suspicious. "Why don't you give Graham a biscuit and ask him about Spinner again."

"Yep. Sure thing."

"And Will? Don't do anything stupid."

She heard Janky's voice in the background. "Isn't that like saying *don't breathe*?"

Will's voice over the phone was sweetly reasonable. "Don't worry. I've got it all under control."

"Well," Annalie said. "Okay."

"I'll keep you posted," Will said, and hung up.

"I think I have to go home."

"Why?" asked Essie.

53

It was later the same evening. Essie and Annalie had tucked themselves away in a quiet corner of the junior common room.

"Because I need to know what's going on and Will never asks the right questions," Annalie said. "And besides, I know he's up to something."

"Like what?"

"I don't know yet." Annalie's fingers were *tacktacking* agitatedly on the desk top. "But whatever it is, I bet it's a bad idea."

"The school will never give you permission to go."

"Then I'll go without permission."

"You'll get into big trouble."

"My dad's on the run from the Admiralty," Annalie said dryly. "I think I'm already in trouble."

"*He* is," Essie said. "*You're* not. At least, not yet."

Annalie thought of the elaborate lie she'd told to try and put Beckett off the scent. It would probably take him at least a few days before he worked out it wasn't true. But once he did…

"Don't go," Essie said. "There's nothing you can really do. And didn't your dad want you both to stay out of it?"

"Yes," Annalie admitted.

"Then shouldn't you do what he wants?"

"Yes, but…that Beckett guy told me all this stuff about my dad, awful stuff, and I need to know if any of it's true."

"Are you sure…" Essie began, then broke off.

"What?"

Regretting that she'd broached the subject, Essie said, "Are you sure you really want to find out?"

Annalie was staring at her, a challenge in her eyes. Essie knew she was venturing into dangerous territory, but could not go back now. "I mean—what if it's true?"

Annalie began to look outraged.

"I'm not saying it is," Essie said hastily, "but maybe your dad wanted to protect you. Maybe it's better not to go sticking your nose in."

"It's *not* true," Annalie snapped. "I know it isn't. My dad isn't like your dad." And she got up and rushed out of the room.

Lolly

Annalie walked toward her dormitory, already ashamed of herself for what she'd said to Essie, but with a horrid feeling creeping through her. Essie loved her father and she'd believed he was a good man—right up until the minute she discovered that he wasn't. What was it Beckett had said? People had secret lives, things they couldn't undo. Was Spinner one of them?

With this troubling thought in her head, she arrived at her own dormitory to a horrible sight: Tiffany and Sandra were standing beside her bed and they had been going through her drawers. Her clothes were scattered carelessly about on the floor, her books were flapping open on the bed and, worst of all, Tiffany had pulled out the suitcase from under her bed and discovered what she had concealed in there.

The two girls looked around as she walked in, their faces both guilty and wicked.

"What's this?" Tiffany asked, holding something up.

It was a doll. Spinner had made it when Annalie was very small, carefully constructing the head, painting the face, creating the jointed arms and legs, the delicate little hands. She was a slightly odd creation, with her face and limbs made of wood and metal, while her rounded body was soft and squashy, but Annalie had loved her passionately since the day she got her. The doll's name was Lolly and, like her owner, she had just one dress, which was a little ragged now. Annalie couldn't bear to be parted from her, but had also known that she could not possibly display Lolly in front of her roommates. One or two of them had cuddly toys that adorned their beds, but Lolly was different. Annalie could see her through the eyes of others, and could not bear to expose Lolly to ridicule. So she had stayed in the suitcase, under the bed—until now.

"Give that back," Annalie said, although as soon as she'd said it she knew it was the worst thing she could do. If she'd kept her cool, pretended it didn't matter...But it was too late now.

"Is this your *dolly*?" Tiffany crooned. "Your very bestest dolly?"

"How sweet!" Sandra chimed in.

"Sweet?" echoed Tiffany, turning to Sandra. "This is actually the worst thing I've ever seen!"

"The worst!" Sandra agreed merrily.

"This is without a doubt the crappiest, ugliest, stupidest doll in existence."

"Can't blame you for keeping it out of sight," Sandra said.

"In fact, I think we should do you a favor," Tiffany said. "Instead of just hiding it, don't you think it's time you got rid of it? I mean, it is the most pathetic thing I've ever seen. Time to cut the cord."

Tiffany marched briskly to the window and began fumbling with the latch so she could throw it open.

"No!" Annalie shrieked.

"It's got to be done," Tiffany said, handing the doll to Sandra while she wrestled with the window latch, which was stiff.

In desperation, Annalie launched herself at Sandra, knocking her to the ground. Lolly was pinned beneath her; the girl cried out affectedly in pain. Annalie struggled with her, fighting to take back Lolly. Tiffany grabbed Annalie around the neck and tried to pull her off Sandra.

Yanked backwards, Annalie lashed out with her feet at Sandra, who dropped Lolly with a howl.

Annalie grabbed Lolly, then twisted like a fish in Tiffany's grip. She broke free then turned to face Tiffany, Lolly in one hand, her other fist raised, ready to take a swing, when she heard a voice from the doorway say, "What is going on here?"

All three of them froze for a moment, then turned to see the house mistress standing in the doorway.

"She attacked us, miss!" Tiffany said instantly, her voice filled with righteous anger.

"For absolutely no reason!" added Sandra.

"Is this your dormitory, Tiffany?" the house mistress asked.

"No, miss," Tiffany said.

"Then I don't need to remind you that other girls' dorms are out of bounds, and for good reason." The house mistress paused, her gaze raking all three of them. "Now, I don't know what's been going on here, but you should know that fighting will not be tolerated anywhere in this school. Do I make myself clear?"

"Yes, miss," droned Tiffany and Sandra.

"Yes, miss," said Annalie.

"Don't let me catch you in here again," the house mistress said, and Tiffany and Sandra darted from the room, giving Annalie a very dirty look behind the woman's back.

The house mistress continued looking at Annalie with an unfriendly expression. "I don't know what it's like where you come from, but this sort of behavior is unacceptable."

"But miss—"

"And so is this level of untidiness. Clean up this mess immediately."

"But—"

"Now." The house mistress gave her a severe look, and left the room.

Annalie slumped onto her bed, pressing Lolly against her heart. The unfairness of what had just happened pierced her. Why should *she* get the blame? It was them who'd come in here, pawing through her stuff, making trouble, but because of who she was and where she came from, the house mistress had assumed that *she* was the troublemaker. A tear slipped out and rolled down onto Lolly's head, but only one. Annalie wiped it away.

"I'm sorry, Lolly," she whispered, smoothing the doll's hair into place.

A sudden movement in the doorway made her look up. Essie was there, hovering.

"I warned you not to mess with Tiffany," she said, tentative, unsure of her reception.

"Yes you did," Annalie said, embarrassed to be discovered like this. She placed Lolly back into her suitcase and slid the case back under her bed, stealthily wiping her eyes.

Essie edged into the room. "I'm sorry about what I said before," she said in a whispery little voice. "I don't know anything about your dad. I'm sure he's a good guy."

"I'm sorry too," Annalie said.

Essie came and sat comfortingly beside her. "I wouldn't have picked you as a doll kind of girl," she said. "I would have guessed cuddly animal."

"Spinner made her for me. I've had her for as long as I can remember."

"My dad gave me Blue Horse," Essie said, pointing to the small grayish toy that sat on her pillow. "Tons of other stuff too. But that one was always my favorite."

There was a silence.

"They're never going to accept me here, are they?" Annalie said.

"Don't worry about them," Essie said, as robustly as she could. "They're just a few stupid bullies."

"It's not just the girls," Annalie said. "It's all of them, the teachers, everyone. They think because I grew up in Lowtown I'm scum."

"Yes, but you're the smartest scum in our class," Essie said, trying for funny.

Annalie didn't smile.

"If anyone belongs here, it's you," Essie said. "And don't you forget it. Why don't you come back to the common room?"

"Just give me a sec," Annalie said. "I need to tidy up a bit."

Essie studied her, still concerned, but then nodded. "Okay."

When Essie had gone, Annalie began sorting through the mess Tiffany and Sandra had made. Some of it went back into the drawers, some of it into the suitcase. A decision had been taking shape in her mind while she talked to Essie, and even while she was fighting with Tiffany, and now it was fully formed. She had to go home, now, tonight. Spinner may have wanted her to stay out of it, but how could she? An Admiralty agent already knew where to find her, and even though he professed nothing but care and friendship, all her instincts told her she could not trust him. She was no longer safe at Triumph.

And Will wasn't safe either. She knew her brother: he probably thought he was being extra smart and extra sneaky and that there was no way he could get himself into trouble. But neither of them had ever been in trouble like this before. Now more than ever, Will needed back-up. And so did she.

She opened the wardrobe and looked at the row of uniforms hanging there: summer, winter, sport.

"I won't be needing you again," she said, and slammed the wardrobe door shut.

Escape

The clock in the dormitory showed it was 5 a.m. Annalie slowly and carefully slid her suitcase out from under her bed. Every shuffle and zip seemed magnified by the silence; every pause in the even tempo of her roommates' breathing made her freeze. But they only stirred, rolled over, and went back to sleep again as she unbuttoned her pajamas and pulled on the clothes she'd brought from home, then slid her suitcase out from under the bed and crept toward the door.

"Annalie, wait!"

She turned to see Essie sitting up in bed.

Annalie put her finger to her lips and attempted to make her escape. But Essie jumped out of bed and hurried after her into the corridor.

"Where are you going?" she hissed.

"Home," Annalie said.

"Then I'm coming with you."

Annalie stared at Essie. "Why?"

Essie blinked back at her, her eyes still slightly unfocused from waking so abruptly. "I might be able to help."

"How?"

"I know how to link. Unlike you. I might be able to help you find out where your dad's gone." Essie eyed the suitcase. "Planning on going for long?"

"I haven't decided yet."

"Then I'm definitely coming. How else am I going to make sure you come back?"

Annalie hesitated, but she knew the longer they stayed there talking, the more chance there was of someone else waking up and catching them. "All right, you can come. But hurry up!"

Essie was soon scampering out of the dormitory in sparkly jeans and sneakers, a bulging pink bag slung across her body, her headpiece emitting patterns of rainbow light. "Ready!" she said.

"Could you be a little less conspicuous?" Annalie pointed to the lights.

"Sorry." Essie switched them off.

The school was silent and spooky as they slipped down the corridor and down the stairs, pattering through dark spaces lit only by the streetlights and moonlight pouring in the high windows. The building would be locked, Annalie was sure, and so would the front gates. But behind the school were those extensive grassy playing fields, and beyond them, fences with railings that would be easy enough to climb.

Heavy doors blocked their way on the ground floor; they separated the dormitory wing from the classrooms, and for a moment she feared they would be trapped there. But then the door swung open under a little pressure—although it let out a fearsome squeak—and they slipped through and went scuttling down the corridor before anyone could come and investigate.

Annalie discovered a more serious barrier when they got to the doors that led out onto the schoolyard and the playing fields. These were locked, and the lock required a key, which was not, of course, in the door.

"Do you know how to pick locks?" Essie asked.

"No," Annalie said. "Do you?"

Annalie jiggled the lock for a moment longer, then went into the nearest classroom. Essie followed her.

This classroom, like all the others, had windows that looked out onto the schoolyard. The tops of the windows were fixed glass, but along the bottom were windows that could be opened to let in fresh air. Annalie opened one.

"We'll never get through there," Essie said. The windows opened from the top, not the bottom; they would have to climb over the metal edge to get out.

Annalie measured the gap with her eyes. "Yes we will," she said.

She squeezed her suitcase through the narrow gap; it only just fit through. Essie wrangled her own tightly stuffed bag through the gap and carefully let it drop to the concrete outside.

"I'll go first," Annalie said.

Climbing up on the nearest desk, she put one leg through the gap, then eased her body through. The window groaned threateningly under her weight as she ground herself, curving, through the narrow gap, scraping skin off her back, and dropped to the ground, knocking the back of her head against the window frame as she went. She cursed and rubbed it, then looked up at the window, where she could see Essie's pale, worried face looking out.

"Your turn," she said.

Essie crept tentatively into the space between the window, maneuvering awkwardly around the tight squeezes. Annalie issued instructions, Essie winced and fussed, Annalie gave more instructions, Essie announced she was stuck. Annalie came up under the window and ordered her through. Essie fell heavily onto Annalie.

"Remind me why I'm bringing you?" Annalie said grumpily as they both clambered to their feet.

"Sorry," Essie said.

Annalie pushed the window shut until she heard it click, then they retrieved their bags and began to run across the dark schoolyard and out onto the wet grass of the playing fields.

They soon came to the tall spiked fence railings that marked the school boundary. Annalie headed for a section furthest from the streetlights, where no one would see them climbing over.

She gave Essie a boost over, then hooked her suitcase over the top of the railing, pulled herself up, clambered over to the other side, unhooked her suitcase, and dropped down into the quiet street. No one was about; it was very early and the streets were empty and silent.

Annalie looked around, trying to get her bearings. It felt strange to be on the wrong side of the railings;

although the girls were allowed to leave the school grounds (under certain strict conditions), Annalie had not yet ventured out, so this was the first time she'd been out on the streets of Pallas since she arrived.

"Now what?" asked Essie.

"We need to get to the railway station," Annalie said, knowing perfectly well that she didn't know how to find her way back there.

"That's easy," Essie said. She accessed her retinal display and her headpiece discoed; she had directions. "It's this way."

As they walked, they began to see the first stirrings of the city coming to life. Late-night revelers stumbled along, or bowled past in pedicabs or electric taxis; there were vans and carts carrying fruit, vegetables, meat, and produce to markets and shops; people in overalls emerged with brooms to sweep the streets clean. Police patrolled too, and Annalie walked past them with her pulse beating in her head, fearful of being stopped, but no one did.

Cafés started to open, bakeries too; she caught delicious wafts of bread and bacon and coffee, and her stomach began to rumble.

"Shall we get something?" Essie asked, looking longingly into a bakery window.

"Let's get to the station first," Annalie said.

"Come on, I'm starving," Essie said, overruling her. She ducked in and emerged with croissants, warm from the oven.

It was after six when they arrived at the main railway station. Here, the business of the day was already beginning: the grilles over doors and shops and ticket counters clanking up, travelers arriving laden with luggage. Lines were forming outside coffee stalls. Annalie joined a group of people trying to make sense of the timetables.

If you needed to travel cross-country, most people took the train, although there was more than one kind of train to choose from. There were very fast trains that could fly you luxuriously across the country in a matter of hours, zooming through tunnels and along elevated tracks, the countryside whipping past in an air-conditioned blur. These were the trains Essie always took. Then there were the other trains, the ones that traveled on the old lines and stopped at every station, fussing and sighing and sometimes stopping in the middle of nowhere for no reason that was ever announced. (Annalie had taken one of these trains when she came to school.) There were express services on the old lines too; they were cheap and fast, but not very comfortable.

"We should take the fast train," Essie said. "They're great—they have movies and cafés and shops—"

"Oh no, it's way too expensive," Annalie said.

"It can't be that expensive," Essie began, using her shell to look up the ticket prices. "Oh. That can't be right, can it?"

"Here, we'll try and get on that one." Annalie pointed: one of the cheap express services was leaving for Port Fine in less than half an hour. They hurried over to the ticket counter, bought tickets, and made their way through the maze of the station to the platform.

It was already busy with yawning workers, eager travelers, laborers, sailors, craftspeople. There were even a few Admiralty uniforms scattered among the crowd.

The train pulled in, a long chain of clanking metal boxes, with glassless grilles instead of windows and stern injunctions warning people not to ride on top of the carriages. The other passengers started surging on but Essie didn't move. "Are you serious?"

"We won't be on it for long," said Annalie. "Come on, or we won't get a spot."

There were no seats inside the carriages and the passengers competed to find room for themselves and their boxes, bags, and equipment. One man fought his way onto the train with a pedicab that barely fit through the door; another hauled cages filled with ducks. Annalie found them a spot to stand near a window, made sure she had something to hang onto, and then stuck there, glaring malevolently at anyone who tried to push them out of the way. The carriage grew fuller and fuller; there were angry words exchanged in the doorways; on the platform, a whistle blew. Then, with a lurch, the train pulled out of the station.

They clanked slowly through rail yards filled with sheds and freight trains. They passed under a bridge and heard a series of thuds and clatters overhead. Essie gave a little shriek. "What was that?" she asked.

"People who can't afford the fares jump onto the outside of the trains and ride on the roof."

Essie looked appalled. "Isn't that dangerous?"

"Yep," Annalie said.

The girls gazed out the window, watching as the unlovely backs of buildings whizzed by. The train was fast, and noisy, and every time it went around a corner the whole carriage bucked, and everyone staggered and fell over.

Annalie remembered the first (and only) time she'd taken this trip. Then, sitting beside Spinner on an old slow-moving train, she'd been both nervous and eager. Spinner had been full of encouragement about all the great things she'd be able to see and learn and do at school. He'd talked about museums and art galleries and symphony orchestras, science labs and libraries filled with great books and the world's knowledge. "You're going to love it," he'd said, smiling in eager anticipation. It had been their last day together. She wondered if she was ever going to see him again.

The train roared and rattled through industrial areas, past shops and houses, and then out into the country. It raced through farmland, past vast rows of wind turbines and the nuclear power station that fed the city. It roared through smaller towns without stopping, some of them living towns, others abandoned for no obvious reason.

The trip took nearly two hours (traveling the other way, it had taken six). The lurching, bone-jarring journey took its toll; Essie, tired by the early start, had to sit down after the first half hour, scrunched up next to her bag. Annalie soon sat down beside her, and unable to see out the window, she began to

69

feel a bit travel-sick (to her own disgust—she never suffered from seasickness).

At last, the train's breakneck pace started to slow. The people in the carriage seemed to wake from their traveling daze and look out the windows. There was an outbreak of noise overhead, and Essie and Annalie scrambled to their feet, struggling against pins and needles, to look out the window. People were dropping off the tops and sides of the carriages and hurrying off out of sight. Annalie knew people were forever getting hit by trains and hurt on the tracks here, but it didn't seem to stop them.

The train was moving through the new part of Port Fine. "So is this where you live?" Essie asked, watching the townscape go by. "It's actually sort of nice."

"This is the nice part," Annalie said. "It isn't where I live."

The train pulled into the station and the girls emerged with all the other passengers into the chaos of the morning. Annalie shook herself, surprised by how relieved she felt to be here.

She whipped her shell out and sent Janky a message: *Tell Will I'm home.*

Lowtown

Essie and Annalie walked through the streets of Port Fine. Essie wasn't used to walking long distances and her feet were soon aching, but she didn't want to complain in front of Annalie, who had the look of someone who'd happily walk all day.

Port Fine was a smaller city than Pallas, but it also felt more chaotic, the streets choked with traffic. Everything here seemed very new, as if the buildings had been put up quickly and cheaply, with no attention paid to decoration. There were no green spaces and no trees, although a few shopping strips cheered things up, and the people seemed busy and prosperous.

People do go on about the slums, Essie thought, feeling rather superior, *but they're really not that bad.*

After they'd been walking for about three quarters of an hour they reached a quite distinct line. The line was a busy road. On the side where they were standing, the streets were smoothly paved, there were streetlights, and all the shops and houses and businesses had power. On the other side was a very different kind of town.

Annalie checked this way, that way, and then darted out into the traffic. Essie scurried in her wake.

"This is where I live," Annalie said with a grin when they reached the other side.

"I never thought it would be so…abrupt," Essie said.

"The emergency government drew a line on a map. Everything on this side was abandoned."

Their progress grew slower now. The roads here were potholed and eroded. In places they had vanished entirely, collapsing into the holes left by damaged infrastructure (burst drains, abandoned metro tunnels) underneath. There were still shops and houses and businesses, but they didn't have centralized power. Wind turbines and solar panels bristled from roofs, wrapped in razor wire to protect them from theft. For every building that was occupied, there were two or three more sliding into dereliction, stripped of everything salable, from taps and doors to electrical wiring, leaving only the rotting shell behind. And even after all this time, you could still see the murky tidemark left by the Flood.

This part of town was just as busy as the new part. There were no electric cars or trucks here; pedicabs—push-bikes with two-wheeled carriages hooked on the back, propelled by wiry men with enormous leg muscles—and handcarts moved people and goods back and forth over rickety-looking boards that covered the worst of the holes. Everywhere, there were things for sale: little stalls sold old clothes, second-hand kitchen implements, reconditioned toys, and lots and lots of outdated tech. People cooked over braziers by the side of the road. Tea was doled out from little carts.

After they had walked another twenty minutes, people started to recognize Annalie.

A woman standing in an empty lot with two goats called out to them. "What you doing back here, girl? Aren't you meant to be at school?"

A few minutes later, a boy on a pedicab cruised past. "Hey Annalie, they kick you out already?"

By now Essie's feet were killing her and she was sure she was getting a blister. "Is it much further?" she asked.

"We're nearly there."

They walked on, and soon they came to what looked to Essie like an old tin shed.

Annalie hurried toward it, a look of fierce excitement on her face. But then they stepped inside.

"Oh no..." Annalie whispered.

The place looked like a bomb had gone off inside it.

Footsteps crunched over broken things, and they saw a dark shape loom up from the back of the shop.

"What are you doing here?"

Bike boy

"I thought you were going to stay at school."

A boy stepped into the light that filtered down from a skylight overhead. He was not overly tall for his age, with a square face and a pugnacious air and the same dark eyes as his sister.

"I had to come and see things for myself," said Annalie.

Will flicked a look at Essie. "Who's this?"

"My friend, Essie." Then she said to Essie, "This is my twin brother, Will."

"Hi," Essie said. "I've never met someone's twin before."

"Uh-huh," Will said, barely acknowledging her before turning back to Annalie. "I told you, I've got everything under control. What're you doing here?"

"I thought about it, and I think I need to be here," Annalie said, with a trace of impatience.

"Does your school know you're here?"

"They've probably noticed we're missing by now," Essie said, exchanging a smile with Annalie, although privately she felt a little sting of anxiety. This was the naughtiest thing she'd ever done, although that wasn't saying very much.

"Won't you get in trouble for running away?" Will said. "Or, what do they call it, going AWOL?"

"Probably," Annalie said. "But this seemed more important."

There was something combative about the way that Will spoke to Annalie that set Essie on edge. She had no brothers or sisters of her own, so she had no real point of reference, but she'd half-expected them to seem pleased to see each other after nearly a term apart. In fact, Will seemed more than a little annoyed to find Annalie here. Not that Annalie was rushing to give her brother a welcoming hug either. Essie wasn't sure what to make of it.

"Did you find out any more from Graham?" Annalie asked.

"Nah, it's pointless. He doesn't know anything."

Annalie narrowed her eyes skeptically, then gave a whistling call. After a moment they heard a rustle of wings and Graham came flying in.

"Allie! Allie! You came back!" squawked the parrot. He landed on her shoulder and began rubbing her face ecstatically with his beak.

"It's good to see you too, Graham. Hey listen, we need to try and find Spinner."

"Spinner lost," Graham said mournfully.

"I know. But you were with him, right, when Spinner got lost?"

Graham squawked affirmatively.

"Where did he take you?"

"I've been through all this," Will said. "He said they went to a noisy house and there was a cat."

"How did you get to the noisy house, Graham? Did you walk?"

"Bike boy took," Graham said.

"You mean Truman? The man who drives the pedicab?"

"Bike boy," Graham agreed, bobbing.

"You never told me that," Will said huffily.

Graham whistled at him rudely.

Annalie turned to her brother. "We need to find Truman."

The noisy house

Truman lived with his old dad in half a house not far from Spinner's workshop. Annalie didn't really expect to find Truman at home when they went and knocked on his door—he worked long hours on his pedicab, mostly on the new side of town.

Truman's dad, who was known as Old Truman, opened the door. It took him a moment to recognize them, but when he did his eyes widened and he beckoned the three of them urgently inside. Annalie had never been inside the house before. It smelled of salt and mildew.

"You shouldn't have come back here," Old Truman told her. "It's not safe for you."

"Why not?" asked Annalie.

"Didn't you hear? They come for your dad."

"That's why I came back. We have to find him."

"You won't," Old Truman said decisively. "Better get yourself on back to school, quick smart."

"But I can't," Annalie said. "The people who are after Dad came after me too. I'm not safe at school now."

Old Truman frowned at this.

"Truman came round to warn me and Dad and help him get away," Will explained. "We just want to know where they went next."

"You'd have to ask him that," Old Truman said, "but you can't."

"Why not?"

"He's gone away for a while."

"Gone where? For how long?"

"Couldn't rightly say," Old Truman said.

Annalie tried to read him. "He's gone until the heat dies down?"

Old Truman tilted his head, as if the answer was yes but he didn't want to say so directly.

"If you know anything, anything at all, please tell us," Annalie said. "We just want to find Spinner."

"Now, don't take this the wrong way," Old Truman said, "but it sounds to me like your daddy's in a whole lot of trouble, and the last thing he needs to be worrying about is you two kids. If you want to help him, the very best thing you can do is go back to that school of yours and make *them* take care of you."

"But—" Annalie began.

"You're Admiralty now," Old Truman said. "You passed their test, you're one of theirs. That can be a bad thing, but it can also be good. Make them protect you. They can do it. Because no one else can."

"I'm not Admiralty!" Annalie protested.

Will gave a little skeptical snort beside her.

"Isn't that what your daddy wanted for you?" Old Truman said. "Be careful picking sides, girlie. Some choices, once they're made, they can never be unmade."

78

It was the same argument Spinner had made; disturbed, Annalie fell silent.

"I don't have a fancy school to go to," Will said. "What should I do?"

"Do what your father told you to do. Keep your head down and don't be an idiot," Old Truman said.

"Can you at least tell us where the noisy house is?"

Old Truman looked baffled. "The noisy house?"

"Dad's parrot said that's where they went."

Old Truman could see how determined she was. He sighed, then said, "I don't hear so good anymore. I don't like going to noisy places. The Crown and Anchor for example—that's a very noisy house. I never go anywhere near it."

The Crown and Anchor was a pub in the Eddy with a fairly alarming reputation. "Thank you, Mr. Truman!" Annalie said, already turning for the door.

"Think about what I said," Old Truman called after her. "Your daddy may not thank you for coming after him. Go back to school while you still can."

"I'll think about it," she said, bursting out into the sunlight and immediately dismissing the advice.

"The Crown and Anchor?" asked Will.

"You got it," said Annalie.

At the Crown and Anchor

The Crown and Anchor was an old sailor's pub with a rough reputation. It had tiled floors and tiled walls, so that every day after closing they could hose away all the spilt beer.

Even at eleven o'clock in the morning the crowd in there was loud and rough. Annalie and Will stood outside the door and argued.

"Leave this one to me," Will said.

"I'm coming too," Annalie said.

"This is no place for a girl."

"No place for a boy either."

Will scowled at Annalie; Annalie glared back. Really she would rather not go in; but if the answers they needed were in there, then she had no choice.

Essie intervened. "Either we all go in, or none of us do. Safety in numbers."

This broke the deadlock. "Okay," Annalie said. "You take the left side, Will. We'll take the right."

She pushed open the door and walked in, Essie so close behind her she was almost treading on her heels.

The room smelled strongly of beer and tobacco smoke and man-sweat, and the voices had that loud, loose, raucous sound that signalled danger, even as they laughed. Heads turned to look at the girls as they moved deeper into the room.

"What have we here?"

"Looking for someone, little girl?"

Although Annalie's knees were shaking, she ignored them and kept walking toward the bar.

The man behind her end of the bar was covered in tattoos that wound up his arms, under his shirt-sleeves, and emerged onto his face, giving his skin a murky cast. He glanced her way as he moved back and forth pouring beers—it was a busy morning—and said, "You shouldn't be in here."

"I was hoping you could help me," Annalie said.

"I'll help you, love," a man standing at the bar said, and his friends chortled.

"I'm trying to find my dad. Spinner. Do you know him?"

"Never heard of him," the bartender said automatically.

"He moors his boat here in the Eddy. The *Sunfish*."

"The *Sunfish*?" repeated someone.

Annalie turned to the man eagerly. "Yes. Do you know him?"

The man's eyes were bloodshot as he stared at Annalie. "Nope." He laughed, as if this was absolutely hilarious.

Annalie turned back to the bartender, growing desperate. "My dad was in here a few nights ago, with Truman the pedicab rider. He had a parrot with him—it got chased by your cat. Don't you remember him?"

"I don't work nights," the bartender said flatly. "Now piss off."

"Please—" Annalie said, but then she felt a hand grip her arm.

"You heard the man. Time to piss off." An unfriendly looking man was glaring at her, his hand gripping her arm so tightly there was no hope of escape. Her eyes took in his fancy waistcoat, his crumpled hat, the colors he was wearing threaded around his arm. He was from the Kang brotherhood. Her heart began to pound with fear. "Come out the back way," he said.

His other hand had a grip on Essie. He escorted them both, frightened and protesting, through the door that led out to the back bar and into the dingy bistro. She tried to catch Will's eye, but couldn't see him through the crowd.

When they were alone in the empty bistro, the man turned her to face him. "Don't you know better than to go broadcasting your business in a public bar?" he hissed.

Annalie stared at him, afraid of what he might be about to do.

"The Admiralty are looking for him, they've impounded his boat. You don't just go shouting about it in front of a bar full of drunks. You don't know who could be listening."

Belatedly, it dawned on Annalie that this man might actually be trying to help her. "Do you—do you know my dad?"

"Yes, I do."

"Do you know where I can find him?"

"Yes."

"Well, are you going to tell me?"

"Nope."

"Why not?"

"For one thing, there's no way for you to get there. For another, it's too dangerous."

"Where's he gone?"

"The Moon Islands."

The Moon Islands were a huge archipelago that stretched over many thousands of nautical miles. No one was quite sure how they'd got their name; some said it was because when you looked at the shape they made on a map it looked a little like a crescent moon; others said it was because to the early explorers, the islands seemed as remote as the moon. There were hundreds, possibly even thousands of islands in the region, which was home to all kinds of strange, scary, and desperate people, from pirates and slavers to religious fanatics. It was also far less homogeneous than its name suggested. Before the Flood, the region had been made up of many sovereign island nations. The Flood had put an end to many of them.

"Can you help us get there?"

He shook his head with a slow smile. "Absolutely not."

"But you helped him—"

"Let's get something clear, sister. We helped him because he paid us. And it cost him dear. Unless you've got a whole lot of lucre stashed away somewhere too, you're not going anywhere."

"But I have to find him."

"The Moon Islands are no place for kids. Stay out of it. When the heat comes off your dad, maybe he'll be back. Or maybe he'll send for you, who knows? But in the meantime, my advice to you is, don't go looking for trouble. All right?"

"All right," Annalie said reluctantly.

The door to the bistro banged open and Will barged through it, looking panicked.

"What are you doing to my sister?" he roared, although his voice squeaked a little.

The Kang man looked at him impassively. "If she's your sister, you might want to start taking better care of her," he said.

"It's all right, Will," Annalie said. "He's trying to help us."

"Let's get one thing straight," the Kang man said. "I haven't helped you. I'm not even talking to you. I don't know you, and I never saw you, and you never saw me."

"Of course," Annalie said. "Sorry."

"From now on, keep your mouth shut. About everything and everyone. No one saw nothing, no one told you nothing. There is only nothing."

"There is only nothing," Annalie said, nodding.

"Cos if the Admiralty even start sniffing in my direction, I'm going to hunt you down and I'm going to cut you," he said, pleasantly, but with perfect seriousness. "All of you."

"Okay," said Annalie.

"Good girl. Now piss off."

Pursued

Will, Annalie, and Essie stepped once more into the seaweed stink of the Eddy.

"Spinner's gone to the Moon Islands," Annalie said. "He paid the Kangs to take him there."

Will's shoulders sagged a little at this news. "You mean he's already gone?" He'd been hoping that Spinner might still be somewhere nearby, and that he might shortly reappear, grinning, ready to fix everything. But if he'd already shipped out, there was little chance of that.

"Looks that way," Annalie said. "But why the Moon Islands?"

"It's a great place to hide out."

They tramped along in silence for a while, mulling it over. Then Annalie remembered something. "Uncle Art lives in the Moon Islands. Maybe that's where he's gone."

Art was one of Spinner's dearest friends. He lived with his family in a rambling old house with views over the sea, on an island called Little Lang Lang (it was between Big Lang Lang and Old Lang Lang). Will and Annalie had spent many summers there, swimming with Art's kids, exploring caves, and hunting for treasure.

"Hey yeah," Will said. "I bet that's where he's gone. Art would help him hide out for sure."

They walked on in silence for a while.

"He's in big trouble, isn't he?" Will said.

"Beckett was talking about jail time."

"But if he's innocent—"

"He'd have to be able to prove it."

"And if he could prove it, he wouldn't have had to run away," Will finished gloomily.

Back at the workshop, they cleared away some of the mess littering the kitchen. By now it was getting on for lunchtime, and everyone was hungry.

"Was that an *actual* Kang?" Essie asked Annalie in a low voice, not wanting to seem ignorant in front of Will.

"Yeah," Annalie said.

"So . . . does that mean you really *do* know gangsters?"

"No."

"But your dad does?"

"I didn't think so, until now," Annalie said, sounding a little testy. She was still a little sensitive about the suggestion that she and her family might actually be gangsters, even though she knew Essie didn't really think that.

They managed to assemble a lunch out of what

the Admiralty henchmen hadn't strewn across the floor, and the four of them—Will, Annalie, Essie, and Graham—sat down to eat together.

"So I guess you girls'll be heading back this afternoon," Will said, when he'd satisfied the worst of his hunger.

"Why do you say that?"

"Well, we know where Spinner's gone now, so job done," Will said.

"Well, not really," Annalie said.

"He's gone to the Moon Islands to lie low for a while. What more do you want to know?"

"I want to know why the Admiralty are trying to arrest him, for a start!" Annalie cried.

"Don't reckon we'll be getting answers to that anytime soon."

"But isn't it driving you crazy?" Annalie asked. "Don't you want to know too?"

"Of course I do," Will said. "But it's pretty obvious Spinner didn't want to tell us."

"Someone must know something," Annalie said.

"I've been asking around," Will said. "If anyone knows, they're not talking."

"Maybe if *I* tried—"

"Annalie," Will said, "I asked, okay? No one knows anything." He paused, studying her. "Don't you want to go back to school or something?"

Annalie fiddled with her water glass.

"You *do* want to go back, don't you?" Essie said.

"I thought you loved it there," Will said, looking at her searchingly.

"Love is a strong word," Annalie said, with a dry little laugh, but before either of them could probe any further, Graham let out an ear-splitting squawk.

Annalie jumped. "What is it, Graham?"

"Black car," Graham said.

His sharp hearing had picked up the rumble of an electric engine; now, they heard it too.

"They're coming back!" Will said.

"How do they know we're here?" Annalie asked.

"Maybe someone's watching the place," Will said.

Essie had a terrible thought. "Give me your shell, quick!"

Annalie handed it to her, and Essie quickly powered it down, then switched off her own shell too. Her headpiece went dark. "If you're on the network, they can use it to track you down."

Will and Annalie looked at each other in dismay. That would never have occurred to either of them.

"We've got to get out of here," Annalie said.

"But where can we go?" asked Essie.

"It's best if we split up," Will said to Annalie. "You take her, I'll lead them away."

"Don't do that, just get away!" Annalie cried, exasperated.

"All right fine. Meet you at the Eddy, okay?"

"Why there?" Annalie asked suspiciously.

"Don't argue, just go!"

The two girls got up and grabbed their bags. "We'll go out the back way. And Will—don't do anything stupid, okay?"

"Never," laughed Will.

The girls hurried out the back door. Left alone, Will began hastily gathering provisions, jamming them into an old army kit bag along with a few useful-looking tools that had been left behind in the workshop. The car was getting closer—he could hear the engine growl as it bumped its way up the street and stopped right out front.

Doors slammed—one, two, three, four. So there were at least four of them. Will crept backwards from the workshop into the living room, careful not to trip over the ankle-turning mess. Escaping through the front door was impossible—he would have to follow the girls out the back way. Behind the workshop was a vegetable garden, backed by a rusting corrugated-iron fence. Over the fence was a maze of houses, some inhabited, some not.

The front door of the workshop creaked, and he heard the first footsteps. No one had spoken a word. Hardly daring to breathe, he crept toward the back door—and then heard a clatter from the side of the house. Someone had tripped over the ladder. That meant they were coming round the back to cut him off.

There was nowhere to go but up.

Will darted toward the stairs and climbed up them, Graham flying ahead of him. He looked around for a hiding place, knowing already that there weren't any. Downstairs he could hear them poking around, looking into cupboards.

"Workshop clear," someone called.

"Kitchen clear," said a second voice.

He heard someone else call, more distantly, "No one here either." They had checked the washhouse too.

There was only one more place to look. He heard the sound of feet coming up the stairs—not so stealthy now. Will dived under the ruins of the mattress, hoping they wouldn't search too thoroughly.

The feet stopped at the door. There was a silence as someone searched the room. Will held his breath. The feet began to move on—then stopped and came back. Will's heart was beating so fast he thought it was going to explode out of his chest. The feet came into the room, toward his hiding place—

"Argh!" The man cried out in surprise as a squawking, flapping parrot came at him.

"What's going on up there?" someone shouted from below.

Will grabbed his chance. He pushed the mattress off himself so it flopped between him and the man, who was still angrily trying to fend off Graham. The man was huge and dark, dressed in a leather jacket, and seemed to fill the doorway.

"You! Stay right where you are!" the man shouted.

Will threw open the sash window and tossed the kitbag out onto the roof of the washhouse, jumping out after it.

"He's here!" the man roared.

The washhouse roof buckled under Will's feet and he feared he was going to go right through it, but somehow it held. The kitbag slid along the tin and dropped off the end, and he followed it, landing on the ground hard, jarring his ankles.

Will glanced back and saw the big man trying to follow him out the window. "Quick—out the back—after him!" the man called.

The men ran out the back door, but Will had a head start. He tossed the kitbag over the top of the fence and squeezed through a gap where the two sheets had come apart. He darted into the back of the house that lay directly behind the workshop—it was empty, its floor half-rotted away, but he knew where it was safe to walk. He scampered through, avoiding the holes and pitfalls, and slipped out the side door. He stopped to listen for a moment. The men had made it through the fence and were following him into the house. A crash and a cry told him one of them had discovered the state of the floors the hard way.

He crept through the hole in the next fence and began threading through the backyards: the one with the rusty swing set, the one with the swimming pool full of stinky green water, the one with the chickens. When he reached the one with the chickens, he stopped again and listened.

"Are they still coming?" he whispered to Graham. Graham took off and did some aerial reconnaissance.

"Look! It's that damn bird!" someone shouted.

"Guess they still are," Will said. He hurried through the muck of the chicken pen, went over to the fence, and pressed the sole of his mucky sneaker on the fence to make it look as if he'd climbed over. Then he scooped up a handful of rocks from the ground and began to pitch them at the chickens.

"Bad Will!" Graham said disapprovingly.

The chickens began squawking, as he'd known they would. He slipped up the side of the house and dived into the bushes to hide.

The men came vaulting over the fence into the backyard.

"Can you see him?"

"Which way did he go?"

"Look—there!"

He heard them climbing the fence into the next backyard. They'd taken the bait. Will slipped out of the bushes and into the street. For a moment he heard nothing, and then there was a growl, followed by a frenzy of barking and shouting and then, horrifyingly, shots were fired. Will kept running, afraid of what he might have done. The backyard next to the chickens held a huge market garden guarded by several ferocious dogs—that's why he'd sent his pursuers in there. He hadn't been expecting guns. He wondered if they belonged to the men who'd been chasing him or the people who kept the garden.

There were no further sounds of pursuit and he hoped that meant that he'd lost them. He crossed the street and slowed to a walk, his heart thudding in his chest. But then he heard the sudden roar of an engine, and threw himself off the footpath into some overgrown shrubbery just as the black car came screeching round the corner. It did a lap of the street, lurching in the massive potholes. Men—bloody but alive—came staggering out from the house with the dogs. The car stopped for them and as they clambered in, the big man himself got out of the passenger seat and scanned the street, his eyes like laser beams. Will shrank down as small as he could behind the bush, fearing that those eyes would discover his hiding place. But the man's gaze traveled on without detecting him, and after a moment, he dropped back into the car and it disappeared up the street.

The Admiralty oath

Safe at the Eddy, Annalie and Essie waited on a quiet back step for Will to arrive.

"He should be here by now," Annalie fretted.

"I'm sure he'll be fine," Essie said.

"You don't know my brother," said Annalie. "He won't have just snuck away and gone a different way from us. He always has to do something smart that'll get him into trouble."

Essie felt the flicker of anxiety. "But neither of you have done anything wrong. Why would *you* get into trouble?"

"What do you think's going to happen to us if they catch us? Our mother's dead, our dad's on the run. They'll probably try and put us in a home. Or worse."

"They might try and send you back to school," Essie joked.

"Maybe," Annalie said. "I just don't trust that Beckett guy. I don't know what he'll do if he catches me again."

"He's not going to do anything bad to you!" Essie said. "He's Admiralty!"

Annalie gave Essie an ironic look. "And?"

"They're the good guys!" Essie said. She quoted the oath that they recited every morning: "*We live to serve upon the sea, upon the land and shore. For order and prosperity we'll fight forever more. We have no fear of water, of tempest, and of wave. The Admiralty protects us all with power strong to save.*"

Essie had grown up on stories of the brave men and women of the Admiralty who'd saved the world from chaos after the Flood. They'd rescued people from floodwaters, brought supplies to the starving, scooped countless refugees from brimming oceans and half-submerged cities. Only the Admiralty had had the ships, the personnel, and the discipline required to hold the world together. It had just made sense for them to form government—after all, no civilian government could rule *without* their support. She knew some people said the crisis had passed and the military ought to get out of government. But even today, the world was still a wild and dangerous place; the ships of the Admiralty were still needed.

"You know that's not actually true, right?" Annalie said. "The bit about protecting us all."

"What do you mean?"

"They don't protect anyone who lives here, for a start," Annalie said, gesturing about her at the Eddy.

"Yes, but—"

"But they're gangsters and illegals and they don't count?" Annalie said challengingly. Then she relented. "You're used to being on the inside. But you're on the outside now. And things are different here."

Essie's thoughts were still scrambling to keep up. She believed in the Admiralty with all her heart: their mission, the great work they'd done and were still doing every day. Work she would do herself one day (although right now she couldn't imagine what that would be). What was Annalie even doing at Triumph if she didn't believe in it too? But she only had to look around her to know that the world Annalie lived in was not at all like her own. So she said nothing.

Annalie looked up and down the street, her brow furrowed. "What on earth is keeping Will?"

Liberated

"Nice save, bird," Will said.

Graham croaked modestly, then gave him a crafty look. "Graham biscuit?"

"Yeah, why not?"

Luckily, he'd remembered to pack the biscuits, although they were now a little smashed. Graham accepted two halves and began nibbling them, holding them in a knobbly but delicate claw, while Will thought about his next move.

It was clear to him now that the Admiralty weren't giving up. They would do whatever was needed to get to Spinner—and that meant lying low was not going to be enough. He needed to get away. And to do that, he needed the boat.

Will knew the neighbors kept an old bicycle near their hen house. They used it to carry eggs and caged chickens to market. He felt a bit bad about taking it, but it would take him ages to get to the port on foot. He sneaked back into the yard, thought about leaving a note, remembered he didn't have any paper, gave up on that idea, and set off.

He was almost killed half a dozen times as he

pedalled furiously through the crowded streets of Lowtown, then hit the more mechanized traffic of the new town. At last he reached the port district, and began pedalling toward the shipyard, where Admiralty ships took on supplies or performed repairs. This was also where they kept impounded boats. Will pedalled around a curve, and suddenly there it was: huge, fenced, and guarded.

An Admiralty patrol class vessel was in port, taking on supplies. Cases were already lined up on the dock, and there were more supply vans arriving all the time. The guards on the gate stopped every van that came in and out, but maybe there was a way to sneak in on one of them...

He watched for a while, then decided to ride on and see what else he could discover.

He followed the fence past large administrative buildings, the dry dock—currently unoccupied—and beyond it, at the far end, were the impounded boats.

Four boats were moored there. One was the *Sunfish*.

Will's heart leaped with joy as he jumped off the bike and raced up to the fence for a look. It was hard to tell from a distance, but the boat didn't seem to be too badly damaged. He wondered what they'd done to disable it, and how difficult it would be to fix.

"The only question now," he said to Graham, "is how to get in."

"Fly?" Graham suggested, with a birdy titter.

The shipyard was surrounded by a chain-link fence. It was high, and there was barbed wire at the top, but it didn't look all that sturdy. Will waited, watching, to see if there were any guards on patrol. After ten minutes, a guard came by, walked the perimeter, then turned and walked back again.

"If I cut a little hole in the fence, I reckon I could get to the boat without anyone seeing me," Will suggested.

Graham made a noise that could have meant anything, but probably *didn't* mean "great idea!"

"Let's go and see what's at the end of the fence," Will said.

He rode along the length of the fence until it came to a rocky point surrounded by water. Where the land ended, a line of spikes stuck out from the fence preventing anyone from climbing past. It was emblazoned with warning signs:

Admiralty Property
Strictly No Admittance
Trespassers Will Be Prosecuted
Danger! Underwater Security Devices
No Swimming, Fishing, or Recreational Boating

Will read these thoughtfully. "What do you suppose the underwater security devices are?"

"Sharks?" Graham said.

"I reckon it'd be easy enough to swim round the point."

"Hate wet," Graham warned.

"*You* don't have to swim," Will said.

He left the bike, grabbed his kitbag, and picked his way over the rocks until he reached the very edge of the point. There was a gap between the large spikes, so he reached through and tossed the kitbag as far round as he could reach onto the Admiralty side. Then he climbed down to the water and jumped in.

The water was cold and his clothes filled instantly, hampering his movements. A current was flowing fast past the point, and he found himself being swept away from the fence and back toward the hazardous waters of the old port. He began to swim determinedly, battling the current until finally he came to land on the Admiralty side of the fence. Wet and gasping, he scrambled ashore and collected the kitbag, then began to pick his way cautiously across the rocks, expecting at any moment that someone might come out and arrest him, but still he saw no one. When he reached the path where the guard did his rounds, he scampered, crouching, toward the berthed boat.

This is too easy, he thought as he slipped in between the boats to where the *Sunfish* was moored. He swung the kitbag across the gap and onto the deck, and then stepped on board after it. Here on deck at least, everything looked mostly untouched. Some of the hatches and compartments were open or unlatched, but there was none of the wholesale destruction he'd seen back at the workshop. He wondered what he'd find below decks.

What had they done to disable the ship? The masts were intact and so were the sails. A quick glance showed him that the mechanisms for moving and setting the sails were all in place. He checked the wheel and saw everything shipshape here too: nothing damaged, nothing missing.

He looked again for guards. There was no one around. No one keeping an eye on the impounded boats. *What would happen*, he thought, *if I just took it?*

He stepped back out on deck and began to cast off the ropes, looking around. Still no one coming. But then he noticed something he hadn't noticed before: in the distance, in front of the administrative buildings, there was a lookout tower. And out on the tower, guards patrolled with binoculars.

He hurried to cast off the second rope. He didn't think the guards had seen him yet. But at any moment they might.

Free of its ropes, the boat began to drift and bump.

Will took the wheel. Although the boat traveled largely under sail, it had a little engine that was used for maneuvering in and out of port, getting about if the wind died down, and generally getting out of tight spots—like the one he was in now. Will pressed the start button, and to his absolute joy, the engine turned over and started to spin.

With one last look around, he opened the throttle and set the boat in motion. The engine roared, the water churned, and the boat began to move. Will steered it forward, trying to keep clear of the boats on either side, but there was something oddly sluggish about the steering. He was correcting the heading, but the boat wasn't responding. With a heavy clunk it clipped the boat on his starboard side, and that collision drove it to port, where it clipped another boat.

That's when Will realized what they'd done to disable the boat. They'd disconnected the steering.

At the same moment, he heard a siren wail across the water. He looked up at the lookout tower and saw sailors up there with binoculars trained on him. They had spotted him.

There was no time to try and fix the steering. The only thing he could do now was keep going.

The boat was still moving forward but he could feel it getting buffeted by the current that flowed around the point. If the boat turned broadside he was in trouble. Worse, its present heading would take it out into the wide bay of the port and the busy shipping lanes, where he risked being caught, or simply mown down by another vessel. He needed to turn the boat—but how?

On the port side he could see sailors scrambling to a pursuit ship, getting ready to intercept. Their boat was fast, light, maneuverable, and powerful. All too soon, they'd be upon him—unless he could think of something.

An idea came to him. He checked his instruments—*wind direction favorable*. Quick as he could, he throttled back the engine and darted out to unfurl a sail and haul it up. The sail flew up—the wind caught it—it filled—and the boat began to turn. Dragged on the wind, the boat began to shift to starboard until they were caught by the current that was moving fast out of the port, round the point, and on into the waters that led to the slums and the Eddy.

Will pushed the engine to full throttle and the boat seemed to leap forward in the water. It was a surprisingly powerful engine when you really opened it up. The only problem was, it drained the battery quite fast, so you couldn't use it for long. Will just hoped it had enough juice to get him where he was going.

He motored along for a while, hugging the shore as closely as he dared. He could not outrun the Admiralty pursuit vessel, but perhaps he could outfox them.

The water he was driving into now, which lay south of the new port, was filled with hazards to shipping. The rocky point he had just cleared marked the end of the new territory, the end of the shipping channel which had been cleared of old wreckage. Beyond lay the remains of the old drowned container yards, with their massive gantries, ship carcasses, and rusting shipping containers; and further south, the ghostly ruins of beachfront hotels and luxury apartment blocks, their expensive ocean views now lapping through their rotting windows, barnacles clustering on their balcony railings.

The water here was immensely dangerous, and for that reason, regular shipping never went anywhere near it; but of course, that didn't mean no one went into it. The waters off the slums were full of boats carrying cargo that couldn't go through the main port with its tax collectors and customs inspectors. Spinner wasn't in the business of smuggling or moving contraband about, but he knew the secret ways in and out, and Will had traveled them with him.

Of course, he had never actually done the steering. And in this case, he didn't *have* any steering.

He was traveling as slowly as he dared now, keeping an eye out for telltale choppy or white water that would signal something lying just below the surface—not that there was much he could do if he saw any. He knew that if he could just get across this first stretch of open water, across the top of the old dockyards, he would reach the first of the drowned beachfront hotels, its distinctive stepped-down silhouette still jutting above the waterline, hide there in the maze of old buildings and do something about the steering. Then he could get back to the Eddy, and find Annalie.

The roar of an engine reached him. Glancing back over his shoulder, he saw the pursuit ship round the point.

There was no help for it. Will opened up the throttle again and went for it. The *Sunfish* leaped forward. Ahead of him, the hotel loomed. He kept on going, knowing there was nothing he could do if something bobbed up in his way. He glanced behind him. The pursuit ship was gaining on him. He looked ahead once again and saw the water seething white directly in his path. He caught his breath in fear, but as he passed over it a wave rolled through and gave him just enough clearance to squeak over whatever it was that lay beneath. He glanced back—the pursuit ship had slowed down a little and was swerving past obstacles.

The hotel was close now: its shadow made the water look dark and sinister. Will pushed the boat as fast as he could for as long as he dared; with no steering, he had no way to adjust his course, and he risked smashing straight into it.

He took one more glance behind him. The pursuit ship was speeding up again, getting ready to come after him. They had followed a slightly different trajectory to Will and he could see they'd managed to drive into a thicket of old pylons and bits of steel sticking up at odd angles, jagged and rusted, with more lying unseen below. They were weaving through the mess, desperate not to lose sight of him.

Will checked his own course—he was still powering toward the gap between the hotel and the next line of buildings just behind it, and he didn't want to risk overshooting. The waves were pushing him in toward the shore. He began to be concerned they would push him too far in and he would miss the gap and smash into the next row of buildings.

Then he heard something crunch, and looking back, he saw the pursuit ship stuck on a projecting spar. It had penetrated right through the side of the boat, holding it fast. The swell dropped away, leaving the boat high and dry, the engine exposed, roaring in the air. They weren't going anywhere.

Hardly daring to believe his luck, Will turned back to watch where he was going. The walls of the hotel loomed up in front of him, the broken windows yawning dark and terrifying. He pushed the engines into reverse; the water boiled around him; the waves slapping between the buildings smacked at the boat; he slowed to a crawl, but still nearly took out her portside on the ragged hotel wall. Gradually, slowly, the *Sunfish* came to a halt in the dank, slimy shadows of the street behind the ruined hotel.

Will switched off the engine and took a deep breath. He'd escaped! Time to reconnect the steering and find his sister.

The boat thief

A harsh squawk made Annalie jump. She looked up, and saw Graham circling down toward her. "About time!" she said, hopping to her feet. "I thought they must've got you for sure. Where's Will?"

"Skeleton Stairs," Graham said.

Annalie stared at him for a moment, then said, "Oh no!" and broke into a flat run. Essie had to scamper to keep up with her.

"What's wrong?" Essie gasped as she ran.

"If he's at the Skeleton Stairs," Annalie said, "it means he's got a boat."

They ran all the way round the Eddy, the full length of the quay, until they reached the very end, where the Skeleton Stairs descended to the water.

There, waiting just offshore, was the *Sunfish*. Standing at the wheel, jiggling with impatience, was Will.

"I got it!" he shouted as soon as he caught sight of them. "I got the boat back!"

"How?" Annalie shouted, pausing at the top of the stairs.

"How do you think?" Will said triumphantly.

Annalie groaned. She started climbing down the green, slimy stairs, as quickly as she dared. When she was at the bottom, she jumped onto the deck. Essie began to descend more cautiously after her, and Graham flew up and perched at the top of the mast.

"You stole the boat?"

"It's not stealing if you already own it."

"Bet the Admiralty aren't going to see it that way," Annalie said.

Will's triumph was turning to irritation. "What would you have done? Leave it there to be burnt or sold? It's not like they were ever going to give it back to us."

"Before this we still had a chance," Annalie said. "But now you've broken into the Admiralty Shipyard and taken an impounded vessel. Now we're criminals too."

Will's face closed. "Not you. Just me."

"Will—"

"None of this has anything to do with you, anyway. You can go back to school. It's like Old Truman said—you're one of theirs now."

"I am *not* one of theirs!" Annalie shouted, fury sparking.

"It's not like you ever cared much about the boat anyway."

"That's not true!"

"You only ever cared about books. The boat was always *my* thing, mine and Spinner's. Now I've got it back, and I'm going to take it to him."

"*That's* your plan?"

"Yep."

"You're going to sail this boat, alone, to the Moon Islands?"

"Yes."

"How are you planning to sleep?"

Will folded his arms. "I'll work something out."

"Do you know how to set the course? Read the charts?"

"Sure."

"Really?"

"How hard can it be?"

"Quite hard, actually," Annalie said. "That's why it was always my job."

Two pairs of dark, determined eyes drilled into each other, neither one willing to back down.

"You can say whatever you like," Will snapped. "I'm going and you can't stop me."

"You won't make it by yourself," Annalie said.

"You think you're so smart, don't you?" Will shouted, pushed beyond endurance. "You always think you know better than me, but you don't. Not about this. I know how to sail this boat and I'm going to the Moon Islands to find Spinner."

Before Annalie could argue any further, an ear-splitting electric squeal interrupted them, and then a voice spoke through a loudhailer. "Attention, unauthorized vessel!"

The voice was coming from above them. Annalie looked up and saw an Admiralty officer and two sailors looking down at them from the top of the stairs. The officer had the loudhailer; the sailors were both armed. "Step away from the wheel and prepare to be boarded!"

Annalie looked at Will, standing at the wheel. Will looked back at her. At once it was quite clear to both of them what was going to happen next.

Annalie leaped for the ropes and cast off, and Will slammed on the engine. Once more, the *Sunfish* leaped forward.

"Switch off your engines now, or we'll fire!" said the voice through the loudhailer.

"They wouldn't shoot at kids, would they?" Annalie said.

Will was too busy steering to answer.

A shot, savagely loud, blasted over their heads, and the children ducked. It didn't seem to hit anything.

"Warning shot," Will guessed.

"Have they got a boat in the water?" Annalie asked. "Can they come after us?"

"They lost one chasing me before. But I'm sure they've got more."

More shots rang out; the bullets whizzed into the water around the rear of the boat, but one or two struck. "I think they're trying to take out the steering," Will said.

"What are we going to do?" said Annalie.

"We're going out the side door," Will said.

Instead of sailing directly for open water, which would have been the quickest way out of the Eddy, Will spun the wheel. The *Sunfish* plunged toward the weedy ruins of the drowned city. There were rat-runs through this labyrinth, secret pathways that would take you safely through the maze and out to sea. Get it right and you avoided the Admiralty and everything that came with them; get it wrong, and you could end up lost, aground.

"Do you know where you're going?" Annalie asked.

"I know what I'm doing!" Will snapped.

Annalie had to trust that he did.

"But I might need you to help us fend off," he added.

Annalie grabbed an oar from a locker and hurried up to the prow to keep an eye out for anything that might loom up in their way.

Will dropped the motor to a low growl and pushed cautiously forwards. The water here was as high as a house above the former street level; they crept between the skeletons of rooftops and the looming necks of streetlights, following the old streets, which in many places were choked with piled debris. These waterways were a maze, but Annalie noticed a dot of colored paint on a corner, and Will turned toward it; other openings had different-colored dots on them; these Will avoided. She realized someone had been through here and marked the way through the maze for those who knew what to look for. Somehow, Will had learned to read what these signs meant.

They were still in the maze when the engine's growl slowed and then stopped. She looked back at Will in dismay.

"Out of juice," he said.

"Now what?"

He squinted up at the sky. It was early afternoon, and the sun was strong, but the battery, they both knew, was slow to charge. "Well, we could wait," he said. "Or we could try and sail out."

"There's not much wind," Annalie said.

"No. Or much room to maneuver."

"But if we stay here we're sitting ducks."

He raised his eyebrows at her. "Then we'd better give it a go then."

He's actually enjoying this, Annalie thought.

Will put the sails up, and they began to tack, carefully. Annalie stood braced at the bow, her oar at the ready. The boat inched forward. Below, she could see fish moving over darker objects beneath. *Weed? Wreckage? Impossible to tell.* The boat surged toward a wall; Will trimmed the sail while Annalie pushed with her oar. The end of the oar skidded off, and the boat kept moving toward the wall, but then at the last minute they corrected course.

Another colored dot on a wall ahead; the boom swung, whistling past Annalie's head; the sails flapped and caught; the boat turned.

This space was even tighter than the last. Glancing back at Will, Annalie could see the tension on his face as he tried to control the movement of the boat.

"There!" he shouted, pointing.

Annalie spotted a huge shape looming out of the water, very close to their bow. She was on the wrong side; frantically she scrambled across to port, and jammed her oar in, pushing with all her strength. The object, rusted metal, might once have been a van. She pushed and she pushed, aware of the weight of the wind in the sails behind her; somehow she managed to exert just enough force—they slipped past unscathed.

"Look!" Will said. "Open water!"

They passed the last few ruinous buildings and sailed at last into the open sea.

Annalie turned to Will. "I don't believe it," she said. "We made it!"

"If we're going to do this," Will said, "you're going to have to start having a little faith."

"Um—excuse me," came a voice from behind them.

Annalie and Will turned.

There, entirely forgotten in all the excitement, stood Essie.

The southern route

"Oh," Annalie said. "Essie."

For a moment no one knew quite what to say.

"She's not coming with us," Will said.

"Of course not," Annalie said.

It seemed quite obvious to both siblings that Essie could not come on the journey.

"But what are we going to do with her?" Will said. "We can't go back now. They'll catch us."

"Yes, but—" Annalie began.

"It seems to me," Essie said, "that we should keep sailing until we can find a safe place to let me off."

"Like where?" asked Will skeptically.

"You've probably got a better idea than me," said Essie.

"We can't just leave you in some strange port by yourself," Annalie said.

"I'll be fine. I'll catch a train back to Pallas," Essie said.

Will nodded decisively. "Sounds like a plan then. Let's get moving. We're going south."

He was already turning the wheel as Annalie

opened her mouth to protest. The sails filled. Annalie turned to Essie. "Sorry," she said.

Essie just waved her hand dismissively to indicate it was nothing, smiling a little too brightly.

Annalie joined Will at the wheel. "What's our plan then?" she asked.

"Well—I thought we'd just go south as fast as we can, try and get clear of the pursuit ships," Will said.

"Can we outrun a pursuit ship if we see one?" Annalie asked.

Will pulled a face. "Probably not."

"Maybe we should find somewhere to hide out for a little while," Annalie suggested.

"We're not far from the mangroves," Will said. "If we pulled in there we could hide out under the trees, work out what to do next."

Annalie nodded. "Sounds good."

They sailed on until they reached an estuary at the mouth of a large, meandering river. Will steered up one of the river's many narrow branches and they dropped anchor where the tree cover was thickest.

"This place stinks," Essie said.

"It's an estuary," Will said witheringly, "it's what they all smell like."

Annalie swiftly changed the subject. "Have you been below? Do we have any supplies?"

"Haven't really had a chance to check the supplies," Will said, "what with escaping from the Admiralty and everything."

The three of them went below decks.

Essie looked around curiously—she had never been inside a boat like this before. It felt a little like stepping inside a doll's house; it was very compact, but the more she looked, the more she saw how well organized it was. In the main room, which she later learned was called the saloon, there was a tiny kitchen and a little table and benches that could fold away when not in use. The walls were lined with cupboards, so everything had a place, although many of the cabinets were unlatched, and the floor was littered with things that had fallen out of them.

"Where do you sleep?" asked Essie.

The cabins were forward, one on each side. One contained two bunks, the other a double bed.

"Spinner slept there," Annalie said, indicating the double bed. "We have the bunks."

"Who gets the top bunk?"

"We take it in turns," Will said.

"We have a roster," Annalie explained. "To stop us fighting."

A further check of all the access hatches and compartments showed the Admiralty hadn't destroyed anything on board, or prized open the skin of the boat to see whether there was anything hidden behind it. They had, however, been through every equipment locker, leaving them a jumbled mess, and must have taken anything they didn't recognize or that looked homemade. There were a number of useful things that were missing, including a device Spinner had rigged up to extract freshwater from seawater. More seriously, the locker that had once held spare parts—for the engine, the steering, the solar batteries, the wind turbines—had been emptied.

"We're going to have to replace those," Will said, as they stood together looking into the empty locker, with its checklist still attached to the inside of the door.

"And that's going to be expensive," Annalie said.

Fortunately they had food and fresh water, although they would need to get more of both before they ventured out into the open ocean.

They decided to spend the night hidden in the mangroves, and then begin their journey in the morning. As evening fell, Annalie got out Spinner's sat nav and began bringing up charts.

"The first thing we need to do is work out which route we're going to take," she said.

"You know," Will said, "you don't actually have to do this."

"Do what?"

"Come with me."

"I do," Annalie said shortly.

"You really don't. I can do this. A lot's changed while you've been away. Me and Spinner have been sailing together a lot, just the two of us. We've been getting along just fine without you."

Annalie went quiet then.

"So you don't have to feel bad about it. Go back to school. It's obviously where you want to be—"

"What's obvious about it?" Annalie said.

Will peered at her, surprised by her reaction. "You love your new school. You're always going on to Spinner about how great it is." Her weekly calls home had been full of all the amazing things she'd done that week. She'd visited museums and worked in state-of-the-art science labs. She'd been on a warship and a submarine. She took her swimming lessons at the same aquatic center where the Swimming World Championships were held. It had all sounded like bragging to Will, and it had made him feel left out and cross. It wasn't that he wanted to go to an Admiralty college—*hell no!*—but there was something about seeing Annalie in that weird, stiff uniform, so far away from them and doing important fancy things, that made everything about home feel wrong. After a while, he'd gone to another room whenever he heard Spinner's shell chime.

"Well of course I did," Annalie said. "How could I tell him anything different? He was desperate for me to go to Triumph. If I'd told him I was hating it, he just would have worried."

"You didn't hate *all* of it, did you?" Essie asked, feeling a little hurt.

"I reckon I enjoyed about as much of it as you did," Annalie said dryly.

"So you *didn't* like it?" Will said. His expression was gradually brightening from hostility into surprise and relief.

"Remember what you said when Spinner asked you whether you wanted to take the scholarship test too?"

"Something like, "I'd rather gnaw my own hand off than go to a stupid snobby school like that"?"

"Well you were right. It *is* a stupid snobby school," Annalie said.

Will laughed and punched her arm. "Told you, didn't I?"

"Actually it's Dux's *leading* stupid snobby school," Essie said with a grin.

Graham chimed in from his perch in the corner. "What snobby?"

"A snob is someone who thinks they're better than other people," Annalie explained. "And they're not afraid to let people know it."

"Bit like you, Graham," Will said.

"Graham not think he better," he said loftily. "Graham know."

Annalie was looking at Will thoughtfully. "There was really nothing for you to be jealous about."

"I wasn't jealous," Will said.

"Really?"

"It just seemed like—"

"Like what?"

"Like that place was changing you."

"Into a snob?" Annalie asked, surprised by the thought. "Did I really seem that different?"

"Getting to be."

"Well I'm not."

Will gave her a sly grin. "Yeah, I see that now. Just as annoying as ever."

Annalie narrowed her eyes at him, but the teasing felt comfortable now. "We should work out which route to take," she said, turning back to the sat nav.

There were two ways to reach the Moon Islands: the northern route and the southern route. Spinner had always taken the northern route, sailing out and across the inner sea, then traveling via the northern lands across and down to the Islands.

"We know the northern route," Annalie said thoughtfully. "If we're going to do it by ourselves, it makes sense to go the way we already know."

"North route," Graham said. "Special biscuit town."

One of their favorite stops on the northern route was the city of Violeta, where they made a kind of biscuit Graham particularly liked.

"The southern route is quicker," Will said.

If you sailed south, you eventually came to the port city of Southaven, and the peninsula that was the southernmost point of Dux. Below this peninsula was open ocean. Roaring winds called the Furies blew from west to east and could send a boat rocketing from Southaven through the rough southern ocean until they reached the Moon Islands. The southern route was plagued by massive ocean storms, huge waves and very high winds. Because of the vast distances involved, it was also possible to overshoot and miss the Moon Islands entirely; if you ended up too far south, the oceans down there were huge and empty, there were dead patches and doldrums, and help was hard to come by.

"It's not quicker if you get wrecked," Annalie said.

"No wreck! Go north!" Graham ordered.

"I bet Spinner's going south," Will said.

The other major risk on the southern route was other boats. The Moon Islands were outside the

Admiralty's control—pirates, slavers, and criminals of every kind operated there, and it was dangerous to go unprotected.

"If Spinner's going the southern route," Will continued, "we should go that way too. How else are we going to catch up with him?"

Annalie looked at Will unhappily. She hated to think that they might go all that way and then miss him because they had taken too long. "But it's so dangerous," she said.

"It's not the worst time of year," Will offered. "The winter storms won't start for two more months."

"There can be storms any time," Annalie said, but her mind was still working. "One reason the northern route is safer is because it's Admiralty controlled almost the whole way."

"They'll be watching out for the boat now," Will agreed.

"If they stop us, it's all over," Annalie said.

"Oh, don't go the southern route," Essie said. "I saw a vid once about a family who went that way by accident and their boat was hijacked and the children were kidnapped."

"That was just a vid," Will said.

"It was *based* on a true story," Essie said stoutly. "It happens."

"And worse things too," Annalie said, "but I don't really see that we've got a choice."

"Isn't there another way? A less obvious northern way?" Essie asked. "I just hate to think of you guys going out there and just—I don't know—disappearing."

"If anyone tried to kidnap us they're going to be disappointed," Will said, laughing. "It's not like we've got anyone to pay our ransom."

"Okay," Annalie said, "it looks like we're going to Southaven. We'd better add wet weather gear to the shopping list."

A cure for seasickness

They set out first thing the next morning. It was a beautiful day to be at sea. The sky was clear with a good wind and the ocean was deep and green and lovely.

"This is what it's all about," Will said to Annalie as they rolled into the swell, a bigger swell than yesterday. This was the life he loved: being at sea, the sun on his face, the wind at his back. It felt good knowing that his sister was there again at his side, although he would never have admitted it to her.

The decision to send them to separate schools had thrown him off balance. If anyone had asked him if he and his sister were especially close (twins, psychic connection, etc.) he would have laughed in their face. It wasn't that he *missed* her when she went away. But her absence changed things. Growing up, he and Annalie had been treated the same. Spinner had expected them to do the same jobs round the house, pull their weight on the boat, help out in the workshop. The two of them had felt like equals. Annalie often had her nose in a book, whereas Will was always desperate to get outside, and their school reports had never exactly been comparable, but that didn't seem to matter—until they turned eleven, and suddenly it did matter, and all Spinner could think about was getting Annalie into that posh school. Annalie, but not Will. He felt oddly cheated by the discovery that Spinner actually did care about academic achievement, as if all this time he'd been hiding something from him.

The Spinner he'd grown up with was a practical man, good with his hands, who loved boats, and Will had wanted to live the same sort of life when he grew up: fixing things, being useful, and spending time on boats. Actually, spending a lot of time on boats. If he could figure out a way to spend all his time on the *Sunfish* and still make a living, he thought that would be just about perfect. But then Spinner sent Annalie away to live a different kind of life: big school, big city, perhaps university and the Admiralty at the end of it. And he'd begun to wonder whether he'd got it all wrong. He'd thought he was already living the best life imaginable. But what if he was mistaken?

The humiliation and injustice of having his sister singled out for special treatment, while his own good qualities were ignored, had been tying him in knots all term. But he felt quite a bit better about it now that he knew she'd hated that school. It made him feel he'd been right about the place from the start: the people were all snobs and there were too many rules. It wasn't the right kind of place for people like himself and his sister. They were better off living their own way, following their own path, back on the boat, the two of them again, equals.

Down in the cabin, Essie was miserably seasick. She'd slept in while the other two got up and got underway, and by the time she'd woken up and looked out the porthole (scratching her mosquito bites) the rubbery mangrove trees had vanished; instead they were moving through a rolling swell, and far off in the distance she could see the line of the shore. They were at sea again.

The whole thing still seemed unreal; she couldn't quite believe that she had run away from school, walked through a slum, been chased by Admiralty men, and was now on a stolen boat heading for Southaven. But at least from Southaven she knew she'd be able to get home easily enough—there were trains from there to Pallas.

Provided she didn't actually die before she got there.

Her stomach churning, she hurried to the bathroom (Will called it the "heads") but didn't quite get all the way there before her stomach contents heaved themselves all over the bathroom floor.

When it was done, Essie crawled up on deck to confess what had happened and ask for a bucket.

"I didn't think," Annalie said apologetically, as she came to help. "We never get seasick."

Annalie hauled up a bucket of seawater from the side and took it below to start sluicing out the bathroom. It took a couple of goes, but soon the floor was rinsed clean.

"Come up on deck," Annalie suggested. "It'll only make it worse sitting down here."

The two girls came back up on deck. Will eyed them, a look of suppressed glee on his face. "You know what the best cure for seasickness is?" he asked.

"What?"

"Come here, I'll show you."

Essie went over to him unthinkingly. To her astonishment, Will grabbed her and flung her over the side of the boat. Essie went down, terrified. She kicked frantically for the surface, her heart beating so fast from the shock that she thought it might actually explode.

Her head broke the surface, but then a wave smacked across her face and she swallowed more water. She coughed and heaved and floundered.

An object smacked heavily into the water beside her. A life preserver had been thrown to her. She grabbed it and clung on, looking mistrustfully at Will, who was holding the other end of the rope.

"How do you feel now?" he yelled.

To her surprise, she discovered that he was right: the plunge into the water *had* cured her seasickness. But that didn't mean she wasn't furious with him.

"I could have drowned!" she shouted.

"No you wouldn't," he said.

He pulled her in, arm over arm. When she reached the side of the boat he put a hand down to her but she refused to take it. "How do I know you won't just drop me in again?" she said.

"Don't be a crybaby," Will said.

Annalie pushed him out of the way and held out her own hand. "Here," she said, and hauled Essie up, with some difficulty.

"Are you okay?" Annalie asked, after they'd both flopped, gasping, onto the deck.

"What would you have done if I couldn't swim?" Essie asked Will accusingly.

Will rolled his eyes in disbelief. "I was standing by with a floaty thing!" he said. "You were never in any danger. Man!"

Will went huffing back to the wheel.

"Still feeling sick?" Annalie asked.

"As a matter of fact, no," Essie said haughtily. "But I still think he should have asked."

Essie sat on the deck and let her clothes dry in the sun, watching both Will and Annalie as they moved about the boat, doing important sailing things, thinking how much she envied their competence. She was impressed by the easy way they moved around the boat, and talked so confidently about routes and dangers, as if they did this sort of thing every day. Watching them steer the boat together yesterday through those narrow channels had been dazzling, daunting: they were like characters from a vid, or a game. She couldn't imagine ever knowing so much about boats, or currents, or being able to handle an oar with such practiced skill. Watching them in action had just made her feel even more useless in comparison.

But at least she no longer felt seasick.

Southaven

The journey to Southaven was trouble-free. More than one Admiralty patrol boat passed them at a distance, but did not signal or come closer, and so they began to think that no one was really looking for them.

They did, of course, take precautions. The huge harbor at Southaven was one of the busiest in the world, and the port authorities ran checks on every boat that entered it. As soon as they checked the *Sunfish* they'd discover it had been reported stolen, so Will and Annalie decided that they would drop anchor in a little bay just up the coast and travel to the city by bus.

"How much money have you got?" Will asked, turning to Annalie.

"A little," Annalie said, fetching out her purse. "Spinner gave me some emergency money, and I haven't had to use any of it yet. What about you?"

"He gave me this," Will said, pulling notes from his pocket.

They pooled their money and looked at it doubtfully. "I don't think it's going to be enough," Annalie said.

"Let me help you," Essie said. "I've got money."

"You need that to get you home," Annalie said.

"No, really, I've got plenty. I've got a creditstream on my shell."

Will turned to her, interested. "What's your limit?"

"I don't really have one," Essie said.

"Why didn't you say so before?" Will asked excitedly.

"Will, it's not our money," Annalie said.

"But if she wants to help us out—"

"She's already in enough trouble without spending her parents' money on us."

"How else are you going to pay for what you need?" Essie asked.

Annalie hesitated. "We can probably find some stuff to barter."

"Won't you need that stuff yourself?"

"Well, maybe..."

"Then let me pay, and I'll worry about my parents later," Essie said.

Will grinned. "Now I know why you brought her along!"

Essie narrowed her eyes at Will disdainfully.

The crowded, wheezing bus took them very slowly from the little seaside hamlet where they'd anchored, over gently rolling countryside, and then made stop after stop through the city of Southaven until it reached the great harbor at its heart.

Southaven, like the city of Port Fine, had been inundated by the Flood, but its position on the international shipping routes was so important that no expense had been spared in rebuilding it. You could still see what the old city must have looked like as you traveled through the city's heights; lower down, everything was new, with flood-proof roads and buildings and mighty anti-flood barriers and sluice gates to protect against high tides and storm surges. There was concrete and steel everywhere, reassuringly massive.

At last they came over the crest of a hill and Southaven port spread out below them, huge and deep, a vast expanse of water, staggeringly full of ships of all sizes and kinds. There were cargo ships and passenger ships, fishing boats and ferries. Some, like the *Sunfish*, traveled under old-fashioned sail; some used high-altitude sails, giant kites that rode the steadier and more powerful winds in the high atmosphere. Others had engines driven by high-efficiency solar, or wind turbines, or wave-power. And there were Admiralty ships, lots of them, from small pursuit ships to large heavy cruisers. Southaven, after all, was the home of the Admiralty's southern fleet.

"There's going to be a lot of sailors down there," Annalie said anxiously, counting the Admiralty boats.

"So what?" Will said. "No one ever notices kids."

They decided to split up: Will to scout for spare parts, Annalie to find provisions. Once they'd bought what they needed, Annalie would take Essie to the railway station and Will would hire a cart to take the provisions back to the *Sunfish*.

It gave Will a great sense of pleasure and purpose to set off on his own through the crowded streets of the port. He'd been to Southaven once or twice before with Spinner, on similar missions—looking for spare parts, or with something to sell—so he had a rough idea of how the town fitted together. He knew there was a group of streets where you could find ships' equipment, from the most basic to the most high-tech. He soon found his way there and began moving from shop to shop, checking prices, comparing quality, eyeing all the lovely gadgets he wished he could afford. He made notes on his list and worked out where all the best deals were, and once he was satisfied he knew what he was going to buy, he turned his attention to the things he was never going to buy: the gleaming shipboard sat navs with their lightning-fast interfaces and dazzling breadth of information.

While the sales assistant was busy elsewhere, he hopped onto a demo model and began to play with it. Idly he keyed in Little Lang Lang Island, the island where Uncle Art lived. At once a map popped up, and Will went closer, zeroing in on the cove where Uncle Art's house was. Then, the obvious thing to do was plot a course there. An array of possible routes popped up, with tools to optimize your search. Will kept clicking and optimising happily, refining the trip for traditional sailing vessels, for the least amount of pirate activity, for coral reefs, debris fields, whales.

I wish there was some way I could save all this, he thought, looking at the beautifully detailed route information with all its supplementary appendices—everything they would need to find their way to Uncle Art's island safely.

Meanwhile, Annalie and Essie had quickly established that the best place to buy the supplies they needed was at the huge, ugly warehouse-style store where they sold things by the box. There wouldn't be a lot of variety, but the prices were inarguable. The boxes, however, would be heavy, so they decided they'd come back later when they'd hired a pedicab.

They had arranged to meet Will in a street filled with shops. Advertisements flashed or were animated in every window, illuminated billboards glowed above the shopfronts, and a news ticker scrolled along the top of a TV studio where you could stand and watch the reporters broadcasting live.

"You know, normally when I'm walking down a shopping street like this, all the shops would be sending me offers through my feed," Essie remarked. She hadn't dared to switch her feed on since she'd realized the Admiralty might be tracking her through it.

"Really?" Annalie said. "All the shops? Doesn't that drive you crazy?"

"Not all of them. Only the ones I'm interested in."

"How do they know you're interested?"

"If I'm on their mailing list, or if I've ever bought anything there. I do get some random stuff though. You buy something for your dad once, and then they're forever wanting to sell you hokey old music and golf-club covers."

Essie hadn't meant to remind herself of her father. A sad feeling settled over her, and she felt the misery

132

of it threatening to overwhelm her again. She looked away, and by a strange coincidence, something caught her eye in the fast-moving stream of the news ticker: *Tower Corp.* She froze, staring up at it. But it was gone too quickly for her to see what the news was, replaced by celebrity gossip and international atrocities and political gaffes, all in a swift-moving jumble.

"What is it?" Annalie asked.

"Something about Tower Corp," Essie said.

"Maybe if you wait it'll come back round," Annalie suggested.

They waited, but it didn't reappear.

"It can't have got any worse, can it?" Essie said.

"Maybe we could ask someone?"

"That would just be weird," Essie said. "I'm sorry, I have to know." She whipped out her shell and headset and switched it on. Chimes rang and kept ringing. She flicked a finger. The newsfeed came up.

Annalie watched anxiously as Essie's eyes scanned the display. She gasped once, and then her face settled into a dreadful, flat expression.

"What is it?" Annalie asked.

"Apparently Dad's been charged with criminal manslaughter, but the big news is my mom's left him for a shipping magnate with pots of money," Essie said flatly. "While I've been offlink she's left me eleven messages. The feeds say they've been together since they met at a charity ball two months ago!"

"The feeds aren't always right," Annalie said. "Maybe you should get in touch with her and find out what she's got to say."

"I don't really care what she's got to say," Essie said abruptly. "Where's Will? We need to buy these supplies."

Will was now talking to the sales assistant about the journey he'd mapped out.

"Planning a career in international piracy, are you?" joked the sales assistant, a young man in his early twenties with a fashionable handlebar mustache.

"Something like that," Will said.

"You know, if you really were going to take a journey like this, in that kind of boat, I'd think about this," the sales assistant said, pulling up more menus and adding parameters and refinements. Still more detail appeared.

"Wow," Will said. "This program is amazing."

"That's why it's the best. So what kind of system are you running at the moment?"

Will hesitated. The boat did have a sat nav, but it was nothing like this one, which could connect to the link from anywhere on the planet, even the open ocean, so you could update data all the time. Spinner had a very old computer in a thick, waterproof case, which ran much older versions of the sat nav programs. They were very basic, and they weren't connected to the links. Spinner always claimed he didn't really need anything else.

"It's old," he said. "But we're thinking of buying a new one. I don't suppose you could let me save this search, could you? If I'm going to convince my dad to buy the new system, it might help if I could show him what it can do."

"Why don't you get him to come in so I can take you both through it?" the sales assistant said.

"My dad's super busy," Will said. "You couldn't just put this on a chip, could you?"

The man's affable smile had disappeared. "No," he said, "I couldn't." And he deleted the search.

Will let out a little moan as the information vanished. He tried desperately to remember as much of the detail as possible but knew it was already sieving away.

"Is there anything else I can help you with?"

"No," Will sighed. "There isn't.'

"Why are you looking so down?" Annalie asked when Will arrived at the meeting spot, laden with spare parts.

"I had all the information we needed to get to Little Lang Lang but the guy wouldn't let me save it on a chip," he said gloomily.

"What do you mean? Where did you find it?"

"I looked it up on a sat nav. You wouldn't believe how much stuff there was! Charts, data, route maps, everything! With all that information the trip would have been an absolute breeze. I don't see why the guy had to be so weird about it. It was only information, he could have just saved it for me."

Essie was looking at him, frowning. "You entered where you're going into a sat nav in a shop?"

"Yeah—why shouldn't I? I didn't tell the guy my name."

135

"You know they say that's the sort of thing the Admiralty monitors, right?"

A horrid cold feeling crept over Will. "They what?"

"There are rumors that the Admiralty monitors all the sat nav programs, so they can check where all the boats are going."

Annalie looked aghast. "We'd better get our shopping done and get out of here."

The three of them went to the big box supermarket and loaded up with groceries, all paid for with a swipe of Essie's shell. Outside, after some bargaining, they found a man with a cart who was willing to take Will and the supplies back to the next town.

"So are you coming?" Will asked, clambering aboard.

"I'm going to take Essie to the station. I'll get the bus back."

Will looked at Essie. "Thanks for buying the stuff for us," he said gruffly.

"That's all right," Essie said.

"Hurry back," he warned Annalie as the cart rolled off.

The girls walked toward the central railway station in silence. Essie brooded; Annalie waited respectfully for her to say something.

At last they reached the great station, and walked in through the large vaulted entrance, wandering toward the information board that displayed the timetable for all the intercity trains. They stood underneath it, looking up. There was a train leaving for the capital in two hours' time.

Abruptly, Essie spoke. "They say my dad's probably going to jail."

"I'm sorry," Annalie said.

"I'm sure he never meant for any of it to happen," Essie said. "But I suppose when something like this happens, someone has to pay." She paused, her face crumpling a little. "She could have stood by him."

"Your mom?"

"As soon as she saw the money running out, she was off." Essie dashed a tear from her eye. "I thought it was bad at school before. It's going to be so much worse now."

"You'll be okay," Annalie said, trying to sound encouraging. "Just tell them if they don't leave you alone, they'll have me to deal with."

"You'll be on the other side of the world," Essie said in a watery voice.

"Not as far as all that, I should think," said a voice.

Annalie turned, and there, to her horror, stood Beckett.

Run

"You've led me a merry dance, young lady," he said. "I'm glad I've finally caught up with you. We have a lot to talk about."

"I've got nothing to say to you," Annalie said, already looking for an escape route, noticing that this time he'd brought backup. Two marines were standing by. There were probably more she couldn't see.

"They're very worried about you two back at Triumph," Beckett said. "Very anxious for your safe return."

"We were about to buy our train tickets actually," Essie said, "so there's no need for you to worry, we can get back safely by ourselves."

"I wouldn't want to risk you getting lost again," Beckett said. "I've got a car standing by to take you back."

"None of this has anything to do with her," Annalie said. "She's just my friend from school and she was on her way back anyway. Why don't you just let her go?"

"That's not strictly true though, is it, Annalie?" Beckett said, with his tooth-baring smile. "She's just paid for all sorts of things she's not going to need at school."

"I made her do that," Annalie said desperately. "She didn't want to, but—"

"None of this is really relevant," said Beckett. "Let's go."

He steered the two girls out of the information hall and toward the front entrance. Annalie's eyes darted about, looking desperately for a chance to escape. "Don't try anything," Beckett warned. "It won't work."

Escape certainly seemed unlikely, with Beckett right behind her, and marines on either side of them. *Where are they going to take us?* she wondered. And what would Will do when they didn't come back? She wished they'd made a contingency plan in case one of them didn't return. She had no way of sending him a message, no way to tell him to get away. She imagined him waiting there at the boat, waiting and waiting while Beckett's men closed in on him.

Suddenly an irate middle-aged lady appeared in front of them, trying to get the attention of the marines. "Excuse me! Excuse me! Could we get some help over here please?"

The marines tried to brush her off, but she wouldn't be brushed. "Those men over there are creating a disturbance and no one's doing anything about it! Over there, look!"

Some men, possibly drunk, were shouting and pushing each other in the midst of some discombobulated travelers. One of them crashed into a stand of water bottles and knocked them flying.

"Sorry ma'am," said one of the marines, "we can't attend to that right now—"

But Annalie, seeing an opportunity, blurted, "Talk to this man! He's in charge of station security!" and pointed to Beckett.

The woman started demanding action, Beckett and his men tried to shake her off, and in that brief moment of turmoil and confusion, Annalie grabbed Essie and they broke into a run. They began weaving through the crowd, dashing and darting and ducking behind as many visual barriers as they could. People stopped to watch them go past, but they were lucky— no one decided to step in and stop them. Annalie spotted a camera as she ran, and realized that a place like this must be heavily monitored.

"We need to get out of the station," she shouted to Essie.

They darted out the great open doors, the heavy thud of boots close behind them. Annalie chose a direction at random and kept running, only hoping Essie could keep up. She saw an alleyway and went running down it; it doglegged around, and came to a dead end. Essie came careering down it after her. "Where now?" she gasped.

There was a door, metal, dented. Annalie yanked it open and clouds of steam billowed out. Not knowing where she was going, Annalie darted inside; Essie followed. They pulled the door shut behind them and moved forward.

It was a huge industrial laundry. Massive washing machines churned in a cloud of steam; dryers roared.

The air smelled heavily of washing powder and bleach and it was very hot.

"Hey!" someone yelled, seeing them, and they ran again, racing past rows of machines and huge trolleys full of grimy sheets and filthy tablecloths.

They found themselves in a loading dock where the trucks rolled in and out; more workers turned to stare at them as they jumped down from the dock and raced out into the street again.

"Do you think we lost them?" Essie gasped.

"Wouldn't count on it," Annalie said. Looking up, she saw a bus coming down the street. "Let's catch that!"

They ran for the bus stop and flagged the bus down, flopping down into two seats near the rear doors.

"Do you know where this is going?" Essie asked.

"Nope," Annalie said. Two stops later she jumped up, grabbed Essie, and they plunged into a busy market.

"Now where are we going?" Essie panted as they wove through slow-moving shopping crowds.

Annalie stopped by a stall that sold accessories. "Hat or scarf?" she asked.

"What?" Essie said, bewildered.

Annalie grabbed two hats with deep brims from the display and paid the first price the stallholder asked for. She pulled one of the hats on, tugging the brim down. "Disguise," she explained. Essie pulled on the other.

When they emerged on the other side of the market, there were a range of different vehicles lined up waiting for fares. "We have to get back to the *Sunfish*," she said.

"Wait," Essie said. "There's two things we need to do first."

The first thing she did was find a cashpoint, where she took out an enormous amount of cash. "Now," she said, when she'd done that. "Give me your shell."

Annalie handed it over, and Essie opened up both the backs. Inside each was a little chip. Annalie's was blue; Essie's gold.

"Ah," Essie said.

"What?"

"You've already got a chip-to-go."

"A what?"

"There are two ways you can pay to use the links. Set up an account and pay it every month, which is what I've got. Or buy a chip-to-go that lasts for as long as it lasts, then you get a new one. This chip," she continued, holding up her own gold chip, "has all my details and information on it. If my shell ever got lost or stolen or I left it on a bus, I could find it again, because it's identifiably mine and searchable. But your chip has no information on it at all."

"So?"

"So as soon as I switch my shell on, if I'm within range of the links, they can find it—and me. But they can't use yours to find you."

"Oh."

"So I need one of those chips."

She ducked into a store, bought a new chip and installed it in her phone. "There," she said, with a grin. "Now I'm invisible."

She dropped the gold chip and ground it under her heel until it was irreparably smashed, then scooped the bits up and binned them. "*Now* we can get back to the *Sunfish*."

"Wait a minute. We?"

"I've made up my mind. I'm coming with you," Essie said. "My mom's run off with some rich guy I've never even met. My dad's in jail. He's probably going to lose the house. And he's going to have to pull me out of Triumph at the end of this term anyway because he can't afford the fees. I don't even know where they're planning to send me these holidays." She took a shaky breath. "I'd rather take my chances with you."

Annalie bit her lip, looking soberly at Essie. But all she said was, "Okay then."

The code

Now, at last, they set a course for the west, and the Moon Islands. Will and Annalie spent a lot of time looking over the charts on Spinner's old sat nav, discussing the best way to go. There were, of course, a million different ways to travel through the thousands of islands that made up the Moon Islands, and neither of them really knew how to decide which way might be best. Their charts were old and inaccurate, and although Spinner had made his own annotations about places he'd been to, there were many places in the archipelago he'd never been.

Annalie and Will studied the routes, arguing this way and that about what looked better. Annalie didn't want to go anywhere that looked too dangerous; Will was all about speed. He wished he could remember more of the route the magnificent new sat nav had conjured up for him, but there were too many unfamiliar place names, and after the first couple of stops he couldn't remember any of it. Eventually, they came to a route that they were both happy with, and programed it into the sat nav. It couldn't chart their position like a more modern sat nav could—they would have to determine their position the old-fashioned way, using instruments and measurements. Spinner's navigation instruments were so old they'd been antiques even before the Flood, and Will had never really had the patience to learn to use them properly, so navigation would be Annalie's job.

Their first day out of Southaven was a beautiful autumn day, perfect weather for sailing, and it felt more than ever like they were going on holiday.

The weather stayed fair for several days. It was easy sailing; they were in open water so there was nothing to watch out for. They had decided to travel outside the international shipping lanes, hoping they'd be less obvious to any Admiralty ships that might be looking for them, so they saw few other boats.

Essie quickly started to get a little stir-crazy. Normally when she was bored she checked her feeds, but that was impossible. Less than a day's sailing out from Southaven they had lost their connection to the links. You needed a powerful booster to connect to the links from the open ocean, and Spinner had never seen the need for such a thing. So there were no more newsfeeds, no more fashion reports. "What do you *do* all day?" she wailed.

Annalie tried to teach her about the boat—words for things, procedures, things she thought it might come in handy to know—but none of it really seemed to stick. Will tried to show her how to fish, but Essie didn't have the patience for it, and she didn't much like fish anyway. Eventually she offered to become the cook, but even that was not enough to fill the long afternoons.

"Here," Annalie said finally, "have some old-school fun," and she handed Essie a worn old pre-Flood paperback. The book, an adventure story about children at sea, had been one of Annalie's favorites when she was younger and she'd kept it, along with a small cache of others, to re-read on the boat whenever things got quiet. Essie looked skeptical, but opened it anyway, and as she did, a piece of paper fluttered out. She picked it up and looked at it curiously. "What's this?" she said.

There was writing on the piece of paper, but it didn't make any sense to her. Annalie recognized Spinner's handwriting.

"I don't know," she said, taking it from Essie.

"Is it a code?"

It certainly looked like a code. The letters were all normal letters, but they didn't form any words that made sense. They had been arranged down the page in small groups.

"It's some kind of list," Annalie said.

"Names?" Essie suggested, looking at the way the letters were grouped.

"There are some numbers too," Annalie said. "Perhaps they're names and addresses."

Annalie studied them a little longer, hoping to spot a pattern that might help her guess what some of the letters were. But she couldn't see anything.

She took the piece of paper up on deck and showed it to Will. "Have you ever seen this before?" she asked.

Will peered at it. "No," he said. "What is it?"

"It's a code. Spinner did it and hid it in one of my books."

146

"Probably just one of those games you used to play," Will said.

When Annalie was younger she'd had a passion for codes and puzzles, and Spinner had sometimes made up coded messages to amuse her, especially during winter when it was too wet or cold to go outside.

"But this is new," Annalie said. "I've never seen it before."

"Maybe he made it for you but you never got around to solving it," Will said.

Annalie shook her head. "I re-read this book six months ago, and it wasn't there then." She looked at the piece of paper, willing it to give up its secrets. "I think this might be something important."

Will yawned his disagreement. "Better go and work out what it says then." And indeed Annalie tried, for the rest of the morning, without getting anywhere.

Later that afternoon, clouds began to mass on the horizon. Will and Annalie watched them as they grew, darkened, and moved toward them.

"Storm," Will said.

Annalie nodded. "Can we get out of its path?"

"We can try." And he did try, but the wind ahead of the storm front had dropped away, and the bad weather was gaining on them.

"We could use the engine and try to outrun it," Annalie suggested.

"Let's save that until we need it," Will said. He studied the storm sagely. "It doesn't look so bad. We can ride it out."

"Better get ready, then."

Annalie took Essie and went below, making sure that everything was safely stowed away, all the hatches battened and all the lockers locked. "It's going to get rough," Annalie warned.

The sky darkened. The wind came, and the gentle camber of the ocean became a violent surging. Waves flung them about, the rain poured down, the wind roared and the air was saturated with salt spray. The watery world threatened to engulf them. The storm raged for hours, and there was nothing they could do but hang on. The boat pitched violently. Graham clung to his perch, shrieking nerve-shreddingly whenever the movements of the boat became too rough. Essie looked terrified. Annalie, wide-eyed herself, tried to reassure her. "We've been through worse storms than this," she said. "We're going to be fine."

The storm beat at them until late into the night, then it passed over and left them alone, and they fell into an exhausted sleep.

The next day was bright and burnished again. The boat had proved itself pleasingly sound—even in that world of water, very little of it had found its way inside. But when Will and Annalie checked their position they were much further south than they had meant to be—the storm had driven them off course, and they were now far from the international shipping channels.

"If that's the worst we encounter on this trip I reckon we'll be all right," Will said, feeling some personal pride in the excellence of his vessel and the quality of his captaining.

"Don't say that," Essie said. "You'll jinx us."

Graham was in a foul temper. "Bad Will. No biscuit. Hate boats. Hate wet."

No biscuit was the worst punishment Graham could think of for someone who'd displeased him.

"I got us through it, didn't I?" Will said, annoyed.

Graham nipped him on the ear before flying up to the top of the mast where no one could reach him.

Less than an hour later, a ship appeared on the horizon. Essie was the first to notice it. "Hey, is that an Admiralty ship?" she asked.

Will pulled out the binoculars, took a look, and swore, then handed them to Annalie. Annalie swore too.

"What is it?" Essie asked again.

"That's not an Admiralty ship," Will said. "They're pirates."

Pirates

Pirate ships did look, from a distance, like Admiralty ships because they had all the same sorts of equipment: gun turrets and grappling hooks and high-tech gear that let them locate and board other ships. They were assault vessels, fast and ugly and built for plunder.

"They won't care about a tiny little boat like this one, will they?" Essie said. "We've got nothing worth stealing."

"A boat's always worth stealing," Annalie said.

"And you'd be worth a fortune for ransom," Will said. "Us, not so much."

"Not any more," Essie said. "My dad's broke."

"Let's get some sail up," Will said. "We'd better try to outrun them."

Will and Annalie put up every sail and began to run before the wind, hoping that if they could make their way back toward the international shipping channels before the pirates could reach them, they might break off their pursuit and return to quieter waters.

"They may not have noticed us," Will said hopefully. But they soon realized the pirates must have seen them. They had changed course and were moving to intercept them.

"Can't we go any faster?" Essie asked. "Why don't you put the engine on?"

"It doesn't go any faster than we're going now," Will said.

"I don't think they're running on wind power," Annalie said, looking back through the binoculars. The pirate ship bristled with ill-assorted turbines and solar panels, an ugly patchwork of some very advanced energy-generating tech, all feeding into a powerful engine that churned the ocean in its wake.

"Where are the Admiralty when you need them?" Will muttered, scanning the horizon ahead. He could see nothing.

In desperation they sailed on. The pirate ship kept coming, inexorably closing the gap between them. At last they grew close enough that Annalie could see individual people on the deck. All of them were armed.

"What are we going to do if they catch us?" she said, turning to Will. "We need a plan."

"If they catch us," Will said, "the best plan in the world won't do us any good."

Graham was perched beside Annalie. "Pirates!" he squawked. "Make Graham parrot pie!"

"No one's going to make you into a pie," Annalie said.

"Yeah, pirates love parrots. Don't you know anything?" Will said.

Essie said nothing. She held the railing so tightly her knuckles were white.

"I'm sorry," Annalie said. "I should have made you go home."

"I wanted to come," Essie said bravely. But she didn't feel brave.

Then, quite suddenly, Annalie saw movement on the deck of the pirate ship. The men were looking about. They heard the distant tang of a loudspeaker, traveling across the water.

"Something's happening," Annalie reported. "I think they're giving orders."

"What sort of orders?"

The men on the boat were moving purposefully about now. They were no longer looking at the *Sunfish.* "I think—I think they're giving up!"

"What?"

Will came over to her and grabbed the binoculars from her, yanking her neck uncomfortably. "Ow!"

She was right. The pirate ship had broken off its pursuit and was changing course.

"What on earth is going on?" Annalie said.

"Pirates go!" Graham squawked, turning somersaults in the air with a chatter of parrot laughter.

"Maybe they decided we're not worth it after all," Essie suggested.

"Maybe someone else is coming this way," Will said.

"A bigger target?" Annalie said.

"Admiralty?" Will countered. "Either way, we'd better get out of here."

Once more they corrected their course to get away from the pirate ship as fast as they could. Annalie kept a lookout as the ship receded, and just before she lost sight of it over the horizon, she saw the answer to the riddle.

It was a cargo ship, propelled by high-atmosphere sails. Everything about these ships, from the cargo on board to the sails that propelled them, was valuable. A ship like that would make much richer pickings than a tiny sailing boat like the *Sunfish*.

"Will they be all right, do you think?" Essie asked.

"They'll be fine," said Will confidently. "Those big boats are armed to the teeth. They have to be."

"So were the pirates," Annalie said.

"Better them than us," Will said. "At least they stand a chance."

Once the pirates had vanished over the horizon, Annalie went to check their position. "We need to keep an eye out," she said. "There's an undersea mountain not far from here. Not much to see above the surface, but plenty below it."

"Might be good fishing," Will said.

"You never know," Annalie said. "Let's try not to bump into it."

"Okey dokey," Will said.

"A mountain?" Essie said. "In the middle of the ocean? Really?"

"The ocean's full of mountains," Annalie said, "much bigger than the ones on land. You do get these rocky uplifts just sticking out of the ocean in the middle of nowhere. There's often a lot of things living around them too—they're like an oasis in the desert."

"You mean like sharks?" Essie asked nervously.

"Sharks, whales, all sorts of things," Annalie said cheerfully. "Don't worry, they're too busy eating each other to be interested in you."

The wind that had propelled them died away again, and the boat sailed on, more slowly now. They kept a lookout for the pirate ship, but it did not return.

It wasn't until the next morning that Annalie determined they were close to the undersea mountain. "Let's go see what's around," she suggested to Essie.

Standing in the bow, Annalie and Essie watched in delight as they crossed paths with a school of flying fish. The fish leaped and soared, their winglike fins lifting them energetically out of the water. Essie was still gazing down into the water, looking for fish, when Annalie lifted her eyes and saw a wholly unexpected sight.

Not far away, white water foamed over what was clearly the rocky top of the mountain. And perched on that rocky top was a boy.

The boy

"Look!" Annalie cried.

Essie looked up and gave a yelp. Even Will stuck his head around. All three of them stared at the boy.

The empty ocean stretched for thousands of miles around them in every direction. The nearest land was many days' journey away, no matter which way you went. Where had he come from?

For a long time the boy stared back at them, without making any movement. Then, slowly, he lifted his arms up above his head. Was he signalling? Or surrendering?

"Oh my goodness," Essie whispered. "I wonder how long he's been there."

"It's all right," Annalie called. "We're coming to get you."

Will dropped anchor with a clatter, and Annalie helped him reef in the sails. Then Will lowered the dinghy and rowed over to the rock. The boy seemed reluctant to move from his perch on the rock, but eventually Will managed to get the dinghy close enough that he was able to clamber in. The boy sat slumped in the dinghy as Will rowed him back; when they got to the *Sunfish*, he was too weak to climb up the ladder and the girls had to help him.

"Let's get him below," Annalie said.

They hooked his arms over their shoulders and carried him down to the saloon. Annalie got him some water and he sucked it down in huge gasping gulps. He drank more and more, until suddenly it came up again in a smelly whoosh. The boy tensed, as if expecting a blow, but it was a dull, instinctual movement, slowed by exhaustion.

"Don't worry about that," Annalie said. "We'll clean it up later. Would you like something to eat?"

Essie jumped up and fussed in the galley, not sure what castaways might like for their first meal back from the brink of death. She offered a banana, a honey sandwich, and a little leftover curry and rice. The boy crammed it all in as if he didn't care what it was.

Annalie watched him curiously. He was terribly thin, his arms and legs like broom handles. He was about the same height as Will, but his hollowed-out face made him look almost like an old man. The clothes he wore—a T-shirt and some long shorts—were ragged and almost colorless. He wore no shoes.

None of them wanted to interrupt him while he was eating, but once he had eaten everything and Essie had brought him seconds and he'd eaten that too, Annalie began.

"What's your name?"

The boy's eyes darted toward her, and then flickered away.

"I'm Annalie, this is my brother Will, and my friend Essie."

"Hi," Will and Essie said.

The boy's gaze darted from one face to another, then around the room. He looked like a wild animal looking for an escape route.

"It's okay," Annalie said. "You're safe now."

This didn't seem to register with the boy at all, and Annalie began to wonder if he could understand them. "Do you speak Duxish?"

Still he gave no response. Essie tried saying hello in a few other languages. The boy showed no signs of understanding these either.

"Maybe," Will said, "we should just leave him alone for a while."

This seemed like a good idea, and the three of them began to get up from the table to give the boy some space. Then, unexpectedly, he said, "Pod."

They all turned back to him with interest.

"Your name's Pod?" asked Will.

The boy nodded, still watchful. "How many on this boat?"

"It's just the three of us," Will said.

"And Graham," Annalie said, pointing to where Graham was snoozing on his perch.

The boy snapped around to look, as if expecting a threat. The sight of the parrot seemed to intrigue him, but he turned back toward the others quickly.

"No master?" he asked.

"I guess I'm the master," Will said, and Annalie gave a splutter of laughter. Will gave her a dirty look.

"We don't have a master," Annalie said. "It's just us."

"So, I'm dying to know," Essie said. "How did you get to be on that rock?"

Pod's face went blank; a silence fell. Will and Annalie exchanged a look, then Will said, "If you want to have a rest, there's a bed in there." He pointed to his own cabin, which had once been Spinner's. With some hesitation, the boy got up and peeped in the cabin door; then he slipped in and closed the door behind him.

Will jerked his head to Annalie to indicate that she should follow him. They went up on deck, Essie following.

"Does anyone else think it might not have been the best idea bringing this kid on board?" Will said, keeping his voice low.

"What do you mean? We couldn't leave him there," Annalie said.

"Well, of course not," Will said. "But who the hell is he?"

"I don't know," Annalie said.

"Maybe he's a refugee," Essie said.

"A refugee from what? We're in the middle of nowhere. The only people who live out here are pirates," Will said.

Annalie's eyes widened. "You think he's a pirate?"

Will shrugged eloquently.

"He doesn't look like a pirate," Essie said.

"What do you think they look like?" Will said.

"Well, tougher. And older," Essie said.

"He looks too nervous to be a pirate," Annalie said. "He looked like he thought we were going to kill him."

"That doesn't mean he might not try and take the boat off us."

Essie looked at Annalie in alarm. "You don't think he would, do you? We rescued him!"

"I'm just saying," Will said, "we don't know *what* he might do."

They were all silent for a moment, thinking about this.

"Let's wait and see what he's got to say for himself," Annalie said.

"Yeah, sure," Will said. "But we've all got to keep an eye on him, right?"

The boy slept all afternoon. That evening, as they were gathering for their meal, the cabin door opened and Pod peeped out.

Annalie noticed him first. "Hey, Pod. Want some dinner?"

He nodded, and came slinking out.

Food, water and rest had done him good; he no longer looked on the brink of death. While the final preparations for dinner were made, he edged toward Graham, watching the bird with great curiosity. Graham saw him coming and flew up out of reach.

"Who this?" he squawked.

Pod blinked in surprise. "It talks?"

159

"Incessantly," Will said. "This is Pod."

Pod watched Graham as the bird flew about the saloon, his face more animated than it had yet been. "So colorful."

Graham's plumage was yellow, blue and green; he was a spectacular beast, and he knew it. Attracted by Pod's attentive gaze, he stopped flying about and came to rest, just out of reach, and then sidled closer to see what would happen. Pod just stood and watched, rapt, as if everything Graham did was a marvel.

"New friend?" Graham suggested.

Pod nodded.

"Graham biscuit?" Graham asked craftily.

Pod wasn't sure how to respond. Annalie handed him a biscuit, and Pod held it out. Graham took the biscuit and ate it with satisfaction, still sizing up Pod curiously.

"We should eat too," said Essie.

The four of them sat around the little table and ate together in shy silence. Will, Annalie and Essie were all still desperate to know more about the stranger in their midst, but none of them knew how to begin. So they chatted about the food until they couldn't think of anything else to say, and all the dinner was eaten up.

Then, abruptly, Pod spoke. "I was a slave."

The others snapped to attention.

Pod's face was expressionless, and he didn't look at them as he spoke. "I don't know where I was born, and I don't remember my parents." He paused. "I remember a village by the ocean, with houses on bamboo stilts, over the water. I remember looking down, looking for fish. I think maybe it was my mother's village, and my sister and me, we lived there when we were little." He paused. "I don't remember how we left that place.

"My first job, I was a diver. My master took us to an old city—there were drowned buildings there, full of old things. They sent us down into the houses to salvage stuff. Metal, mostly."

"Stuff that was worth money?" Annalie said.

Pod nodded. "Sometimes we had to go right under the water. We had a hose to breathe through, but it didn't always work."

"What happened when it didn't work?" asked Essie, already horrified.

"You drowned." Pod paused. "They were okay masters. They gave us food. But you had to go down under the water, had to work. Couldn't say no. Say no, get taken away, never seen again." He paused, swerving away from this topic. "Diving's no good anymore. The good stuff, the easy stuff, it's all been taken. Only the deep stuff's left. Too hard to bring out, no money in it no more. So they sold us.

"Next job, we worked on a farm. The day we arrived, there was a huge sign by the gate with pictures of all the fruit and vegetables and grains we were going to be growing and my sister said, 'Look at all that food! We going to paradise!'

"But there was salt in the ground. We were supposed to be fixing the soil, making it grow food again. But it was hard work—work all day in the fields until you're exhausted, in all weather. They said they'd feed us out of what we grew, but nothing grew right.

Things died or grew up stunted. Nothing tougher than salt. So we got hungrier, started working slower, and the masters got angrier cos they got big contracts to fill. In the winter, people were falling down and dying on the ground. We heard if you died there, they'd smash you up and put you in the dirt. Fertilizer."

Essie's hand flew up to cover her mouth.

"Eventually the farm went broke," said Pod. "They sold us on. We got put on a boat, very bad boat. People were crammed up in the dark together for weeks. Lots of people got sick and died. And then we stopped."

He paused. "You ever seen them floating palaces? Huge boats, all white and shiny. Rich people live on them."

"Oh yes!" Essie said. "You mean cruise communities. My uncle and auntie live on one. They're cruise ships, but you live on them permanently, and they just go round the world, stopping at nice places along the way."

Pod listened, unsmiling. "So we stopped at one of them. Bosses come down. They're looking for girls to work as maids. They need two hundred, and they choose all the prettiest faces. They chose my sister. She didn't want to go without me. I said to them, take me too, I'll do any work you want. But they only wanted girls."

"Hang on," Essie said, her face red. "That can't be right."

"What can't?"

"They wouldn't use slaves on cruise ships."

"My sister's a slave. They bought her."

162

"But—those ships are extremely expensive to go on!"

"Someone's making good money then," Pod said. "That crew, they're slaves."

Essie looked away, mortified.

"Perhaps your sister was lucky though," Annalie said. "If the cruise ships are nice, maybe they're a good place to work."

"Maybe," Pod said, looking skeptical.

"But, wait, you mean *none* of the staff are getting paid?" Essie asked, not willing to let it go.

"Here's how it works," Pod said, his eyes blazing. "Someone sold me to my first master. He paid money for me, so I owe that money to him now, I got to pay it back. So I work and work until I pay the money back. But there are always costs—food, clothes, lodging. So my debt never gets any smaller. Every time I get sold on, it all starts again. New boss, new debt."

"So probably your sister *is* getting paid, but her wages are going to your master to pay her debt," Essie said.

"Maybe," Pod said dryly. "Never seen any wages myself."

Essie was still looking baffled and outraged. Will intervened. "So anyway, what happened to you? How did you wind up here?"

"That boat, I was on it for a long time. They sold some boys, not me, I don't know why. Then one day, we got boarded by pirates. But they can't find nothing on board. One of them says to me, 'Where they hide the good stuff? Where's the tech at?' I say only thing

163

worth stealing on this boat is me. He says no way. Slaves are too much trouble. I tell him I'll work hard. But he says he don't believe in hard work, that why he's a pirate."

Pod laughed, surprisingly.

"So I told him I'd show him the good tech, but only if he took me with him. So I showed him and he said, "Call that good tech?" but he took it anyway. And he took me with him.

"So now I got a pirate boss and a new job. I didn't know nothing about boats, had to learn pretty quick. They show me something once, I got to remember it first time. Pirates don't like to repeat themselves. The pirates did what pirates do: jack ships, strip the tech, sell it off. I did what they told me to do. Tried not to get in anyone's way. As jobs go, it wasn't so bad. Food was good. The captain though—he was the worst boss ever. He thought everyone was plotting against him. He got all wound up about it, started hearing voices, thinking someone was gonna kill him, steal his boat, steal his money. The others kept saying, 'No boss, it's okay boss, no one's trying to kill you,' but he doesn't believe them.

"Then one day he works it out: my master is the one. So the captain chops his head in half with a machete, and then he started coming after me, but the other guys said, 'He's not a bad kid, you don't need to kill him too.' So the captain said, 'Fine, I won't kill him, but he's not staying on my ship.' And he tossed me over the side."

The others gaped at Pod.

"I was lucky though. One guy threw a big plastic bottle over the side when the captain wasn't looking, I floated on that pretty good. After a while, I saw some white water. I thought maybe it was land. Wasn't really land though. Just rocks."

"So, how long had you been there when we came along?" Will asked.

"Three days," Pod said. He looked at the others with an air of defiance. "So. Now you know."

What to do about Pod

For a while, no one knew what to say. Pod's story was like some kind of dark, horrible fairy tale. Eventually Annalie spoke.

"The pirate ship you were on," she said, "what did it look like?"

Pod frowned, and then described the very ship that had almost attacked them. "We saw them!" Annalie said. "They came after us but then they went after something bigger and left us alone."

Pod looked critically around the boat. "Yeah, slim pickings here. Not much to sell. But if you see 'em again, run fast as you can."

"You don't suppose they're coming back for you?" asked Essie, looking worried.

Pod shook his head. "They think I'm dead." A silence fell. Eventually, Pod spoke, a half-nervous, half-defiant look in his eye, "So, what are you going to do with me?"

Annalie, Essie and Will exchanged looks. It was the same question they'd been asking themselves.

"What do you want us to do with you?" Annalie asked. "Do you want us to take you home?"

"Where's that?" said Pod dryly.

"You could go to the Admiralty," Essie said. "Slavery's illegal. You could make a report. I'm sure they'd do something to help you."

"I don't suppose you have any papers?" Annalie asked Pod.

Pod shook his head.

"Then there's no point going to the Admiralty. If you don't have papers saying where you belong, they'll put you in a refugee camp to wait for resettlement," Annalie explained.

"That wouldn't be so bad, would it?" Essie asked.

"No one's actually resettling refugees," Will said scornfully. "The governments all say they've got enough people to deal with already."

"But—" Essie began, then stopped.

"The Admiralty's no good," Pod said, and spat on the floor. Essie stared at him, disgusted. Realising he'd done something wrong, Pod wiped the spot with his foot, shamefaced. "Admiralty," he muttered. "Never helped anybody."

Annalie turned to Will and Essie, looking for ideas. "We could drop him off at a decent-sized port," she suggested. "Somewhere he might find work, or help?"

"There are charities," Essie said. "They might be able to help you work out where you came from. Help you find your family."

"My family sold me," Pod said dully. "They don't want me back."

"Well, maybe not," Annalie said. "But I'm sure we can find someone who can help you."

167

Pod nodded. His fieriness had died down into a hopeless passivity. "Wherever you want to take me, I go," he said.

Pod's true colors

They sailed on. The weather remained fair, and the days passed. After telling his story, Pod returned to an inscrutable silence. Annalie saw that he had learned to keep his head down and move through the world as frictionlessly as possible. But this did not mean he receded into the background. Unlike Essie, who had decided sailing really was none of her business, Pod was always watching Will and Annalie as they worked; in no time, he seemed to have absorbed as much as he could from them about sailing the boat, and had started lending a hand, unasked, whenever he saw the need arise.

Will was aware of this, and he didn't like it. He didn't disbelieve the story Pod had told them; growing up in Lowtown he'd met many people who'd had similar experiences. After the Flood there had been huge numbers of displaced people on the move, looking for somewhere safe to live, and nowhere near enough countries willing to take them all in. Many of them ended up in refugee camps, where vast numbers of people still resided, forty years later. Some had put themselves into the hands of people smugglers who could get them into wealthy countries like Dux. Without proper papers, many of them ended up trapped in shantytowns and slums like Lowtown, illegal, living on the fringes, always at risk of being deported. Others ended up as slaves, working for no pay, doing desperate and dangerous work in some of the most terrible corners of the world. Sometimes they were lucky; they got away and were able to make a new life for themselves.

What worried Will was what Pod *hadn't* told them.

How had he really got himself adopted by pirates? That part of the story didn't quite ring true to Will, and he wondered if Pod was really the hard-working innocent he said he was. Back in Lowtown, Will knew boys who lived on the fringes of the brotherhoods, and could imagine nothing better than to join. The brotherhoods were secretive, hierarchical, and violent—entry was not simple. You had to prove yourself trustworthy, and that sometimes meant doing terrible things to show you were up for anything and willing to follow orders. Pirate crews, he thought, must be similar. Had Pod *really* been adopted by a pirate? And what had they made him do once he joined the crew? Will wasn't sure he believed Pod's story, and he wasn't ready to trust him yet. He found Pod secretive and unreadable, and Will worried that at any moment Pod might show his true colors and kill the three of them, or sell them as he had been sold, and take their boat for himself.

One day Will noticed Pod examining the solar panel that powered the auxiliary engine. They hadn't had any reason to use the engine since Pod had come aboard and it was possible Pod hadn't realized that there *was* an engine. Until now.

"What are you looking at?" Will asked suspiciously.

"Solar—what's it for?" asked Pod.

"It doesn't work," Will said untruthfully. In fact it ran all sorts of things that needed power, from the sat nav to the kitchen stove. Essie used it to charge her shell, although she had not been able to link since Southaven.

"I seen one like this before," Pod said. "I could help you fix it."

"I can fix it myself, thanks," Will said.

Pod slunk away without another word, leaving Will more suspicious than ever.

Later that day, Will said to Annalie, "Are you keeping an eye on him?"

"What for?"

"I saw him today poking around one of the solar panels."

"So?"

"So, what's he doing getting into the workings of the boat?"

"I think he's trying to learn more about it. He wants to help."

"You sure about that?"

"Why are you so paranoid?" Annalie said, exasperated.

"We already know he was a pirate. We've got a boat, and he's got nothing. What's to stop him from taking it?"

"He wouldn't do that," Annalie said firmly.

"I'm not so sure," Will said. "I'm not letting him

out of my sight."

Annalie rolled her eyes.

The good weather held; they completed their crossing of the open expanse of ocean. Annalie steered them toward the Astramans, the island group that was one of the westernmost outliers of the Moon Islands, where they would take on fresh water and supplies.

"We made it through the Furies," she said to Will, smiling, as the top of a mountain appeared on the horizon.

"Easy!" Will said, and laughed. "The worst of it's behind us now."

Astra Nostro, the second largest island, had a port and trading post. Unfortunately, there was also a small Admiralty base there, so they decided to bypass Astra Nostro and go to Astra Semla, a smaller island, which their charts told them had fresh water. Although the Astramans were far from Dux's territorial waters, the Admiralty maintained a base there—one of many around the world—so they could patrol inside the island archipelago if the need arose.

The most obvious route would take them directly past Astra Nostro and on to Astra Semla, but neither Will nor Annalie wanted to risk coming to the attention of any Admiralty ships, so they took a longer route, circling a smaller island and looping around to Semla, which lay to the east of Nostro.

"I bet the fishing's good around here," Will said,

as they sailed around the rocky coastline.

"You want to throw a line in?" Annalie asked.

"Actually I was thinking I could do some spearfishing—maybe look for shellfish too."

"That's a good idea," Annalie said. "If you got enough, we could barter."

Will loved to fish, and loved to dive even more. He used a mask, but didn't bother with a snorkel, just held his breath while he dived under the water.

"I can drop you off and you can have a dive while we take the boat into harbor and get the supplies," Annalie said.

For a moment, Will let himself get excited about diving a new site. But then he realized that if he got off the boat, he would be leaving the girls alone with Pod. "Forget it," he said.

Annalie looked baffled.

"We should all go to get the supplies. There'll be time for diving later." When Pod was safely off the boat.

Essie began assembling a shopping list as they drew closer to Semla Harbor. "How much cash do you think I'll need to take?" she asked.

Will was aware of Pod listening attentively.

"Don't take too much," Annalie said.

The wad of notes Essie had got for them in Southaven had been divided up and hidden in different places around the boat. To Will's relief, the two of them disappeared into their cabin and closed the door while they dealt with the money.

When the girls emerged again, Annalie turned to

173

Pod. "So, we'll be in Semla Harbor soon."

Pod nodded, expressionless.

"I think they're meant to be pretty safe, the Astraman Islands."

Pod still said nothing.

"When we get there, I thought we could go into town and see if International Flood Relief have an office there, or the Charitable Sisters."

"Brothers in Harmony are good too," Essie offered. "They have excellent second-hand shops."

"We'll find someone who can help you," Annalie said.

Pod just nodded again. It was obvious he didn't want to go. Annalie looked guiltily at Will. But Will didn't feel any guilt. He wouldn't be able to relax until he knew the pirate's apprentice was safely off his boat.

They sailed into Semla Harbor and docked at the water station. The fees were high, but not outrageous (it rained a lot on Semla). All of them were glad to step ashore. They had been at sea for weeks now.

"The ground feels so weird," Essie said. "It's so *flat*."

"Will, do you want to fill the tanks and mind the boat while we take Pod into town?" Annalie asked.

Will hesitated, torn between his desire to stay and protect the boat, and his unwillingness to let his sister go off with Pod. But before he could decide what he thought, Pod spoke: "I'll go now. Thanks."

Pod turned swiftly and began to walk away.

"But—" Annalie began.

"I thought we were going to give him some money," Essie said.

This was news to Will, but he said, "Let him go. He can handle himself. He doesn't need you fussing round him."

"But he hasn't got a *cent*," Essie said.

All three of them watched him go, Annalie in sorrow, Essie in awe, Will with a sense of growing relief.

"Well, that's that then," Will said briskly. "Let's get what we came for."

Will pumped water into the tanks, then they all went into the small town to buy supplies.

"Look," Annalie said, pointing. The shabby little post office had a sign advertising that it was an office for International Flood Relief. "He'll be able to get help there." She kept hoping she'd see Pod. But he had vanished.

"You know," Annalie said, as they walked back through the little market with their provisions, "we don't need to get out of here straight away. There's still time for some diving."

Will grinned at her. "You girls want to come?"

Annalie shook her head, and Essie said, "Are you kidding? There's *signal* here!" She waved her shell happily. "I have weeks of catching up to do."

"Your loss," Will said.

They sailed out of the harbor and back toward a

likely looking bay Will had spotted on the way in. Essie and Annalie arranged themselves on the deck while Will kitted himself out with his dive bag, mask and speargun.

"Don't drown," Annalie said.

Will made a face at her and jumped overboard.

The water here was lovely and warm and a beautiful color. He stroked strongly away from the boat and looked down into the swarming, flickering life below. The sea was full of fish, all colors, all sizes. For a long time he just swam about, enjoying the sights, without any thought of using his speargun. After a while his swimming took him toward the rocks, which were deliciously clustered with shellfish. He swam over and prized some off with his dive knife. He thought he saw an even denser bed of them further away and swam on, then swam again. Soon, his dive bag was laden with the freshest shellfish, but when he stuck his head up to work out where he was, he discovered that he was much further from the boat than he'd thought. A current was working down the side of the island and it had swept him away from the *Sunfish*. He could see it, but it was going to be a long swim back. He was just contemplating whether to begin that swim now or dive for a bit longer and swim back later when he heard an odd whistling sound, and then something landed wetly and heavily upon him. Startled, he went under and came up spluttering to discover he was entangled in something.

That something was a net. He fought to get it off, thinking it must have been floating in the water, but then he heard a little croak of laughter.

"Hey boy, doing some poaching now?"

He struggled to turn toward the shore, still encumbered by wet nylon webbing, and saw, to his horror, two young men standing on the rocks above him. They were bare-chested, in the Astraman fashion; one had a shark tattoo, the other was tattooed with something clawed and crabby. Both were looking down at him with hostility.

"I'm sorry," he called, treading water. "I didn't realize."

"You think you sorry now?" Shark said. "You ain't seen nothin' yet."

Will struggled to free himself. Crab pulled on a rope attached to the net and it pulled tight around Will. They began to haul him in. He kicked and struggled, trying to get his arm free, to reach his knife, to maneuver the speargun into a position where he could use it. But his head kept getting pulled underwater, flushing him with panic, making it impossible to do anything.

He glanced back at the *Sunfish*, desperately hoping the girls might have seen him. But they were so far away he could barely see them on deck; what hope was there that they could see him?

He crashed painfully into the rocks, and the two young men began to haul him up. He was dragged up, kicking, scraping himself in numerous places but as he came level with them he managed to wave his speargun about and fire it.

The shaft flew, but flew wide. The young men shouted in astonishment. Crab grabbed the speargun from Will and tossed it behind him into the scrub, while Shark said, "Oh, you in *big* trouble now." They dropped him hard onto the rocks, and Crab pressed his knee into Will's chest, while Shark pulled out a knife of his own, a big, ugly-looking hunting knife.

"I think you got something that belongs to me," Shark said. He took Will's dive bag, opened it, and showed it to Crab. Crab chuckled. "Didn't anyone tell you this place is for locals only?"

He tossed the dive bag aside, then came at Will's neck with the knife. Then, quite suddenly, something flashed across Will's line of sight. Shark grunted and fell back, then Crab, who was still kneeling on Will's chest, toppled too.

Pod was standing over him, brandishing the speargun. He'd swung it once, twice, clouting the two men across the head. He darted to where Shark's knife had fallen from his hand and picked it up.

Will scrambled to his feet. Shark was still lying on the ground, groaning, clutching his head, but Crab was on his feet, coming back for another go.

"The speargun," Will shouted to Pod.

Pod tossed him the speargun. Will caught it and slipped another bolt in, his hands shaking, before training it on the men. Pod and Will moved toward each other, as if they were a team.

"I won't miss this time," Will warned.

Will and Pod began to back away over the rocks.

Shark moaned. Crab turned to check on his mate, and Pod hissed, "Run!"

Pod ran up the rocks like lightning and Will followed. There was lush green foliage above the rocks, with a well-trodden path between rocks and scrub. They ran along it as fast as they could, back toward the *Sunfish*.

When they got close enough, Will started shouting, "Hey! Hey!"

He could see the girls still sprawled on the deck. Essie was cruising the links, Annalie reading a book.

"They're coming," Pod reported, looking back over his shoulder.

The men were still after them, one of them with blood running down his neck.

"Annalie!" Will roared, "Essie!" and at last Annalie looked up and turned in every direction until finally she spotted him jumping and waving as he ran along the shore.

"We're going to have to swim for it," Will said as he neared the boat and began clambering as fast as he could down the rocks.

"I don't swim," Pod said.

"I thought you were a diver?" Will shrieked.

"Doesn't mean I can swim."

They reached a rock ledge that projected over the water. Below, the waves swooshed in and out. Will looked down, then back. The men were still coming and, worse, he saw them shouting to someone. He looked over his other shoulder and saw another man coming from the other direction.

"Time to learn!" Will shouted, grabbed Pod and leaped into the water with him.

Down they went, down and down, then bobbed up to the surface. Pod grabbed Will and started frantically trying to climb up him to get out of the terrible water.

Will fought back, and they wasted precious moments floundering at each other. Then a soft plop sounded near them.

"Oi!" Annalie shouted.

The life preserver floated almost within reach. Will and Pod paddled toward it, then Pod grabbed onto it desperately and clung on. The girls hauled him in, leaving Will to swim the fastest he had ever swum in his life. Pod scrambled up the ladder, Will went up behind him, and they had barely got themselves over the side and onto the deck before Annalie gunned the engine and sent the *Sunfish* roaring out of the bay.

On deck, Will started to giggle. "That was a close one."

"Who were those guys?" Annalie asked. "What did you do?"

"Locals," Will said. "I guess fishing isn't allowed."

Pod was still sprawled on the deck where he'd flopped, still catching his breath, his face gray. Now he surged to his feet and grabbed Will angrily. "Never do that again!" he shouted.

"What?" Will said. "You mean the water? Mate, I had to. They would have caught us."

"You never do that again," Pod said ferociously, shaking him. "Ever."

"You tell him," Essie said.

"Okay, I'm sorry!" Will said, feeling ganged up on. "Man!"

Pod let him go, still glowering.

"Nobody likes being tossed in the water," Essie said unapologetically. "You've really got to stop doing that."

Annalie, Will and Essie all turned then to look at Pod.

"So...?" Annalie began, speaking for them all.

"Those men," Pod said. "They followed you from the market. They thought you were easy pickings. So I followed them."

"Why?" Will asked, astonished.

"You saved me," Pod said awkwardly. "I owe you."

"No you don't," Annalie said. "But thank you."

"What were they going to do to us?" Essie asked.

Pod shrugged, brushing the question away.

"So now what?" Annalie asked.

Pod looked down, clearly very uncomfortable, then back at Annalie. "Maybe I can help you get where you're going," he said.

Annalie looked at Will. Will raised his eyebrows at her and shrugged.

"Okay," Annalie said.

And then, for the first time, Pod smiled.

Pod joins the crew

As they left the Astraman Islands behind, Annalie spotted an Admiralty boat patrolling the waters they had just left. This was probably just a coincidence, but it gave Annalie an uncomfortable feeling. How certain could they be that they weren't still, somehow, being tracked? Luckily the patrol boat did not seem to see them, and they left the Astramans without any further trouble.

From now on the sailing would be trickier; the seas of the Moon Islands were full of hazards, from rocks and reefs to dangerous currents and shipwrecks. Spinner's sat nav had charts, but they were old—some were even pre-Flood—and couldn't be relied on. That is, the islands were mostly in the right place, but some of them showed pre-Flood towns and coastlines that were now underwater. Others had been updated to show the present waterline and depths. But what they didn't show were the other things they needed to know: where to buy water or get a mast repaired; where the movement of the ocean currents deposited sea junk, from lost shoes to whole shipping containers. They might not mention the whirlpool that sometimes appeared at high tide off a particular island. They certainly wouldn't show the lighthouse that wasn't really a lighthouse, but a trick designed to lure boats onto rocks so the islanders could strip their contents.

"Now that we're here we're really going to have to work together as a crew," Will told the others as they sat at dinner, the night they left the Astramans behind. "Pod will have to work with me to get up to speed on everything, and Annalie, you'll need to make sure you stay across the navigation."

"Yes boss," Pod said. The others looked at him and realized he was not joking.

"What do you want me to do, boss?" Essie asked, more facetiously.

"Just keep doing whatever it is you've been doing," Will said.

Essie stuck her tongue out at him.

Now that Pod was a part of their crew, they realized they were going to have to try to get to know him. Essie, overawed by the story of his traumatic upbringing, didn't have the first clue what to talk to him about, so she plied him with food instead. She had an idea that he must have grown up eating bread made with sawdust, moldy rice, and roasted rat, so it was up to her to introduce him to all the nice things in life, as if that might make up for the deprivation of his early years.

Annalie wasn't sure what to talk to him about either, but she noticed how his eyes followed Graham around the cabin, and that gave her an idea.

"Did you know Graham's more than forty years old?" she said to Pod one day.

Pod looked surprised. "He doesn't look that old."

"He is though. He was part of an experiment into animal communication, before the Flood."

"Is that how he learned to talk?"

Annalie nodded. For the first time it crossed her mind to wonder how Spinner had come to own an experimental parrot who had once been part of a scientific study, and whether it had anything to do with his former life as a scientist. "My dad rescued him. They've been together ever since."

For a moment they watched Graham, who was hard at work tending his feathers.

"He's normally much livelier than this, even though he's an old bird," Annalie said. "But he's really missing my dad."

The longer Graham spent away from his home and Spinner, the more he seemed to lose his spark. The bird had always been a bracing presence, deploying a stream of opinions, squawks and insults, but as the voyage continued he had begun to sink into himself, spending more time huddled on his perch with his back to the room.

"He's sad," Pod said.

"You know," Annalie said, "it'd be good if you tried to make friends with him."

Pod's face was caught between eagerness and doubt. "What do I know about birds?"

"There's nothing to know," Annalie said. "You just have to pay him attention. Tell him how clever and handsome he is. He loves all that stuff."

Pod was good at following orders. As the days

unfolded he courted Graham, offering him biscuits, talking to him, praising him, carrying him about, laughing at his birdy jokes. They even began to develop their own private jokes about the other people on the boat.

Will didn't like the feeling that Pod and the parrot were laughing at him behind his back. "I think I preferred it when Graham was miserable," he said.

The journey proceeded uneventfully for the next few days. They saw other boats from time to time—fishing boats, small mixed cargo ships, even the odd passenger vessel—but no one gave them any trouble or even seemed terribly interested in them.

Soon they arrived at the Millinni Islands, a group of almost a hundred islands varying in size from quite large to little more than specks of rock. One of the Millinni Islands had a volcano on it, and the view as you sailed into the strait was spectacular. Essie, perched in the bow, was taking pictures of the volcano with her shell when something caught her eye.

She put her camera down, stared, could see nothing, looked back at the picture she'd taken, and zoomed in. Then she hurried back to where Annalie was standing with Will, checking some details on the charts. "I think I saw an Admiralty boat," she said.

"Where?"

"Up ahead." She showed them the photo she'd just taken. They all peered at it. "Look. There."

"Are you sure?" Will asked.

Annalie studied the photo then looked at the chart, comparing them. "If that bit there is this bit here," she said, "there's a bay they could be hiding in. Coming up the strait we won't see them until we're right on top of them."

Will looked at the chart and could see that Annalie might be right.

"Why do you think it was Admiralty?" he asked.

"Doesn't that look like their flag?" Essie said, pointing at a sliver of color on the picture.

"It could be," Will admitted.

That was enough for Annalie. "So what shall we do?"

"Better be on the safe side and go round the outside," Will said.

They changed course, taking a wider path around the island, although Will remained skeptical that it really had been an Admiralty boat.

They saw some fascinating things in the Millinnis. They came across a floating village in the calm waters between two islands. Houses had been built on rafts constructed out of natural and recycled materials. The rafts were lashed together and linked by walkways, and as they sailed by they saw kids leaping in and out of the water, swimming and playing like frogs, while the adults came and went in little boats. These people watched them go by, and some waved; they were neither hostile nor overly curious.

"Look," Essie said, "the islands on either side are completely covered with crops." Although small, the islands were like market gardens, filled with fruit trees, vegetables, and other edible crops.

"Maybe they decided not to waste their land on housing," Annalie said. "I think a lot of these islands won't grow anything any more because they're salt-affected. Maybe they put the village out to sea so they could cultivate as much of the land as they could." Annalie sighed. "Wouldn't you love to live somewhere like this?"

Essie shuddered. "Too wet."

"You sound like Graham," Annalie laughed.

Another day, still in the Millinnis, they spotted the patrol boat again, sliding past the tail end of another island, still a long way off.

This time it was Will who spotted it. "Guess you were right," he told Essie. "There they are again."

Annalie frowned. "Do you think they're follow-ing us?"

"They don't know we're here," Will said. "They're just patrolling. It's what they do, being a patrol boat."

"Hmm," Annalie said thoughtfully.

They passed a number of islands that had clearly once been alive, but were now dead, graveyards for the skeletal, storm-battered trunks of palm trees. Others were still lush, green and tropical.

They continued on through the Millinnis, safely navigating several tricky passages. As they were about to clear the island group completely, they saw, yet again, the patrol boat cruising nearby.

"There they are again," Annalie said.

"We'll take cover until they're gone," Will said.

He took them into a rocky inlet and they waited there, watching as the patrol boat sailed to the end of the island group, then performed a slow arc, turned around and began cruising back the way they'd come.

"What are they doing?" Annalie wondered.

"Patrolling," Will said, with a roll of the eyes.

"Why here? It's so quiet round here."

"Maybe pirates have moved in. The good news is they didn't see us. Let's get out of here in case they decide to come back."

They left the Millinnis behind them and sailed out into the open sea again.

That night, over dinner, Annalie expressed her concerns.

"That patrol boat," she began, "don't you think it's sort of funny it was hanging around the Millinnis like that?"

"Not really," Will said. "Why?"

"Well, for one thing, they don't really patrol the Islands that much. That's why there are so many criminals here. But they seemed to be patrolling those islands pretty thoroughly."

"Not that thoroughly," Will chortled, "they never noticed us."

"Well, we got lucky," Annalie said. "But they were spending a lot of time hanging around those islands, don't you think?"

"What are you getting at?" Will said.

"Do you think they were looking for us?"

Will stared at her, his color rising. "How would they know where we are?"

"Do you think they noticed that search Will did back in Southaven?" Essie asked, catching Annalie's drift.

"They couldn't trace it back to us," Will said, his face now very red. "I didn't give the guy any information."

"You did optimize the search for a boat just like this," Essie said. "And they knew we were in South-aven. There can't have been *that* many small sailboats leaving for outlaw country that day."

"You've got no reason to think that patrol boat was looking for us," Will argued, but he also had a creeping sense that he might have unwittingly led them into danger. "They could have been looking for anyone. Could be pirates. Could be just a coincidence."

"I think we need to change our route," Annalie said.

"No," Will said. "This is the best route. It's the quickest. You agreed with me, remember?"

"I know, but—"

"After we leave here we're not even following the route from the sat nav," Will said, exasperated. "I couldn't remember the rest of it. We'll be going a different route anyway."

"Yes, but not that different," Annalie said. "I think we need to take another look at it, maybe go somewhere they really won't be expecting—go south, or north—"

189

"That will take weeks longer," Will said. "If we take too long, we could miss him!"

"But if they catch us—"

"They're not going to catch us!" Will shouted. "I'm the captain of this boat and I say we follow the original route!"

For a long, terrible moment, Essie and Pod looked at Annalie, waiting to see what she would say next. Will could feel his control over the voyage teetering, and he hated Annalie for it.

She drew a breath—her mouth opened—there was a moment's pause. Then she said, "Okay."

Will turned to Pod and Essie. "Okay?" he said aggressively.

Pod gave Will a nod. Still on his side.

Essie looked dismayed. She turned to Annalie, but Annalie was looking at her hands. "Okay," Essie said.

"Right then," Will said.

Dinner ended in silence.

That night, when the girls were in their bunks, Essie asked, "Why did you back down like that?"

"Because it wasn't worth fighting about," Annalie said.

"It wasn't? But what if you were right? What if they know where we're going, and they catch us?"

"I don't know that they *are* following us," Annalie said. "It was just a feeling. And Will's right about one thing—if we take too long, the whole journey's pointless."

Essie thought for a moment. "Remember when we were back in Port Fine, you told me you didn't trust Will because he always wanted to do the dangerous thing, not the smart thing?"

Annalie didn't reply for a while. Then finally she said, "I did say that."

"Then why did you let him say that he was the captain of the boat?"

"Because he needs to believe that he is."

"But he isn't," Essie said.

"Then who is?"

"Well, you are, obviously."

"No I'm not," Annalie said. "I didn't come on this trip because I thought it was a good idea. I mean, it all happened so fast, for one thing. But the main reason I came was because I knew he wouldn't make it on his own. Apart from anything else, he can't tell one end of a sextant from the other. He needs me."

This seemed, to Essie, to prove her point, but Annalie did not agree.

"I couldn't do this without him, either. I couldn't sail this boat single-handed. The thing you have to understand about him and me is, I'm happy to be part of a team. But he can't be, unless he thinks he's the boss. So let's just let him think that."

"Yes, but what if he's wrong about this?"

"We're all sailing blind out here. His guess is as good as mine. So why not let him decide?"

Essie would have much preferred to see Annalie cut Will down to size. But she could see now that perhaps Annalie had a point.

191

She just hoped Annalie's suspicion about the route was wrong—otherwise they were sailing into big trouble.

Mangoes

There were many strange sights in the Moon Islands. One day they sailed near a large island that stood alone and unneighbored, some distance from any other island groups. It was thickly forested and there was one tree in particular that caught Annalie's eye.

"Look!" Annalie cried. "Mangoes!"

A huge mango tree, laden with fruit, was clearly visible from the sea. The others all came to look.

"I've never seen a mango tree," Essie said. "Big, isn't it?"

"That one's huge," Annalie said.

"Hey Pod, you ever eaten a mango?" Will asked. Pod shrugged.

Annalie looked at the others. "Do you think anyone lives there?" she asked.

"You want to go and get some mangoes?" Will asked.

"Don't you?" Annalie said, grinning.

Annalie and Pod took the dinghy and rowed it over to the island. It was lush and beautiful and smelled strongly of overripe fruit. It didn't take them long to find the tree, and they got busy picking the ripest mangoes and placing them carefully into the bags they'd brought with them.

Just as Annalie was beginning to wonder whether they'd picked enough and it was time to go back, she heard something substantial making the upper branches rustle. At first, the thickness of the foliage meant she couldn't see what was making the noise, and she began to feel frightened, because whatever it was, it was big.

Then a face appeared in the trees above her, and another, and another. The faces had dark, intelligent, human eyes, but they were covered in long red fur.

They were great red apes.

Annalie had seen pictures of them but had never seen a live one. There were a few surviving in zoos, but it was believed that they had died out entirely in the wild. Annalie stared at them in astonishment. What on earth were they doing here, on an isolated island in the middle of nowhere? Pod had frozen in fear, but now she saw him looking about for something—a rock, a stick—his hand reaching for a weapon.

"Don't!" she said. "They won't hurt us if we don't threaten them." She hoped this was true. She knew they were likely to be territorial.

The trees around the mango tree started rustling. Apes were swinging in from all over. Most of them stayed up high, but two of the biggest swung down to the lowest branches, face to face with Annalie and Pod.

"Hello," said one of the apes. The voice was strange, an electronic sing-song, and the accent was not Duxish. "We welcome you."

"Can you help us?" said the second.

The island, it turned out, had been a wildlife sanctuary and scientific base. Before the Flood, apes had been rescued from zoos, bushmeat markets, and logging camps, and brought here to be observed, preserved, studied, and returned to at least a version of the wild.

Some of the apes had been caught up in the scientific fad for making animals talk. They had been fitted with headsets that translated their thoughts into words, and sent these words to vocal simulators housed in collars around their necks. The younger apes had not been born until after the Flood, but the older apes had handed the translator units down to a new generation so they could share their new language. The apes had created epic ballads about their ancestors and their many paths to this island, which they regarded as a little paradise on earth. These ballads could take all night to recite, but now the apes had a problem.

The collars used longlife batteries. The apes knew how to recharge them, but the science station had lost power after a storm the previous year, and they could no longer recharge their batteries. One by one, the collars were failing. There were now only two of them left, and the apes were desperate to recover their voices before it was too late.

They showed a wondering Annalie and Pod through what remained of the science station where they had grown up. Although the apes themselves preferred to live outdoors, they were proud of the place that had given them the gift of speech, and had looked after it carefully.

"Where did the scientists go?" Annalie asked.

"They leave after Flood, in boat," the ape said. "They say they come back, but they don't come."

"Can you fix?" asked the second ape.

"Is it all right if I bring my brother here?" Annalie asked.

"You want to give a solar panel to some red apes?" Will said.

"We may not need to," Annalie said. "Their equipment hasn't been properly maintained for forty years—it may just need fixing. Won't you come and have a look at it? If you get everything working again we won't need to give them a solar panel."

"But if we can't fix it, we'll have to give them something or they're likely to tear our arms out of their sockets."

"Come on," Annalie wheedled. "They're great red apes. They're meant to be extinct. And they can *talk*! Don't you want to at least meet them?"

Will had always been mad about animals, the wilder the better. As captain of the *Sunfish* he knew he ought to be guarding their precious supplies just in case, but this opportunity was something he couldn't resist.

"Okay, let's go," he said.

Essie didn't want to miss out either, so Will and Essie both got into the dinghy with Annalie and Pod, bringing Will's toolbox and a few spare parts.

"So did this lab used to run on generator power?" Will asked, once the apes had showed him around.

"Yes!" the ape said. "The genny! Broken."

"If we can just get you some power, you can recharge these batteries again," Will said. "Then you'll be able to speak."

Will examined the generator, then clambered all around the station checking connections and cables, replacing a damaged solar cell, fixing this, repairing that. When he was done, he shouted to Pod, who was standing by the main switch. "Okay, try it now!"

Pod flicked the switch and the science station sprang back to life: power, lights, humming appliances.

The apes hooted excitedly.

"How did you know how to do all that?" Essie asked, impressed.

"Spinner taught me," Will said casually, although he was secretly rather thrilled that he had been able to get it working again. He hadn't been at all sure he'd be able to pull it off.

Annalie watched as the apes extracted batteries from their collars and put them in a charger, their great leathery fingers showing a surprising delicacy. The charging took a long time, but at last, at long last, the indicator light on the charger flipped from red to green. The batteries were ready. The apes put the batteries back in their collars and put them on.

"I speak!"

"Here I am!"

"I am me!"

Words began carolling out of the apes, and they began to sing and dance and hoot and roar, magnificently.

"Essie, do you know how to work those old computers?" Annalie asked. The scientists had left some of their computers behind—big blocky-looking antiques—and she had found microphones in the same supply cupboard as the battery chargers. "If they still work, we can show the apes how to record their songs and stories, and then none of it will be lost."

It took Essie a while to find the right switch to turn the computer on, and longer again to wrestle with the unfamiliar operating system, while Annalie looked for a hole to plug the microphone into. Seeing this, one of the very oldest apes came to join them. "Recording," she said. "Scientists make recording."

"Did you make recordings?" Annalie asked.

"Yes. As a youngling."

Essie was still trying to make sense of the interface. "Where do you suppose they've hidden the apps on this thing?" she asked.

"Your department," Annalie said ruefully.

A red arm reached past Essie and a long, strong

finger began to type, slowly and steadily. To Essie's astonishment, the recording program opened.

"I can't believe you remember the key command after all this time," she said.

"We don't forget," the ape said.

Essie turned and found herself gazing into the old ape's eyes. They were dark, solemn, but also very lively; for a moment she felt a deep sense of kinship and affinity with the old ape, as if she were an eccentric long-lost aunt.

When they left the island of the great red apes, celebrations were in full swing.

"Do you think they'll be all right?" Essie asked, as they sailed away.

"They've done okay so far," Annalie said. "So long as the generator doesn't die on them again."

"Wouldn't surprise me if they worked out how to fix it all for themselves," Will said. "Did you see how they watched me? They're pretty smart."

Only Graham was unimpressed. "Monkeys?" he squawked derisively. "How smart can they be?"

Breaking the code

All the next week, they sailed quietly through empty ocean.

Annalie spent her time trying to crack the code Spinner had left for her in her favorite book. She knew there were some tricks to decoding a message. You could look for three-letter words that appeared a lot—they'd probably be either "the" or "and". One-letter words at the beginning of a sentence were probably "I". In the middle of a sentence, they were more likely to be "a". Starting with these clues, she tried to build a key, but she got nowhere. There were three-letter words in the document, but she couldn't work out which might be "the" and which might be "and"—if that was even what they were. And if the code was, in fact, a list of names and addresses, these tricks would not be any use to her at all.

Essie sat down with her and looked at the jumble of letters. "Making progress?"

Annalie shook her head. "Not really."

"I was never very good at this kind of puzzle," Essie said.

"Codes are often pretty simple," Annalie said.

"You just need a key to unlock them. There are simple codes, where you just shift all the letters round by one or two. You know: A becomes B, B becomes C, that sort of thing. They're easy to use, but they're also easy to crack, so they're not really very good as codes if you want to keep something secret."

"You don't suppose this is one of them?" Essie asked.

"I don't think so," Annalie said. "It could be a random code. You reassign all the letters of the alphabet randomly, without following a pattern."

"How do you crack those?"

"Well, really you need the key."

"Oh."

"Although sometimes it isn't random," Annalie said. "Sometimes another document is the key." Inspired, she jumped up. "Where's the book?"

"What book? You mean the one we found this in? On my bunk."

Annalie raced to fetch the book and began jotting and circling letters excitedly. "There's a kind of code where you start with the first letter of a book," she explained. "That first letter becomes A, the next new letter is B, and so on, until you've gone all the way through the alphabet. It's a random code, completely unbreakable, unless you have the book in front of you."

Annalie worked her way through the pages until she had a complete key.

Then she set to work decoding the message.

Finally, she sat back. "It's a list of names and addresses," she said.

There were four names on the list: two men and two women, and the addresses were widely dispersed. One was on the east side of the Moon Islands; another was beyond the Islands in one of the far eastern nations; another was on a mountain in the far north; and the last address was in the island continent in the south, which had closed its borders decades ago.

"Do you know who any of these people are?" Essie asked.

Annalie puzzled over them. "I don't think so."

They showed the list to the boys. Will didn't recognize any of the names, but he was interested by the fact that one of the addresses lay in the Moon Islands.

"Maybe that's where Spinner's going," he suggested.

"I thought you thought he was going to see Uncle Art," said Annalie.

"I didn't know about this, though, did I?" he said, still studying the list. "What's the one thing you notice about all these addresses?"

"They're all in terrible places?" Essie suggested.

"Exactly," Will said. "And most of them aren't even proper addresses. They're directions for how to get to places. Whoever these people are, they're living in places that are really hard to find." He thought for a moment. "Hey Annalie, get the charts, will you?"

Annalie went and got the sat nav. Will opened the giant world chart and found the approximate locations of the four addresses. They were almost as far

202

flung as it was possible for them to be, with thousands upon thousands of miles between them.

"I'm pretty sure," Will said, "that we've never been to any of these places."

"No," Annalie agreed, "and that's kind of surprising, because we've been to a lot of places with Spinner."

"Almost like he was staying away from them," Essie said.

They were silent for a moment, looking at each other.

"Who are these people?" Annalie asked.

"And why was it so important to keep their names and addresses a secret?" Will asked.

"The first time Beckett came to see me he wanted the names of Spinner's friends and where they lived," Annalie said.

"What did you tell him?"

"I made stuff up," Annalie said. "I knew there was something not right about him."

"Do you think," Will said, "that this list is what the Admiralty's looking for?"

Annalie nodded. "We have to keep it safe."

"So what does this mean for us?" Essie asked. "Are we going to try and find the people on this list instead?"

Will and Annalie looked at each other, considering. "We don't know who they are," Annalie said.

"They must be important," Will said.

"But maybe not in a good way," Annalie said.

"If we ever find an island with some signal I can search them," Essie said. "See if there's any info about them on the links. It might help us work out where to go."

"Good idea," Annalie said.

"You may not find much," Will said. "I bet there's not much about Spinner."

"Everyone's on the links somewhere," Essie said airily.

"Well, for now we know nothing about these people," Annalie said. "I don't think we should go looking for them just yet. We know Uncle Art, we know we can trust him. I think we should stick to the original plan and go and find him. Will, do you agree?"

"Yeah," Will said, nodding. His mind was still stuck on the idea that this list might not be a list of friends after all. But if they weren't Spinner's friends, who were they?

"Hey," Pod said. "Maybe Graham knows them."

Annalie was embarrassed it hadn't even occurred to her to ask.

"Hey Graham, come here. We want to ask you something," Pod said.

Graham flew obligingly down to the table. "Do you remember someone called Dan Gari?" Will asked. "Might have been an old friend of Spinner's?"

Graham fluffed his feathers up. "Who?"

"Dan," Pod said. "Gari."

Gaham rarked, then said, "Danny Boy."

"Who is Danny Boy?" Pod asked.

"Danny Boy very grumpy. Didn't like Graham," Graham said. "Called Graham Birdbrain. Graham break *one* instrument, Danny Boy never forgive."

"What kind of instrument?" Annalie asked.

"Musical instrument?" asked Pod.

Graham made a rude noise. "No. Science."

"Danny Boy was a scientist?"

Graham bobbed up and down.

"What about Sola Prentice?" Annalie asked, moving to the next name on the list.

"Sola," Graham said. "They call her Sun."

"Of course they did," Will said dryly.

"Long hair, like a rope. Sun very sweet. Always say 'Hello, Graham! Like a biscuit, Graham?'"

"And was she a friend of Spinner's too?"

"Yes. Good friend. Always had good biscuits."

Pod took the hint and got Graham a biscuit.

"Pod good friend too," Graham said, stroking him briefly with his head.

"What about the other two?" Annalie asked. "Ganaman Kiveshalan and Sujana Kieferdottar?"

"Can't talk," Graham said, spraying crumbs. "Eating."

They waited while Graham finished his biscuit. "Vesh and Suj. Vesh had cowboy hat. Suj big fat lady. All Spinner friends. At night we sit and look at the sky. Lots of stars. Sing songs, Spinner play. Vesh used to say 'nothing else to do out here'."

"How come we never met any of them?" asked Annalie.

"Long time ago. We live in the desert then," Graham said. "Allie and Will not born. Then one day Spinner and Graham leave. Never see desert friends again."

"What was Spinner doing in the desert?" Annalie asked.

"Work," Graham said.

"Like, fixing stuff?" Will suggested.

"Was it anything to do with the Department of Scientific Inquiry?" asked Annalie. This was the department Beckett belonged to; he'd said Spinner had worked for them as well.

"Just work," Graham said huffily, annoyed by a question he couldn't answer.

They looked at each other. "Well, at least we know they were all friends once," Essie said.

"And that one of them wore a cowboy hat," Will said. "It's not a lot to go on, is it?"

"Maybe Uncle Art will know more," Annalie said. "When we get there, we can ask him."

"When we get there, we can ask Spinner himself," Will said.

Later that evening Will was standing watch when Pod came and joined him on deck. The stars were out and they looked up into them in silence for a while.

"Your dad," Pod said finally. "He a bad man?"

"No," Will said. "He's a good man. But he's in trouble."

"What kind of trouble?"

"The Admiralty are after him. They say he stole something, but he didn't. He's hiding out here in the

Islands and we're on our way to meet him." Will couldn't help noticing it all sounded much clearer and more definite when he said it than it actually was.

"This is a bad place," Pod said. "Moon Islands. A bad place full of bad people. Why did he make you come out here?"

"He didn't make us come," Will said. "We decided to come."

"We?"

"Me and Annalie. Essie wasn't meant to come, that was more of an accident."

"You're not safe out here. You got no idea," Pod said. "Why'd you want to come?"

"The Admiralty took our boat," Will said. "We had to get it back and give it back to our Dad."

"A boat's a good thing to have," Pod said. "Worth money. But why bring it here, where so many people want to take it away from you?"

Will stared at Pod, an uncomfortable feeling trickling down his spine. "We needed to find Spinner," he said.

"What if you don't find him?"

The uncomfortable feeling was spreading, expanding. It was doubt. "We'll find him," he said. "I know we will."

Pod fell silent. Will wished he would go away and stop asking him questions.

After a while, Pod spoke again. "I don't remember my dad. Had plenty of bosses. Don't miss them much." He laughed then, a slightly scary laugh. "One day, though, I want to find my sister."

Will looked at him, unable to see much of his expression in the starlight. "Yeah?"

"Find that floating palace. Get her back."

"How would you do that?"

"Don't know how. But someday."

The Blue Room

For a skinny boy, Pod had a big appetite. With four of them aboard (plus Graham, of course) they had begun to run low on food much sooner than Essie had anticipated. "Perhaps he's making up for lost time," she said, when she brought the problem to Will and Annalie's attention.

"We're going to have to find somewhere to take on more supplies," Will said.

They gathered around the sat nav to check the charts and plan a course change.

"What about here?" Will said, naming a small group of islands to the south.

"Don't go that way," Pod said. "There's pirates down there."

Will pointed to another set of islands, further off course but still within striking distance. "What about here? Know anything about these ones?"

Pod shook his head, but Annalie brightened.

"Oh!" she said. "That's where the Blue Room used to be!"

The Blue Room was a famous sea cave on Kapa Island. The only way into it was via the sea, through a small opening that would admit a rowboat, but nothing bigger. Inside it was said the water glowed with a beautiful, slightly eerie blue light, which flooded in from a much larger hole below the waterline. Before the Flood the Blue Room had been a famous tourist attraction, and people had flocked there and lined up for hours for a chance to row in and out and see the blue water glow.

"I thought it was all underwater now," Will said.

"I'm sure it is," Annalie said sadly. "Still the chart says there's a town there. We have to go somewhere, may as well go there!"

They changed course and sailed for Kapa Island. Kapa was quite a substantial island, one of a group of three that had had a long and varied history: inhabited by cannibals, valued and fought over for its spices, annexed by one colonial ruler after another, until it became part of the international tourist trade, when there still was such a thing. Now it was quiet, isolated by the Moon Islands' dangerous reputation, its water supply damaged by salt.

They reached Kapa and sailed down the famous coastline, where a few old billboards still clung to the cliffs, pointing the way to the Blue Room and announcing the names of long-vanished bars and restaurants.

"I wish I could have seen it," Annalie said wistfully.

"Me too," Will said. "Remember that bit in *Three for the Sea* where they go there and find treasure?"

Three for the Sea was Will's favorite book, one of the few he could be bothered reading all the way to the end.

"Don't go getting ideas," Annalie said, with a grin. They sailed a little further.

"I reckon we're getting close now," Will said, watching the signs. "Reckon if you put a mask on you could dive down and find the entrance?"

"That sounds like a really bad idea," Annalie said.

"Wait a minute," Will said. "Maybe we don't need a mask."

A sign had been newly painted directly onto the cliff above the sea. It said:

The Blue Room
Visiting hours change daily
Inquire at Kapa Village for tickets

Beside the sign was a small circular opening in the rock, big enough to admit a dinghy. A pontoon floated outside it, and it looked like someone had begun building a ticket booth on it, but hadn't yet finished the job.

"It can't be," Annalie said.

"Looks like it can," Will said gleefully. "Who's coming?"

"But shouldn't we buy tickets?" asked Essie.

"Who from?" Will said. He was right—there was nobody about. "Come on. We'll be in and out before anyone notices."

They anchored the *Sunfish* at a safe distance in the bay, then took the dinghy in toward the cave entrance. Pod had to be persuaded to come with them—he said he wanted to stay behind to guard the boat, but eventually he confessed he didn't like water-filled caves.

"Come on. It's one of the wonders of the world," Will said. "You can't miss this."

Will rowed them all toward the crevice, which looked dark and rather forbidding.

"Are you sure about this?" Essie asked. The swell was washing up and down; it seemed there was a chance they might get smashed into the rocks as they attempted to go through.

Will waited for his moment; the dinghy washed safely through the gap; and suddenly they were in a magical world. The cave opened up above them, huge and dark; all around, the water was glowing with a vivid blue light. It was strange, eerie, unearthly.

"What's making that light?" Pod whispered, looking spooked.

"Who cares?" said Essie, gazing around her in delight.

"I could tell you the scientific explanation, but why spoil it," Annalie said. "It's so *beautiful*."

"How can it still be here?" Essie asked.

"Some smart local must have made a new hole," Will said appreciatively. "Good on them."

"Pity no one's ever going to get to see this, buried out here in the middle of the Islands," Essie said.

Suddenly, the glow vanished.

"What's happening?" Essie said, frightened.

"Look," said Will, pointing back toward the entrance to the cave. Something was casting a shadow across it—an enormous shadow.

"What is that?" Annalie cried. "Could it be storm

clouds?"

Will rowed the dinghy back toward the entrance. Cautiously they peered out through the gap.

Moored outside was something huge and white, so high it blocked the sunlight. It was a cruise ship.

Blue Water Princess

"What is that doing here?" Will cried, looking up the towering face of the ship. It had anchored behind the *Sunfish*, and dwarfed their tiny sailing boat.

A fleet of little boats started to appear from around the headland, where the town was located. The cruise ship blasted its horn in greeting, a huge sound that rolled out over the water, and the little boats honked and tooted in reply.

While most of them went whizzing over to the great cruise ship, one of them came over to the children's dinghy and pulled up right alongside them. It was a small boat with a little motor on the back, with two ancient men in it, one steering, the other standing in the front.

"You want to see the Blue Room?" called the front man. "Very reasonable prices! I tell you all about the history. Quick, we take you in now, before the crowds!"

"Thanks," Annalie said, "but we're heading for the town." It seemed prudent not to tell him they'd already been inside.

The man changed tack. "You need somewhere to stay? Go here, tell them Astos sent you, they give you very good rate." The man leaned across the water to hand Annalie a card advertising a guesthouse and spice shop. "The best rooms, best views, very cheap. Try the spice cake!"

Then the second ancient man gunned the engine and they roared away to chase the rest of the little boats.

The cruise ship had released its own floating pontoon with a long companionway. The gates opened up on one of the ship's main decks, and a great stream of passengers started tromping down to cluster on the pontoon while officers of the ship, dressed in shiny white uniforms, haggled with the people in the little boats. Soon, the passengers were clambering into boats, brandishing their shells to capture every moment.

The dinghy returned to the *Sunfish*, and the four of them watched the flotilla ferrying people from the cruise ship to the Blue Room and on around the headland to the town.

"What's a cruise ship doing in the Moon Islands?" Will said. "I thought none of them came here anymore, because it was too dangerous."

"I guess nobody told them," Annalie said.

Will turned to Pod. "You ever see a boat like this in the Moon Islands before?"

"Yes," Pod said. "Once. I need to get on there."

"You can't," Annalie said. "They'd never let us on board."

"The boat that took my sister looked like that. Maybe she's on board."

"Sorry Pod, but there's no way you'll get on that ship," Annalie said.

"Yes there is," Essie said. "You just have to act like you belong. I bet I could get you on board."

Annalie turned to stare at Essie in astonishment. "Are you serious?"

"Trust me, it'll be easy. Look how many people are getting on and off. If we go into town we can follow them on when everyone else is getting back on board the ship. Pod can ask about his sister, and then we'll get off again. We won't get into any trouble." Essie looked at Pod, who was still wearing the ragged clothes he'd come aboard in. "We might need to get him something better to wear though."

While Pod was tidied up and made presentable in some of Will's clothes, they sailed around and anchored in the bay beside the town.

"Are you sure this is a good idea?" Annalie asked, as Essie and Pod were getting ready to climb into the dinghy. "What if someone questions you?"

"I'll make something up," Essie said.

"But what if he finds his sister?"

"We'll take her with us," Will said.

"But—" Annalie began, then gave in. "Be careful. And don't take too long."

Will, Pod, and Essie took the dinghy into town. They quickly separated so no one would see them together; Will went to buy supplies, while Essie and Pod followed the tourists. Essie was wearing her headset for the first time in weeks, colored lights twinkling. She checked her shell optimistically—still no signal. All around them tourists were wandering, looking very out of place: the rich of the new world poking around the ruins of the old world.

"Now what?" Pod said, tense.

"Now we act like everyone else," Essie said.

They found a marketplace filled with stalls selling everything from spices and T-shirts to baked goods and ancient pre-Flood souvenirs. Essie bought Pod a T-shirt with the slogan, "Don't be blue, see the Blue Room", and made him put it on. For herself, she bought a souvenir necklace (also blue) and put that on. Then she bought them both a box of baby spice cakes, and headed back to the beach.

There, a white-uniformed steward was busy mustering boats for the passengers who were ready to return to the ship. Essie went up to him. "Hi," she said brightly, "I think my parents went back already."

"No problem," said the steward, "the next boat's leaving shortly."

They went and stood with the rest of the passengers while they waited for another boat. Pod twitched and fidgeted until Essie had to remind him to relax and not look so suspicious. She held out her shell to an older couple who were standing nearby. "Could you take our picture?" she asked. The older man was happy to oblige, and Essie and Pod posed while the man took their picture. "Thanks!" Essie chirped, accepting her shell back.

The boat arrived then, and the passengers climbed aboard, Essie and Pod among them. Pod looked sick with nerves.

"What did you think of the Blue Room?" the older woman asked as the boat moved out.

"I thought it was lovely," Essie said. "So blue."

"It *was* blue," the woman agreed. "Really lived up to its name."

They smiled at each other and then returned to silence.

The boat tootled back up the coastline and the cruise ship loomed up ahead of them, huge and white. Essie read the name on the side: *Blue Water Princess*. She'd heard of the *Blue Water* line: there were a number of them, named aristocratically in order of size. The largest of them was the *Blue Water Empress*. Essie wondered briefly what they'd do for a name if they decided to build a bigger one.

At the pontoon, another officer stood with a checklist. Essie felt a tremor of nerves; this was where it could all go wrong. They climbed out with the others onto the pontoon and joined the queue.

The people in front of them gave their names, were ticked off the list, and allowed up the companionway. When Essie reached the officer in charge she said, "I don't think I'm on your list. We weren't going to come and then we changed our minds and it was all such a rush we didn't get on the list."

"Name?" the officer asked.

"Essie Kudos. And this is my brother Paul," she said calmly.

The officer added their names to the bottom of the list. "I hope you enjoyed your visit," he said, already turning to the next in line.

Essie walked up the companionway, fizzing with excitement, and then stepped onto the cruise ship itself. The decks were wide and sunny, with chic coordinating deckchairs and sun umbrellas as far as the eye could see. A series of swimming pools in interlocking shapes and different depths sent up an azure dazzle. People reclined in bikinis, in sunglasses, in shorts, in caftans, sipping cocktails or eating hamburgers or salads made with tiny prawns served in huge glasses. There were staff everywhere, fetching and carrying and mopping and serving. Restaurants, cafés, bars, and shops lined the pool area. It was a gorgeous, lustrous, floating world of consumption and pleasure.

And this had been Essie's world until very recently. These people, the kinds of people who could afford a trip like this, were her people. Her father, the property developer, with his deals and his connections and his many business interests, had generated this sort of wealth and given his family this kind of life—until it all went wrong. Now her father's empire was collapsing and her mother had gone off with a new rich man. Essie had no idea where she would fit in with their lives when she finally stepped off the *Sunfish* and returned home.

Looking at her luxurious surroundings, Essie felt so many conflicting things all at once it made her dizzy: how very lovely all this was; how wrong it was that a privileged few should live in luxury when so many more were so very poor; and how superior she felt knowing she was on a super-important secret mission; but mostly she felt how nice it was to be able to live like this and how sad she felt that that was probably all behind her now.

"Come on," she said abruptly to Pod, "let's see what we can find out."

Nearby, they saw a young woman in a gray uniform appear with a mop and bucket to clean up someone's spilled drink. When she was done she slipped away through a plain door marked *Staff only. No admittance.*

Pod watched this, then turned to Essie. "It's probably better if I do this alone," he said.

"Sure," Essie agreed. "Meet me back here as soon as you can."

Pod nodded, and followed the maid.

Outside on the deck, everything was painted a crisp, nautical white and blue, with accents of sunny yellow, but inside the service corridor was a dingy gray, lit with the cheapest lights. There was no natural light here. Pod hurried along it, knowing he shouldn't be here, hoping he wouldn't encounter anyone self-important enough to question him.

He caught up with the maid with the bucket. "Can you help? I'm looking for someone."

The maid gave him a fearful look. "Ask a steward," she said, and scurried away. Waiters pushed past him, carrying trays. He passed huge kitchens, banks of stoves, vast clean-up stations, and noticed that some of the workers scrubbing pots and scraping plates wore only a jacket over their normal clothes. Just past the kitchens, a row of hooks held some spares and he helped himself to one, dropping a jacket over his tourist T-shirt and rendering himself instantly invisible.

Another maid went past, and he followed her. "'Scuse me," he said. "I'm looking for someone, I think maybe she works here. Can you help me?"

The maid looked at him in surprise, then beckoned to him to follow her. She took him into a cleaning station. It was filled with cleaning gear of all kinds, floor to ceiling, and another maid sat at a work station in the middle of the room, monitoring a scrolling list of jobs that needed to be done. The maid pushed Pod behind a high shelving unit, keeping him out of sight of the woman at the workstation, then dropped her bucket back in the bucket area. "Deck C122 clear," she called to the woman at the monitor, then collected Pod and took him down to the back of the room, where a group of exhausted-looking maids were sitting on benches.

"You say you're looking for someone?" the maid asked.

"Yes," Pod said. "My sister. She went away to work on a boat that looked just like this one."

"What's her name?"

"Blossom."

The maids all looked at each other as they mulled over the name, but eventually all of them shook their heads.

"How long ago was this?" one of them asked.

"Maybe a year ago," Pod said.

221

"I've been here two years," the first maid said, "I don't know anybody called Blossom. You sure it was this boat?"

"It looked like this," Pod said.

"Honey, they all look like this," the maid said sympathetically. "What's your name anyway?"

"Pod."

"Shamela," the maid said. She looked at him curiously. "Where'd you come from anyway? You just start here?"

"Not exactly," Pod said cautiously.

"You don't work in the kitchen?"

"I'm just looking for my sister," Pod said.

"Hey, Dodo!" called the maid on the monitor. "Glass broken on D40."

"Coming boss!" One of the other maids got up.

"Hey," Shamela said, "spread the word, huh? Maybe someone knows this boy's sister."

Essie was settled comfortably in a deckchair. Bliss! There was signal. It had been weeks since she linked in and she had forty voice messages and more than four hundred unread mails to wade through.

Most of the voice messages were from people trying to find out where she was. Friends at first. Then school. Her mother. Her father's lawyer. Lots more messages from her mother and the school.

Her mother: "Essie? It's Mom. Call me back."
Beep.

"Essie, I need to talk to you. Call me back please."

Beep.

"Essie, can you switch your shell on please? It's really important that I speak with you."

Beep.

"If you're getting any of these messages can you call me please? Now."

Beep.

"Essie, it's me. The school keeps calling me. They're threatening to expel you if you don't come back. Enough is enough. It's time to come back now."

Beep.

"All right Essie, you've made your point. You're angry at me, I get it. But you know I'm not actually the bad guy here. I know you worship the ground your father walks on, but there are things I could tell you... Anyway, no need to get into all that now. Just call me, please. Or if you won't call me, call *somebody*. Everybody's worried about you."

Beep.

She didn't sound worried, Essie thought. More annoyed that her daughter was causing trouble at an inconvenient time.

There were more messages from her mother but she didn't listen to the rest. She thought she had a fair idea what they'd say. Instead she turned to her mail. At least three quarters of it was pleasant fluff—pictures taken by her friends, songs and movies and all that—but then, buried among it, she found a message from her father.

It had been forwarded by her father's lawyer while he was still in jail, some weeks ago (the

223

company had eventually agreed to pay his bail—an astronomical sum—and he was out again, under very strict conditions, while he awaited his trial date). He wrote:

My dear Essie,

You must be thinking the worst of me right now, and I can't blame you for that. What happened was terrible, and I feel terrible about it. It's all more complicated than they say in the newsfeeds and I hope one day I can make you see things from my point of view. But I'm not writing this to justify myself. I'm writing to beg you to come back to us.

I don't know what made you run away from school. I hope it wasn't because of me and all my troubles. I know it can't have made things easy for you. But even if things have been tough, you have to give it another try. The school will take you back, I'm sure I can make that happen. Don't worry about the fees. I don't know what your mother told you, but I won't let anyone take you out of Triumph. You deserve the best, because you're smart and kind and you're the sort of person the Admiralty needs. So you don't have to worry about being sent away.

They told me about the money, too. As you probably know, they're freezing all my assets, but I'll try and keep that line of credit open for as long as I can, so if you need it, you can use it. They told me you were last seen in Southaven, with another girl who'd also run away from Triumph. I have

224

to hope she's really your friend and she's not just
taking advantage of you. I wish you'd let someone
know where you are and what's going on. Why
did you run away? Where are you? Why have you
switched off your shell? We've been trying to locate
you but they say your shell's gone dead. Please let us
know what's going on. I won't be angry, I just want
to know that you're safe. I have a lot of time in here
to worry about your welfare, so please put me out
of my misery and get in touch! Even if it's just to let
me know you're okay. And remember that wherever
you end up, whatever has happened, if you want to
come home, just pick up your shell and I'll arrange
it, I promise.

Please know that whatever happens with the
trial, and whatever happens between me and your
mother, I will always love you, and I will always
do my best to look after you. I'm still hopeful that
everything's going to work out okay. But even if it
doesn't, know that I'm always your loving dad, and
I'll try my best to take care of you.

I hope you can forgive me. Please come home.
Dad

Essie had to hide her face behind a drinks menu
when she got to the end of the mail so no one could
see her cry.

She had known, sort of, that they must be wondering where she was. But until now she hadn't really let
herself think about it. Now she realized that they must
be frantic with worry. She had been gone for weeks

without a word, and they had no way to contact her or even locate her. Guilt sideswiped her.

Essie spent several minutes trying to compose an email to her father, reassuring, explaining, justifying, but everything she wrote seemed wrong, or gave away too much information. Eventually she wrote:

Dear Dad,

Please don't worry about me. I'm okay and Annalie is a true friend. I'll send word when I can. Hope to be home soon.
    Love Essie.

"Hey, sister boy," the maid called Dodo said, and beckoned to Pod.

He got up and followed her out into the service corridor, where two young maids were standing with a trolley filled with neatly folded towels and tiny shampoo bottles. One of them looked at him, and her face brightened with excitement. "Hey, I know you!" she said.

Pod recognized the girl too. "Karmon, right?"

"Yes!" She was giddy with excitement. "We were on that slave hulk together, you and me and Blossom. That boat was the worst!"

Pod nodded, almost feeling faint with anticipation. "You seen Blossom?"

"We *were* together," Karmon said. "First six months or so. We were on the same boat at first, but then we got separated. We both started out on *Blue Water Duchess*, then they moved me here, to *Blue Water Princess*."

"Is she still there?"

"Far as I know," said Karmon.

"How's she doing?" he asked eagerly. "How do they treat you on these boats?"

"They're good places to work," Karmon said, a little too emphatically.

"Truly?"

"Ain't the worst job I had," Karmon said, and laughed.

"Food's okay," the other maid said. "Work's okay. No danger. Just hard. Long hours."

"Long hours," Karmon said. "And we never see land. Trouble is, costs are high on a job like this. Uniforms, food, cabin, water. I got me an even bigger debt now. Your sister too, prob'ly."

The story was too familiar to make Pod very angry, but still it rankled. "But she was okay, the last time you saw her?"

"She's okay. Don't worry." Karmon paused, looking at him curiously. "So are you working here now? Got a job in the kitchen?"

"Not exactly," Pod said. "Hey, you ever see Blossom again, you tell her I'm doing good now. And tell her I'm looking for her, okay?"

"What do you mean you're doing good?" Karmon stared at him, her eyes widening. "You *free* or something?"

The maid in charge of the monitor had come out to see what all the chit-chat was about. "Hey," she said, "why ain't you working?"

227

Karmon and the other maids scrambled. The maid from the work station glared at Pod. He hurried back the way he'd come, shedding his kitchen hand's jacket, and went out onto the deck to find Essie, his head pounding with excitement.

He hadn't found his sister, but he'd found the next best thing: he knew the name of the ship she was on.

Essie was still sitting in her deckchair when he emerged into the sunny dazzle of the deck. She was deeply immersed in her shell and didn't seem to notice him until he was standing right in front of her.

"We're good," he said. "Let's get out of here."

Essie nodded and they were about to head back to the companionway that led off the ship when the sound of a siren split the air.

At first the people around them merely seemed startled, but then an alarm began to blurp, loudly and repetitively, in a way that seemed guaranteed to prevent rational thought. The passengers looked variously startled, disgruntled, confused. Only the staff made it clear: they looked terrified. Something was going on.

"What's happening?" asked Essie, grabbing a steward.

"Nothing to worry about," he gabbled, "everything's under control. Now please return to your cabin and stay there until you hear the all-clear."

Essie and Pod stared at each other and ran as one to the gate.

Too late: the companionway was being raised.
There was no way off the ship.

Pirate submarine

"How do we get off this thing?" cried Pod. "I don't know," Essie said. "It's too far to jump."

"I'm not jumping," Pod said.

"Maybe there's another deck below this one. It wouldn't be so far—"

"I'm not jumping," Pod insisted.

"We have to get off somehow!" Essie said.

They were interrupted by a scream. They turned; passengers were running to look over the opposite deck. Pod and Essie ran with them, and saw something in the water below them.

It was a long, curved metallic shape floating just above the waterline, bristling with guns and turrets. Inflatable boats were deploying from it, filled with men carrying big guns, and other men in diving gear.

"That's a pirate submarine," Pod said.

"A what?" said Essie.

"They put mines on the bottom of the boat. Captain don't hand over the boat, company don't pay the ransom, they blow it up," said Pod flatly.

Essie looked at him in horror. "We *really* need to get off this boat," she said.

With a blast, water cannons began to roar, pouring torrents of water off the cruise ship and down onto the submarine and its submersibles. The submersibles scooted out of range of the water cannons, and when they were visible again to the people up on deck, their cargo of divers had vanished—presumably somewhere under the boat.

"Where do you think Will and Annalie are?"

"Hopefully, where we left them," Pod said.

Essie began to run toward the stern of the boat, in the vague hope that they might be able to see the *Sunfish*. They reached the back deck and looked out. There was no sign of them.

"Oh, what are we going to do?" wailed Essie.

"Look," Pod said. He dragged Essie over to a map of the ship that had been posted on the wall with many detailed instructions about what to do in case of emergency. "Where are we now?"

Essie looked frantically around her. "Um... we're on this deck," she said, pointing.

"There's another deck here," Pod said, pointing to another deck below the one they were on. "Let's get down there."

They ran to the nearest stairs, but the crew were busily locking them down. "Return to your cabin!" they shouted.

"But our cabin's down there!" Essie said.

"Go via the main stairs."

"But these are right here! I promise we'll be quick!"

The crewman unlocked the gate, let them through, then slammed and locked it behind them. Pod and Essie clattered down the stairs. At the bottom, the gate was already locked.

"Hey!" they shouted. "Help!"

But there was no one nearby. The deck was littered with overturned deckchairs, abandoned magazines, lost shoes and tumbled towels.

"Help!" they shouted, rattling the gates.

At last a crewman stuck his head out, looking pale and frightened. "What you doing there?" he called.

"We're trying to get to our cabin, can you let us out please?"

"We're locked down!"

"*Please!*"

The crewman dashed out, unlocked the gate, and set them free. As he did so, a stream of armed men came pouring from a *Staff Only* door.

"Get off the deck, quick!" the crewman said, and fled back to where he'd come from.

Essie and Pod ducked for cover as the armed security guards spread out and took up positions, looking over the sides. None of them seemed even slightly interested in the two children: all their attention was on what was happening in the water.

"How hard do you suppose it would be to launch a lifeboat?" Essie whispered. She could see one, not far away. The instructions for its use seemed very detailed.

"Hard," Pod said.

There was a shout, and the security guards began

to fire. The noise was deafening. Orders were barked, and they heard radios squawking, then the guards closest to them were running forward.

"Come on," Pod said, and started running in the opposite direction.

Something was clearly happening at the front of the boat; the sound of gunfire grew more intense and there was more shouting.

Essie grabbed two lifejackets and handed one to Pod.

"No," he said.

"You want to get off this boat or not?"

They scrambled into the life jackets, fumbling with clips and straps, and headed to the observation deck in the stern.

A security guard was standing there, monitoring the approaches. Fortunately he had his back to them and they avoided being seen.

"We'll have to go over the side," Essie said. "Don't want any of them to see us."

"No," Pod said. "'Specially not the pirates."

They peered over the sides. The water cannons were still blasting—if they jumped directly into the path of one they would get pummelled. They crept along the deck, afraid that the security guards might return at any moment.

"Here," Essie said. "We have to do this, Pod. It's the only way."

Pod knew she was right. So he did what he'd learned to do years before when he'd been sent down into some flooded factory with only a leaky hose to rely on. He made his mind go blank, and focused on doing the very next thing that needed to be done. That was the trick: take this step, then this step, then this step, and not think about it.

He climbed up the rail. He held on. He took Essie's hand. He let himself fall.

Into the churn

A nd oh, how far it was. So far and so far, falling with his stomach traveling at its own separate and sickening pace, and then he hit the water, his body ready to keep flying down into the terrifying green, but the life jacket had other ideas. It smacked him in the chin as it pulled him back up to the surface and he was floating awkwardly and Essie was beside him.

"Swim!" she gasped, and began breaststroking awkwardly, hampered by her life jacket.

Pod paddled with his arms as best he could.

It was mayhem above them, mayhem in the water. The water cannons still roared and he could hear the whine of the motors on the pirates' inflatables. They had jumped into the water on the landward side; the submarine was on the other side, so they could not see what was going on. An inflatable roared past, only meters from Essie's face, the pirates in it spraying the upper decks of the great cruise ship with gunfire. Gunshots pinged down into the water all around them and Essie screamed in terror, afraid she might be caught in the crossfire, but the inflatable roared off and the shooting went with it.

Then, from the other side of the boat, they heard a thud, and then, a moment later, they felt a shockwave roll through the water around them. The huge cruise ship barely moved.

"What was that?" Essie asked. "Do you think they detonated the mine?"

"We'll soon find out," Pod said grimly.

They swam, even more desperately than before, both of them aware, from different sources, that sinking ships could suck you down with them. (Essie had seen a tear-jerking movie about a famous historical shipwreck; Pod had heard first-hand stories about the wreck of a slave hulk.)

Behind them, the cruise ship's horn boomed out, three blasts, and then a new roar was added to the mix.

Pod glanced back. "They're starting their engines!"

The water cannons shut off. The great propellors began to turn. The water boiled.

Essie and Pod kicked frantically, getting nowhere fast. All around them they could feel the water churning. Very slowly, the great ship began to move.

"It could still pull us in!" Essie shrieked, and the two of them kicked and thrashed and stroked some more.

The cruise ship, huge, white, slightly scarred, moved off into open water. The churn moved with it.

Essie and Pod stopped paddling and dangled there in the water, held up by their life jackets.

"Now what?" Essie said.

They were still a long way from shore, and there was nowhere to land. This part of the island was edged with cliffs

Then, from around the headland, came a welcome sight.

The *Sunfish* was sailing toward them.

Links

"A pirate submarine?" Will exclaimed. "Really?"

"And armed security guards," Essie said. "That's a new thing for cruise ships."

"I don't think the submarine made it," Pod said.

There was floating debris in the water; it looked like the submarine had been seriously damaged, if not destroyed entirely. They had decided to steer clear of it and swiftly left Kapa Island behind.

"I found some things I think you should see," Essie said, when they were out in open water once again.

While Pod had been searching for his sister, Essie had made the most of the *Princess'* signal and done some searches. She'd begun with the four names on the list.

"I found a few references to them," Essie said, "but none of it's recent. In fact, most of it's from before we were born."

She flicked through the little she'd found: young men and women attending university, winning medals, publishing scientific papers, appearing in campus musicals, performing with long-vanished bands, smiling from long-ago news stories. The most recent entries were fifteen years old. Then nothing.

"They've *all* gone underground," Annalie said. "Every single one of them."

"Yes. But I did manage to find this," Essie said.

It was a photograph, slightly fuzzy, showing seven people standing on some elaborate steps outside a building. They all had Admiralty kit bags, although they were not wearing uniforms. There was a man in a cowboy hat, a woman with long red hair in a plait, a big woman, and a thin, dark-eyed man, older than the others, with a dark coif, already threaded with silver.

"It's Spinner!" Annalie said.

"Is that them?" asked Will excitedly.

"It has to be them," Essie said. "And look. That's the guy who tried to arrest us in Southaven."

His face was less grooved and his hair was much fuller, but it was recognisably Avery Beckett. He was on a higher step than the others, positioned between Spinner and a third woman.

"Who do you reckon that is he's standing next to?" Essie asked.

"I think—" Annalie began.

"That's our mother," finished Will.

The twins leaned in closer. The woman was young and lovely, smiling at the camera. She had the same thick hair as Annalie, Will's square jaw. The two of them studied the fuzzy image, trying to trace themselves in that unfamiliar face.

"So that's what she looked like," Annalie murmured.

"You don't remember her?" asked Essie.

"Don't remember her, never seen a photo of her," Will said. "She died when we were babies."

They were all quiet for a moment. Then Pod whistled. "Hey, Graham. Come look at this."

Graham flew down and cocked his head on one side as he studied the picture. Then he began to squawk with excitement and fly round and round Pod's head, words escaping him.

"Yep. He recognizes them," Will said.

"I recognize the building too," Essie said. "They're on the steps of the Ministry of Science. See?"

She'd found a second photo of the Ministry of Science to compare it with. It was a very old building with the same elaborate marble staircase the seven young people were standing on.

"I wonder where they're going," Will said.

"The desert?" Pod suggested.

"I searched "Ministry of Science" and "desert" but I didn't get very far," Essie said. "Mind you if it was top secret, I wouldn't expect to find much."

"I can't believe you found this much," Annalie said. "It's amazing."

"Searching the links is what I do," Essie said modestly.

Later, Essie took Annalie aside. "There's something else I wanted to show you," she said, activating her shell again. "After I recognized him in the picture I thought I'd look into that Avery Beckett guy too.

240

There was *heaps* of stuff on him."

He was, as he said, an agent of the Admiralty's Department of Scientific Inquiry, and was listed with a name and photo on their personnel page as Head of the Special Investigations Section. The description of what the department actually did was brief and vague.

Next, Essie showed her a news article that had appeared six years ago in the *Daily Herald*, one of Dux's main newsfeeds.

VICTORY IN INTERNATIONAL PIRACY FIGHT
The Admiralty has smashed an international smuggling ring trading in stolen technology with the arrest of pirate captain Ambo Suz Mila, 35, and his confederates. Suz Mila has been charged with conspiracy to steal, transport, and sell top-secret technology taken from the Admiralty's Department of Scientific Inquiry, and also with using that technology to carry out acts of piracy against vessels traveling through Allied Federation of Nations waters.

The investigation into the pirates has been conducted over a period of eight months, and culminated this morning in a dawn raid on Moombass Island, one of the Moon Islands, where the pirates had a heavily fortified compound. The Admiralty team overcame strong resistance to penetrate the compound, coming under heavy fire, without sustaining any serious injuries. The pirates attempted to detonate the compound to destroy the evidence of their activities, risking the lives of the family members and children also living there, but they were prevented from doing so by the swift action of the Admiralty team. The team then made numerous arrests and recovered a large amount of stolen technology, weapons, and other contraband items.

"The theft of naval technology represents a grave threat to the ongoing security of everyone who lives under the Admiralty's protection," said Commander Avery Beckett, who headed the operation. "These people are ruthless, and they'll stop at nothing to steal the technology that helps us keep people safe. By smashing this ring, we've struck a blow against the pirates who want to steal from us, and made the high seas a safer place for all of us."

The technology recovered includes experimental communications equipment and a new kind of propulsion engine. Although the details of this new engine remain classified, Commander Beckett noted that this new-generation high-speed engine would make pirates virtually impossible to catch.

"The recovery of this technology was of the highest priority for our team," he said.

The Admiralty leadership has commended Commander Beckett and his team for the surgical precision of the successful operation. The accused, who come from non-Federation countries or are non-documented persons, have been transported to Dux to await trial.

"Yikes," Annalie said, when she'd finished reading. "That guy's even more hardcore than I realized."

"Wait until you read this," Essie said.

242

The second article she showed her was much longer. It was a feature article that had been published on a newslink called *Uncover.*

"What's *Uncover*?" asked Annalie.

"It's an independent investigative newslink published out of Barbassa," Essie said. Barbassa was a small, mountainous, landlocked country that had never seen the need to join the Admiralty's Federation of Allied Nations and maintained a lofty neutrality to the squabbles of the world.

DEATH ON MOOMBASS

They came in the pre-dawn darkness: four landers from the Admiralty warship *Defiance*, each containing an operational team of five men. They slid silently onto the beaches at 4.54 a.m., weapons ready, and moved up the beach and into the trees. Their target was a large encampment, protected by armed guards and an electric fence, where as many as two hundred men, women, and children lived together. To the Admiralty, this camp was a pirate base and a vital link in the international tech-theft network. To the two hundred people who lived there, it was the only home they'd ever known.

Team A's mission was to disable the electric fence. Team B was responsible for taking out the guards. Team A found the electric fence was non-functional and penetrated it easily. Team B found there were no guards on duty. The four teams entered the compound at 5.14 a.m.

Less than an hour later, the encampment would be in flames, with scores of the inhabitants dead, injured,

or missing, including forty-two children. And yet
the Admiralty team who carried out the raid, led by
Commander Avery Beckett, was officially praised for
its "surgical precision".

What really happened that morning on Moombass?

Hulk Harbor is the largest refugee camp in the world.
In the immediate aftermath of the Flood, desperate
people from all over the world set out in boats to
escape the rising waters. Some of them were escaping
from coastal regions that disappeared under the sea,
some from the ghost countries that were completely
immersed by the Flood. Still others came seeking
refuge in those fortunate countries that had escaped
the worst effects of the Flood.

Many of these ships were unsuitable for large
groups of passengers, poorly provisioned, or had
been damaged by the floodwaters, and in one of
the great heroic acts of the post-flood period, the
Admiralty found and escorted all these refugee
ships to safer waters. A place was found for them
in the great Bay of Kinute, on Tappa Island, off the
north-east coast of Dux. But plans to repatriate these
refugees came to nothing. Many of the refugees no
longer had homes to go to; others were unwilling
to return to countries rendered destitute by floods.
Some nations closed their borders completely. Many
more would accept only a small number of refugees
in any given year. Waiting lists for the richest
countries are now decades long. Hulk Harbor—a
collection of rusting, barely habitable boats,

floating in the filthy junk-strewn water of the Bay
of Kinute—has become a permanent floating home
to millions. Generations have been born there, with
little hope of escape.

Some of these refugees have taken matters
into their own hands. Giving up on any hope of
resettlement through official channels, they are
leaving Hulk Harbor and finding their way south,
to the Moon Islands. Although this low-lying part
of the world was the hardest-hit by the Floods, for
many people, it is their one hope of salvation. New
communities are springing up there, unconnected to
national governments or authorities. The Admiralty
call it "a vast zone of lawlessness." The people who
live there see it as a kind of freedom. But it can be a
perilous freedom.

There is no doubt that piracy represents an ongoing
threat to the security of international shipping. The
Admiralty have long used this threat to justify their
continuing presence at the heart of government.
However, independent analysis of crime statistics
over the post-flood period shows that the number
of attacks currently grouped under the heading of
piracy has been either steady or falling over the last
ten years. These statistics are difficult to verify, as the
Admiralty and government keep the details secret "for
operational reasons." However, it does seem clear that
the trend in international piracy is downward. The
public, however, believes that piracy is increasing, and
is increasing in sophistication.

The Admiralty has carried out a number of well-publicized raids on pirates and technology thieves over the last five years, with the stated objectives of reducing international piracy and smashing the trade in stolen technology.

However there are persistent rumors that the technology making its way out of the Admiralty and onto the black market is not all being stolen by spies or pirates. Some say it is being provided by secret elements from within the Admiralty itself. These deep cover operatives are supplying new technology to pirates, creating an atmosphere of lawlessness and fear. The law-enforcement arm of the Admiralty then cracks down on these pirates, without ever seeming to uncover the source of the leak that let the technology onto the market in the first place.

Moombass began as one of these crackdowns. But something went wrong.

The electric fence around the camp on Moombass ran off a wind turbine generator. The Admiralty have argued that the presence of an electric fence indicates that the camp was a fortified compound. Residents say it was largely defensive; the electric fence had been put up to deter ordinary looters.

There had been a celebration in the camp the night before the raid. A young couple had got married, and everyone had joined in the celebrations, which went until late into the night. When the marines broke into the camp at first light, the vast majority of the inhabitants were sleeping it off.

Accounts differ about exactly what happened next.

The official Admiralty report, written by Commander Beckett, states: "My men disabled the electric fence and entered the compound. We were fired upon by an unseen shooter and we immediately took cover and returned fire."

An eyewitness living on Moombass tells a different story. He says: "I woke up and saw a terrifying face looking in at me through the window of my house. It was a marine in helmet and combat goggles. He had a gun trained on me and my wife. We thought we were dead for sure. He chased us outside, and when we came out we saw they were emptying all the houses around us. I could see the people stumbling out, some of them still half-asleep. A couple of us were angry and started shouting back at them. That was a mistake. We started shouting, and then they started shooting."

The eyewitness estimates that at least fifteen people were shot in that initial exchange.

Another eyewitness recalls: "They started going from house to house, tearing everything apart, knocking over the furniture. You could hear things going crash, smash. People's precious possessions, being smashed to bits.

"Then a man came and spoke to us. He was wearing a uniform and I saw his name on it—Beckett. He held up a picture—I didn't know what it was exactly—some piece of high tech. He said, 'If you want all this to stop, you'd better tell me where to find this. Or I'll tear this place down to the nails and screws.'

"At first no one said anything. Maybe they didn't know what that thing was. I certainly didn't know.

Then finally Ambo says, 'I'll tell you where it is. Please don't wreck our town.' The man called Beckett took him away."

According to the Admiralty's report, Ambo Suz Mila, 35, was discovered hiding in his home with an automatic weapon. When marines attempted to enter the property to search it, he fired on them. The marines managed to subdue him and take him into custody, despite fierce opposition. When they searched his home they found a number of stolen items hidden there. Subsequently, Suz Mila would be charged with a range of offenses, and accused of being the ringleader of the operation.

But what was the nature of this operation?

The waters around Moombass were once rich in marine life. The sudden change in sea level caused the fisheries to collapse, but since then Moombass has seen a revival of its fish stocks. For the people of Moombass, fish is an increasingly important part of their livelihood. The Moombass fishing fleet is small—only five boats—and just one of these is suitable for traveling long distances. This boat has become the island's lifeline, transporting a part of its catch to the busy market at Gomba Island, which sells new, old, and reconditioned tech as well as fish. Over the last few seasons, the Moombassans have begun making improvements to their fishing fleet. One of the things they bought was a device that could help them locate fish. Another was a better engine for their boat, so they could get their catch to market faster.

The Admiralty alleges that these items were important new technologies stolen from Science Special Projects. Moombassan witnesses insist that none of these items were hidden in people's homes. They had been bought openly, and were being used as part of the day-to-day business of the fishing fleet. They deny that there were large caches of weapons in the compound or on board the fishing boats, although each captain did keep a gun or two on board for self-defense.

"Every pirate claims to be a fisherman until you find the automatic weapons in the hold," said Commander Avery Beckett at a press conference.

"We're not pirates. We're just families, trying to live our lives. Old people and parents and children trying to get by," said a Moombassan woman.

Today, the future is uncertain for those who remain on Moombass. Their largest boat has been impounded as evidence, making it almost impossible for them to continue trading with Gomba. But still they hang on, hoping to rebuild. What choice do they have? They have nowhere else to go.

When Annalie had finished reading, Essie looked at her expectantly. "Do you think it could be true?"

"Which article?"

"The long one, obviously."

"Sure," Annalie said. "You hear about stuff like that happening."

"*Really?*" Essie asked. "Marines going into people's camps and just shooting unarmed people?"

"*I've* heard stories like that," Annalie said.

"Well I haven't!" Essie said, upset. "The Admiralty *I* joined wouldn't do stuff like that. They wouldn't let someone like that work for them either."

"But he *does* work for them."

Essie looked at Annalie angrily. "We both went to Triumph so we could get into the Admiralty one day. How could you go to school, knowing you'd have to do active service, if you already knew they did things like this?"

"I was never all that keen on going into the Admiralty at all!" Annalie said. "It seemed like a—necessary evil. That's the way Spinner made it sound. If you want to go to university and do something important with your life, you need to go to an Admiralty school."

"That's all it ever was to you? Something your dad made you do so you could get on in life?"

"Well, what was it to you?" Annalie asked.

"The mission—the oath—I believe in it. It's important," Essie said, unable to express herself clearly.

Annalie could see her distress. "I know you believe it. Lots of people do believe it. And of course the Admiralty do good work. Of course they do."

"They do," Essie agreed, somewhat appeased.

"But in an organization as big and complicated and powerful as the Admiralty, it's probably not surprising there are a few rotten apples." This was the sort of thing she'd heard Spinner say; it was the closest he'd ever come to direct criticism.

"If that article's even half-true, then Beckett's a bit more than a rotten apple," Essie said.

"Right," Annalie said soberly. "Let's hope we never run into him again."

A sighting

Their next stop was an island that was a major staging post for travelers. It had a reputation for being rough and wild, but they hoped that as long as they were careful they'd be okay.

They didn't plan a lengthy stop: it was decided when they landed that Pod would fill the water tanks, Will would go and look for the spare part he needed, and Essie and Annalie would look for food. They would only be in port for an hour or two.

Pod stood at the watering station, listening to the water as it poured from the hose into the tanks. Graham was perched on the railing beside him, watching the world go by.

"Nice town," he squawked. "Trees."

It *was* a nice town, spreading around the wide harbor, a jungly mountain rising up behind it.

"We stay here? No more sea," Graham suggested.

"Can't stay here. Bit more to go," Pod said.

"Pod and Graham stay here."

"Don't you want to see Spinner?"

Graham let out a shriek.

"Then we got to stay on the boat a bit longer.

252

Be patient."

Graham whistled to let him know what he thought about being patient. "Spinner bad," Graham grumbled. "Go away too long. No biscuit."

"He misses you too," Pod said. "I'm sure he wants to get you back."

"See Spinner again, Graham bite nose off!" he said defiantly.

Pod had filled the first of his tanks. He put the hose into the second tank and screwed the lid securely back onto the first tank, keeping a watchful eye on what was going on around him. The port was a busy one, and all three water-pumping stations were occupied by different boats. There were two men standing nearby, not doing much, and Pod was trying to decide whether they looked suspicious or not, when he heard Graham let out a great musical squawk. He turned in time to see Graham taking off, wings flapping at a great rate, shrieking "Spinner! Spinner!"

"Graham!" he shouted. "Come back!"

But the bird had already vanished into the crowd.

Essie and Annalie had treated themselves to hot, flaky sausage rolls, golden-brown and warm from the oven, as well as the usual much less interesting provisions, and were walking back toward the boat.

"Have you thought about what you'll do after all this is over?" Essie asked.

"You mean, after we find Spinner?" Annalie said.

253

"Well, we'll give him the boat back. And then I guess we'll take it from there."

"Do you think he's going to want to keep you and Will with him?"

"I don't know," Annalie said. "He'll probably keep Will. But he might want me to go back to school."

"Is that what you want to do?" Essie asked.

"I don't know if they'd even have me back," Annalie said.

"Oh, they'd have you back," Essie said. "You don't have to worry about that."

"You reckon?"

"You were one of the smartest people in our year," Essie said. "They'd have you back like a shot."

Annalie was silent for a moment as they walked along. "What about you? What will you do?"

Essie felt a wave of sadness wash over her. "I don't know. Mom said she couldn't afford to keep me at Triumph any more, but then Dad said he was going to make them take me back. I don't know how much leverage he's going to have if he's a convicted felon." Her eyes filled with tears at the thought of her dad humiliated, diminished, locked away with dangerous, violent criminals.

Annalie looked at her sympathetically. "We'll work something out. Maybe they'll take us both back." She paused. "Back to locker inspections and cleaning our boots with a toothbrush."

"Climbing ropes in sports."

"Fun people like Tiffany."

Essie laughed through her tears. "So much to look forward to."

"We could always switch to piracy."

"There'd be a lot less rules."

Annalie shot her a more serious look. "Well, whatever happens, there'll always be a place for you on the boat, you know."

Essie gave her a little smile of gratitude.

Pod finished filling the water tanks in an agony of uncertainty. He knew he should be chasing after Graham, but he couldn't leave until the tanks were filled and paid for—and even when they were, he didn't want to leave the boat unprotected.

Will came back, carrying spare parts, as Pod was paying for the water.

"Problem," Pod said. "Graham took off."

"Stupid bird," Will growled.

"I think he saw your dad."

Will stared at Pod for a moment, frozen to the spot, then turned to look wildly at the crowd. "Did you see him?" he cried. "Where did he go?"

"Only saw Graham flying off after him. He went that way." Pod pointed.

His heart pounding, Will ran. Could it really be true? Spinner, here?

"Did you ever used to watch that vidshow *Below Decks*?" Essie asked.

Annalie shook her head.

"Oh, it was the best show. It was all about young Admiralty sailors and officers going to sea for the first time. There were heaps of them: *Below Decks: Courage, Below Decks: Victory*. There was even a *Below Decks: Triumph*."

"Really?"

"They didn't shoot it on the real ship. I'm sure most of it was done in a studio, although you couldn't tell. *Below Decks: Courage* was the best—it was the first one, the others were all spin offs. It looked so exciting, being on a battleship and doing your service. Having adventures, doing good deeds, saving the world. There was a lot of romance too, which I wasn't so keen on, not when I was little anyway."

"And you thought that's what it would really be like?"

"Well, I hoped," Essie said.

"The reality is probably a lot less fun," Annalie said.

They walked in silence for a moment or two.

"What do you think will happen to us if we don't go back to Triumph?" Essie asked.

"I guess, eventually, we'll go somewhere else."

"My parents always told me that if you didn't go to the right school, get into university, make the right kind of start, you'd never get anywhere. Do you think it's true?" Essie asked.

"The world's full of people who don't go to good schools *or* university, and they still lead interesting, valuable, important lives," Annalie said firmly, although she felt much less certain about this than she sounded.

Essie considered this. "I don't care about valuable and important. But I'm hoping for interesting."

"What do you want to do when you grow up?" Annalie asked.

"I hadn't really worked that out yet," Essie said.

Annalie stopped suddenly, and caught Essie's arm. "Look—is that a uniform?"

Almost as if their talk of the Admiralty had conjured him up, they saw an Admiralty marine standing in a doorway, looking about as if she was monitoring the street.

"Is she looking for someone?" Essie asked.

The two girls looked at each other, suddenly full of dread. "We need to get back to the boat!" Annalie said.

Will had stopped running, out of breath, and was now walking down the main street, calling, "Graham! Where are you?"

It had occurred to him that even if Spinner *were* here, he probably didn't want someone walking down the street hollering his name for anyone to hear.

He had been through the market, pounded his way up and down the main street, and was now getting deeper and deeper into dangerous territory. The people around here were looking increasingly scary, and he didn't feel safe. But what if Spinner was here somewhere? He'd shipped out with the Kangs—perhaps he was hiding ashore with them too.

He spotted a bar with a Kang mark beside the doorway. It seemed to have no actual door, as if it never closed; inside it was a smoky, beer-smelling cave. He was just plucking up the courage to go in when Graham came flapping down and landed beside him.

"Graham! There you are! Pod said you saw Spinner."

"No Spinner,' Graham said mournfully. "I follow, I lose, I find. But he not Spinner. He say, Go away!"

Will looked at the disconsolate parrot, his own heart sinking. He hadn't realized until now how desperately he'd been hoping to find Spinner, to know that their journey was finally over and he could hand the responsibility back to him. "You're sure it wasn't him?" he asked.

Graham swung his head from side to side. "Same Spinner hair. But no Spinner. Then I get lost."

Will let Graham sit on his shoulder as he began the long trudge back toward the boat. "How did you get lost? You only had to fly back to the port. You can *see* it from here."

Essie and Annalie ran down the boardwalk to where Pod was waiting. "We need to get out of here," Annalie said. "There are marines on the streets.'

"Looking for someone," Essie added. Pod looked at them sharply. "Didn't see no Admiralty ships when we come in," he said.

"No," Annalie said, "but they're here. I don't like

it. I think we should get out of here as soon as we can. Is Will back yet?"

"Not yet," Pod said, and explained what had happened. Annalie stared when she heard Spinner's name.

"We should go and look for them!" Essie said, catching her excitement.

"Too many of us running around," Pod said. "Everyone'll get lost."

"You're right," Annalie said. "We're better off staying here. Let's get ready for a quick departure."

Graham was grumbling. "When go home?"

"I don't know," Will said. "Soon."

"When soon?"

"Like I said, I don't know."

"Spinner lost. Will take Graham home."

"They wrecked our home, remember?" Will said in gloomy rage. "We don't have anywhere to go back to."

He turned a corner, and as he did so, a figure stepped out into the path directly in front of him. Will almost collided with the man who was not in uniform, but had something of an Admiralty look about him.

The man smiled and his lip curled up to reveal sharp teeth. With horror, Will recognized the man who'd chased him out his own bedroom window back in Lowtown.

"Hello, Will," said Beckett. "Long time no see."

Beckett again

Will turned to run, but hands gripped him firmly. Two marines had come up from behind and grabbed him. He struggled and wriggled, trying to wrench himself free, but the men were too strong for him.

"Graham!" Will shouted. "Tell Annalie!"

"Catch that bird!" Beckett roared, but Graham was too quick for them. He soared up into the sky and flew away.

"Cuff him," Beckett said, and one of the marines zip-tied his wrists together. "Now, if you know what's good for you, you're going to tell us where to find your father."

They walked Will down toward the port. Will expected them to take him aboard one of their ships, but there were none lying at anchor in the harbor. Instead they took him to the office of the harbormaster. He realized they were outside the Admiralty's jurisdiction here; they didn't operate a base or even have an office in town, so the harbormaster's office was the next best thing.

He tried surreptitiously to see whether the *Sunfish* had left harbor. When he sent Graham to warn the others, he'd meant they should get away and save themselves while they still had a chance. This, he thought, was really rather noble of him; but he also felt sick with fear about what was going to happen next.

They sat him down on a hard visitor's chair. Beckett relaxed in the harbormaster's chair, across the desk from him, while the marines went to wait outside the door.

"You've been hard to catch," Beckett said. "I thought we'd track you down a lot sooner than this."

Will gave him an unfriendly look and said nothing.

"Well, here's how it's going to go. I already have you in custody. It won't be long until I find your sister and that boat of yours. When I do, I'm going to confiscate the boat—again." He smiled horribly. "Then we're going to dismantle it down to the smallest joint and rivet. We're going to break it down until there's nothing left of it, just in case the item I'm looking for is still aboard. Okay? That's the first thing I'm going to do.

"Then, I'm going to charge you and your sister with breaking into an Admiralty facility, stealing a boat from our custody, and unauthorized exit from Dux. I'm going to charge your sister with kidnapping that girl you've got in tow and fraudulently obtaining money from her father's account."

"We didn't kidnap her!" Will said, forgetting he had intended to say nothing at all.

"But you did steal her father's money, didn't you?" Beckett said, his smile gleaming. "Be assured of this: you'll be spending the rest of your teenage years in juvenile detention, and so will your sister. She can forget about going back to Triumph College. That's done with. She'll be sent to the girls' facility in Oates Lake, and you'll be at the boys' facility on Mount Staggar or Fort Beacon."

Oates Lake was an industrial town on the shores of an old, dry salt lake. It was hot, remote, and harsh, famous for its colonies of prisons and its toxic-waste dump. Mount Staggar was a boys' prison next to a mine; really, it was a labor camp, and a dangerous one. Fort Beacon, on the other hand, was a prison where the boys were kept locked down twenty-three hours a day.

Will gulped, reminding himself to stay tough. "Prove it," he said.

"That won't be difficult," Beckett said. He smiled, letting the idea of prison sink in for a moment. "But you can still make all this go away. You can save yourself and your sister. You just have to tell us where your father is."

"I don't know where he is," Will said. "And that's the truth."

Beckett studied him thoughtfully. "Well, that's not really very helpful, is it?"

"It's true. He could be anywhere—he didn't tell us where he was going. We were just looking for somewhere to take the boat and lie low," Will said.

Beckett considered this for a moment. "I guess it's the kind of thing a couple of kids might do," he conceded. "Sail off into the wild south with no plan at all." He paused. "Once I give the story of your capture and arrest to the newsfeeds, I hope, for your sake, it'll flush your father out of hiding. If he takes the bait, all the better for you. If he doesn't, I've already told you what's going to happen. And I'll let you think about what kind of loving father would stand by and let all that happen to his kids."

Beckett waited for a moment longer to see if Will would crack, then pushed his chair back and got to his feet. "I'm going to go and find your boat and arrest your sister now." He went to the door and smiled at Will. "Do have a think about all I've said."

He tapped on the door, and was let out. The door was locked again behind him.

Left alone, Will looked openly around the room as he hadn't quite dared to before. There was a window, but it had bars on it. He examined it anyway, in case there was some chance of squeezing out, or jiggling the bars loose. But they were set quite firmly in the wall, and there was no chance of squeezing out between them. Plus he still had his hands zip-tied behind his back.

He went to the harbormaster's desk and found some scissors. Rather awkwardly, (it was hard to use scissors with your hands behind your back) he managed to cut himself free. He looked around the room again, rubbing his wrists.

One window, barred.

One door, locked and guarded.

No other way out.

Then he glanced up. There was an access hatch in the ceiling.

Excitement bubbled up inside him. The hatch was at one end of the room, above some filing cabinets. He crept over to it and climbed up very carefully, trying not to make a sound. From the top of the cabinet he could push the hatch—it lifted—but he wasn't tall enough to pull himself inside it.

Cautiously he hopped down again and picked up the visitor's chair. He placed this on top of the filing cabinet, then climbed up beside it and stepped ever so carefully onto it. The legs slipped slightly under him, and the metal gave a boom. Will froze, waiting to see what would happen, but no one came in. Hurrying now, he stepped up onto the chair, lifted the hatch and wriggled through the narrow space into the ceiling.

It was almost dark under the roof, and hot, and full of grit and dust. But there were cracks of light visible here and there: the roof above him was tiled. He planted his feet carefully on the beams, and pushed at a roof tile. It lifted easily; he slipped it out, placing it carefully down beside him, then lifted out another and another, until he'd made a gap big enough to climb through. He poked his head out into brilliant daylight and looked around at a landscape of rooftops and chimneys, satellite dishes, solar panels and humming turbines. He let himself out onto the tiles, then skidded down the roof. He managed to stop himself just in time and clung to the gutter, his heart thumping, as he looked for a way down. There was another, slightly lower roof nearby—he stretched out a foot and stepped down onto that, hoping for a drainpipe he might climb down. The one he found looked rickety, as if his weight might rip it from the wall with a horrendous noise that would bring everyone running. Eventually, he decided to let himself down over the side, hang and drop.

The landing was painful, but only for a moment or two. He set off at a run, back toward the place where he'd left the *Sunfish* moored.

But as he approached, he could see the berth was empty. The *Sunfish* was gone.

Shipwreck Alley

Will came to a halt, not sure what to do next. He'd hoped that the others would manage to get away. But he couldn't help feeling bereft.

"Hey!" someone hissed.

Will looked around, and to his immense relief, Pod stuck his head up from a hiding place behind the water-pumping equipment and beckoned to him. Will scampered over and dived in next to him.

"What happened?" he gasped. "Where are the others? Where's the boat?"

"Admiralty's everywhere," Pod said. "When Graham said you were captured, Annalie took the boat and got it out of the harbor. I waited with the dinghy in case you came back."

"So where's the dinghy?"

"That way," Pod nodded toward the boardwalk. "Let's go."

They looked out cautiously. The coast seemed to be clear. Will followed Pod down the boardwalk to the far end where a number of dinghies and rowboats were pulled up on the beach. Will saw, with a sort of pride, that Annalie had rigged their dinghy with a motor (usually they just rowed it about). The boys dragged it down the beach, pushed it out, and were away.

The motor roared as they bounced out of the port. Pod was at the tiller; he seemed to know where he was going. The wind made conversation impossible. Will watched all around him for the Admiralty ship he knew must be nearby, but there was no sign of it.

They skimmed round a headland, and there was the *Sunfish* waiting for them, Essie and Annalie keeping an anxious lookout. While the boys secured the dinghy and climbed aboard, Annalie hauled up the anchor.

Will hurried to the wheel. "Let's get out of here!"

The winds were too light to be of much help. Will powered up the engine and the boat began to move. Annalie was beside him, checking the charts.

"There's a clear passage ahead," she said, pointing. "Don't go west—there are rocks."

They motored as fast as they could toward the open channel ahead of them—but then, from the other side of the bay, an Admiralty destroyer came gliding into view.

"So that's where they were hiding," Will said.

"They've been lying in wait for us," Annalie said.

"Can we outrun them?" asked Essie.

"Are you kidding?" Will said.

He corrected his course, veering away from them, although he knew there was no way he could avoid them. They were on a course to intercept and they were faster and more powerful than the *Sunfish*.

"What can we do?" Annalie asked.

An idea came to Will. "This," he said. He spun the wheel and turned west.

"Where are you going?" Annalie shrieked.

"Where they won't follow us."

"But they call this Shipwreck Alley!" Annalie said.

"Lucky we're not a ship then. We're just a little boat."

Annalie looked at him aghast, then took a deep breath and turned to the others. "Okay. Essie, I need you to go up the front and keep a look out for rocks. Pod, you do the same. Will, I'll try and talk you through it."

Annalie looked at the chart while Essie and Pod scrambled to the front and hung over the boat's edge, looking out for obstacles.

Their path lay between two islands—the passage seemed deceptively wide, but there were fringes of rock not far below the surface.

"Stay on this line," Annalie said, checking their position.

"Roger that," said Will. "What are they doing?"

Annalie looked behind her. "They're changing course."

The *Sunfish* motored forwards.

"I see something up ahead!" Essie called. "Right!"

"Do you mean it's *on* the right or I should *turn* right?" Will shouted.

"On the right!" Essie shouted.

Will corrected. The boat motored on.

"Another big one coming up on the portside," Annalie warned.

268

Will corrected again. "What's that Admiralty ship doing now?" he asked.

Annalie looked around again. "I've lost them."

"What?"

The Admiralty ship had disappeared from view. Annalie realized where they must have gone. "I think they're circling around behind the island," she said. "They must be going to try and cut us off."

"We'll see about that," Will said grimly. He increased speed.

Essie, at the front, yelped. "Rock! Left! Big one!"

They veered.

"There's a very tight passage coming up," Annalie warned. "Slow down."

"Just tell me where to steer," said Will determinedly.

"You need to come round to port."

"Coming round."

"You're overshooting."

"Correcting!"

"We're going in too fast!"

"Too late now!"

"Rocks!" shouted Essie.

They sailed into a narrow channel. Rocks loomed on both sides. The boat powered on, rising and falling over the fast-running current.

Will gripped the wheel, Annalie tracked their position, Essie gripped the railing in front, hardly daring to look.

"Turn left!" Essie shouted.

A rock loomed above the water, directly ahead. Will turned the wheel. The boat began to turn, but not fast enough. They struck. The boat gave a shudder, and then turned, tearing, across the rock with a noise that made Will's heart freeze. But they hadn't stuck. They were still moving. "Someone go below and have a look!" Will shouted.

Pod went below. There was a rip in the wall of the starboard cabin, and water was pouring in. The sight of all that water surging in, completely uncontrolled, paralyzed him. He had no idea what to do next.

Suddenly Annalie was there at his side. She grabbed one of the pillows off the bed and stuffed it in the hole, squishing it in with her foot. It was surprisingly effective at slowing the flow of water. "There's nothing more we can do about the hole now, we'll have to try and fix it later. Get the pump going, quick. Then shut the cabin door. It might help contain the water."

While Pod got the pump working, Annalie went back on deck.

The channel had widened again and Will was steering more calmly. "We're out of the worst of it," he said.

"Rocks on the right!" Essie called.

"There's a big hole in the hull," Annalie said.

"Below the waterline or above?"

"Right about on it. There's a lot of water coming in. Pod's getting the pump going."

"We can't fix it now," Will said.

"I know. But we're going to have to fix it soon, or it could sink us."

As they motored on, they saw a dreadful sight: the Admiralty boat slid into view. They were traveling at full speed and were once more on an intercept course.

"Should have known they wouldn't give up so easily," Will said. "Is there anywhere else we can get to quickly? Our motor's not going to last too much longer."

Annalie studied the charts. "They've cut us off. We have to go that way, along that route there, there's no other way out. We're cut off from the rest of the Islands by the Emperor Reef."

"The Emperor Reef?" Will repeated. "Is that where we are?"

The island group they were passing through was protected by a huge coral reef, hundreds of kilometres long. Once it had been one of the wonders of the world, but then the Flood had killed it. Now it was just a barrier to shipping.

The two islands they'd passed between stood almost as a gateway to the reef—it lay to starboard, not far from their present position.

Will leaned over the chart, studying it. "A destroyer can't get across the reef until they get all the way up to here," he said, tracing the route that led to the break in the reef, a long way to the north, where most ships crossed. "That's why all the shipping routes go that way."

Annalie was studying the charts too. "But maybe there's a place where a little boat could get through," she said.

They put their heads together, searching—and there it was.

"A channel," Will said.

"Can we make it there?" Annalie asked.

It was still a long way to their north. They would have to race the destroyer to reach the channel first.

"We have to try," Will said.

He changed course and pushed the engine to full.

They surged forwards on their new heading, the destroyer following implacably. They crossed the open water, heading for the distant reef.

"I don't think we're going fast enough," Annalie said, looking back.

"We can't go any faster," Will said.

"They're gaining on us!"

"You know, that really isn't helping."

They pushed on and pushed on, the huge boat in pursuit of the tiny one. The destroyer was soon level with them, easily matching their pace, but then the reef came into view.

"Water's getting shallower," Annalie said.

"Shallow enough to lose them?" Will asked.

"Not yet."

They powered up the outer edge of the reef, Annalie watching closely for the gap, the destroyer stalking them from the deeper water.

"There!" Annalie shouted.

Will turned the wheel, and they slid into the channel through the reef.

Annalie turned to watch what the destroyer was doing. "I think we caught them by surprise!" she called. "They're still going forwards."

"It'll take them a little while to turn around," Will said. "Are they launching small boats?"

"Not yet," Annalie said.

Will kept motoring on, determined to put as much distance as he could between them and the destroyer.

"Wait! I see them! They're coming!" Annalie cried.

And they came: two inflatable boats with big powerful motors, very like the ones the submarine pirates had used, each with a complement of marines. The inflatables came bounding across the water, eating up the distance between the destroyer and the *Sunfish*.

"Are they armed?" Will asked.

"What do you think?" Annalie said.

"We got any weapons?" asked Pod. He had returned to the deck.

"Spinner doesn't believe in that sort of thing," Annalie said.

Pod made a rude noise.

"We'll just have to try and outrun them," Will said.

"Have the batteries got enough juice in them?"

"I guess we'll find out," Will said.

The inflatables were in the channel now, gaining on them all the time. When they drew closer, they heard a voice distorted by a loudhailer. "Attention *Sunfish*! Turn off your engine and prepare to be boarded."

"Like hell," Will muttered, and kept right on going.

The voice on the loudhailer repeated the command.

"Do you think we should do as they say?" Essie said.

"Give up now?" Will said, laughing.

273

The voice on the loudhailer said, "Attention *Sunfish*! This is your final warning! If you do not turn off your engines, we will board you by force!"

"You give it a red-hot go," Will shouted.

One of the inflatables came surging up alongside them. The marines on board were standing ready with ropes and grappling hooks. "Grab an oar!" Will yelled. "Fend 'em off!"

Annalie and Essie both grabbed oars as the inflatable pulled in alongside them. Ladders and grappling hooks swung up, and the girls took wild swipes at the marines, trying to stop them hooking onto the boat. Annalie smashed at one who'd managed to hook a ladder over their railing; the marine fell back into the water and Annalie grabbed the ladder and tossed it over the side as one of the inflatables pulled back to recover their injured comrade.

The second inflatable swung round the other side of the *Sunfish*. Annalie could see the man with the loudhailer now. His face was turned toward them, his eyes invisible behind mirrored sunglasses. "Attention *Sunfish*, if you continue to resist, we will designate you a hostile vessel and we *will* use force."

Annalie shouted at him across the small gap. "We're just kids! Look at us! Do we look like a hostile vessel to you?"

"Prepare to be boarded," said Mr. Loudhailer. The second inflatable came in, ladders and hooks at the ready. Then suddenly the inflatable's engine seized and fell silent.

The marines looked around in confusion. The engine's operator stood and pointed. "Him!"

Annalie turned to see Pod holding Will's speargun. To her utter astonishment, she realized that Pod must have fired a spear into the engine and scored a direct hit. He was already loading a second spear into the gun and ducking over to the other side of the boat to take aim at the other inflatable.

"Hostile!" someone shouted.

Shots rang out.

Annalie dropped to the deck, not believing the marines would actually fire on them, and saw Essie and Will do the same.

Only Pod stayed on his feet. He shot again, and missed.

"Pod, get down!" Will called.

But Pod took no notice. As the second inflatable came after them, Pod put one more bolt in the speargun. More shots rang out. Pod fired. Incredibly, he hit his target. The second engine sputtered into silence.

The *Sunfish*, still at full speed, kept motoring on. The inflatables, both engines damaged, quickly dropped behind. Will jumped to his feet and took the wheel again. The channel through the reef was narrow and twisty. It would be a poor sort of victory if they outran an Admiralty destroyer, only to run aground on the reef.

Pod let the speargun fall to the deck. "We're safe now," he said. He seemed dazed.

Annalie got to her feet, a strange light-headed feeling coming over her, as if the world was moving too fast. "Is everyone okay?"

"We're going to be in so much trouble," Essie said, scrambling to her feet.

Will looked at Pod, giggling giddily. "I can't believe you took on the Admiralty with a speargun," he said.

"Will," Annalie said, "why are you bleeding?"

Will looked down questioningly. There was blood streaming down his leg and running into rivulets on the deck. He found a tear at the bottom of his shorts; below it, his thigh had been laid open and was gushing blood. "I think I've been shot," he said.

Holed

Seeing the blood made the bullet wound a reality. Will's legs gave way beneath him and he slumped to the deck, groaning.

The others ran to him.

"How deep is it?" Annalie asked. "Is it serious?"

There was so much blood it was hard to tell.

"We should take him below and clean up the wound a bit so we can see what we're dealing with," Essie said.

Will seemed to be going into delayed shock, but his mind was still on the job. "Is someone steering the boat?" he asked.

"I'll steer," Pod said.

Pod took the wheel. Essie and Annalie helped Will down into the saloon. For a moment Annalie was shocked to see there was almost a foot of water sloshing around down there. Then she remembered they'd been holed. She felt her brain begin to freeze with panic as she struggled to decide what to deal with first. The gunshot wound? The hull? The need to get away from their pursuers?

"Are we sinking?" Essie asked in a frightened voice.

"I don't feel so good," Will groaned.

Annalie wanted to burst into tears. But then she reminded herself that there was no one else who could get them out of this now. It was all on her shoulders. And the first thing she had to do was convince the others that she knew what she was doing, otherwise everyone would start to panic.

"Essie," she said, in the calmest voice she could manage, "can you take a look at Will's wound while I work out what to do about the hole?"

Together, the girls hoisted Will on the table, then Essie went to fetch the first-aid kit while Annalie went back to the starboard cabin for another look.

The water was still pouring in through the rip in the cabin wall, surging with the swell. It was scary seeing the water rushing into the boat. She knew that a hole this size could take on enough water to sink it very quickly, and if they were forced to abandon ship here it would be disastrous. She stood there for a little while, trying to gauge how much water was coming in. The pump was puttering away, pumping the water back out again. If it was coming in faster than the pump could pump it out, then they had a problem. She decided that the water didn't seem to be getting a lot deeper; the pump would hold it for now.

She came out of the cabin and went to see how Will and Essie were doing. Essie had washed the excess blood off Will's leg, although more kept pouring out.

"I think the bullet's hit him in the thigh, gone through the muscle, and come out the other side," Essie said. "See, there's a smallish hole here and then—"

"A big mess out the back," Annalie finished grimly.

"That's good though, isn't it?" Essie said. "You don't want the bullet to be stuck in there. I don't think it hit the bone either."

"Do you know first aid?" Annalie asked hopefully.

"No," Essie said. "But I love doctor shows. Did you ever watch *Frontier Hospital*? People are always getting shot in that."

"Do you think you can stop the bleeding?" Annalie asked.

"I'll disinfect the wounds and keep applying pressure, then get a dressing on it. Hopefully that'll do the trick," Essie said.

"Okay," Annalie said, already moving toward the stairs so she could go and talk to Pod on deck. Then a sudden silence fell.

"What was that?" asked Essie.

"The engine just stopped," Annalie said. "We've run the battery down."

"Does that mean the pump's out of power too?" Essie asked.

"It has its own," Annalie said, "but I don't know how long it will last."

She hurried up on deck. Pod turned to her anxiously.

"We need sails," he said.

Annalie set the sails and the *Sunfish* began to move again, more slowly than before.

She picked up the binoculars and looked back the way they'd come. The two inflatables were still in sight, dead in the water, and further off she could see the shape of the destroyer on the horizon. They would certainly be sending more boats to recover their comrades; whether they would send more boats after the *Sunfish* was another question.

"Do you think they'll keep coming after us?" Annalie asked.

"I would if I was them," Pod said.

"Yeah," Annalie sighed. "Me too."

"We got to keep going," Pod said. "Get some distance between us and them."

"I agree," Annalie said, "only we've got a hole in the boat."

"Oh," said Pod. "Yeah."

He began to look sick as he remembered the hole and the water gushing in.

"I've been down for another look," Annalie said. "There's a bit of water coming in, but the pump's still managing to keep up. We could stop now and try to patch the hole. Or we could just keep going until we find a safe place to stop on the other side of the reef, and hope the pump doesn't break down in the meantime."

If Will had been at the helm he would have had very certain views about what they should do next; they could have discussed it, argued, and then thrashed out a solution. But this was Pod, and the look he was giving her made it clear that he expected her to know the answer.

"What do you think we should do?" Pod asked.

Annalie hesitated for only a moment longer. "I think we should keep going."

They sailed on through the narrow channel in the reef. The water below them was so shallow they could see the sandy bottom. The reef stretched out around them, bleached, white, broken, a desert beneath the water. But as they came toward the end of the channel, and the far side of the reef, Annalie began to see signs of life: a few sprays of color, shoals of fish. She wasn't sure why conditions on this side might be different, but here there were glimmers of the old beauty. Perhaps life was returning after all? She hoped so.

Essie came hurrying up from below. "The pump's stopped working!" she cried.

"The battery must have run out," Annalie said. "We'll have to pump it manually." She ran down and found the water was rushing in through the hole. The water level had risen alarmingly. She fitted the manual arm to the pump and began pumping. "This is what you have to do," she told Essie. "Pump as hard as you can."

Essie, wide-eyed, took her place and began to pump.

Annalie had hoped they might be able to run to an island to take stock and deal with the damage, but that would not be possible now. They had taken on too much water to risk continuing and pumping it out manually would be slow. They were going to have to deal with the hole right now, or there was a good chance the boat might actually sink.

Before she went back on deck, Annalie went forward to check on Will. She found him sitting on the bench seat, his injured leg propped up, wrapped in a thick wad of bandages. He was very pale and he

281

was obviously in pain. The water slopping around their calves was tinted with blood.

"How do you feel?" she asked.

"Bit terrible actually," he said.

"Does it hurt?"

"Well, what do you reckon?" Will said.

"Have you had any painkillers?"

"Yeah, but they're piss-weak."

"Do you think the bleeding's stopped?" Annalie asked.

"Mostly," Will said.

"He needs to rest," Essie called from the cabin. "I tried to make him go and lie down but he wouldn't."

"Cabin's full of water," Will reminded her.

"There are *two* cabins," Essie reminded him back.

"We've taken on a lot of water," Will said.

"I know," Annalie said. "But I'm going to deal with it. Don't worry."

"We should be bailing the boat out. I'll get a bucket—" He was already levering himself off the bench. Annalie pushed him back into place, noticing a fresh bloom of blood welling onto his dressing.

"I've got this," she said. "Stay put. We need you to get better."

She hurried back up on deck. "Okay," she told Pod. "Let's have a look at this hole."

They anchored and furled the sails, then rigged up a little platform on ropes, and Pod lowered Annalie over the side to see the damage.

The rock had gouged a rip into the hull as long as her forearm, and the area around it had been pushed in by the impact. It was a substantial hole. She put her fingers into it and felt the water rushing past them. She thought she'd better check that this was the only hole. She took a deep breath and dived under the water, the salt making her eyes sting. There were a few scrapes in the paintwork lower down, but no more holes.

She surfaced. "Pull me up!"

Pod hauled her back on deck. "How's it look?"

"Not great. There's a tear in the hull. It's about this long." She measured with her hands.

"Can you fix it?"

Nothing like this had ever happened to her before. What did you do when you were holed, alone, in the middle of the ocean?

A story came back to her. She wasn't sure if she'd heard it as a sailor's yarn, or read it in a book, but she remembered a story about a holed boat, miles from anywhere, with little hope of rescue. "I heard a story once about someone who wrapped their hull in a sail. It kept enough of the water out for them to get to the next port."

"How, wrapped in a sail?"

"I mean they got a sail and swam under the boat with it," Annalie said. Even as she said it, her stomach churned at the thought of it: the great hull, the huge, wet flapping sail, the risks of getting tangled as you tried to swim under the boat. The price of failure.

Pod turned to look at the sails. "Would that work?"

"They wouldn't be telling the story if it didn't," Annalie said. "But I wonder if there's something else that might work better than a sail…"

Ideas were coming to her piecemeal, half-remembered bits of conversation, things she'd read. "I think we've got some waterproof sheeting somewhere," she said. "Useful for all sorts of emergencies."

She went to the locker, opened it, and discovered that there was indeed a large piece of plastic sheeting folded there.

"Now we just need to attach some lines to it and get it in place," she said. Pod and Annalie hurried to attach lines to the corners of the plastic sheet. Pod's fingers were shaking; he was having trouble fitting the lines through the cringles and tying them. "It's going to be okay," Annalie said, noticing this. "As soon as we get this in place, and get it pulled tight over the hole, I can start making some repairs and we'll be absolutely fine. The boat's not going to sink."

Pod nodded, still attaching his ropes.

"Ready?" Annalie asked.

"Ready," Pod said.

They went forward with the tarp and dropped it into the water, then hauled on the lines to try and drag it into place. It stuck and wouldn't spread out.

"Haul her up," Annalie said, "let's try that again."

They dragged it back up, threw it out once more, and tried to haul it into place. Again, it tangled and stuck. They tried poking it with boat hooks and oars but could not get it into place.

"This is not working," Annalie said.

"It'll work," Pod said. "Try again."

"Annalie!" Essie's voice floated up from below.

"There's a lot of water coming in now and my arms are getting really tired!"

"This is hopeless," Annalie said. "I'm going in."

Pod looked helplessly at her, his face twisted with fear and something more. "I should go," he said.

"But you can't swim," Annalie said. "Anyway, it's my boat, my idea. I should go."

"You're brave," Pod said.

"Or stupid," Annalie said, with a nervous laugh. She got ready to jump over the side.

"Hate wet!" Graham squawked from the rigging. "Allie drown!"

"I hope not," Annalie said, and she jumped, before she could change her mind.

It's not that far, she told herself, treading water beside the boat. *It's really not that far.* But she could feel the pull of the current and the waves rolling beneath, and the thought of having to swim right under the hull seemed terrifying, now that she actually had to do it.

"Coming down!" Pod yelled, and released one end of the plastic sheet. She grabbed it, then tucked it into her waistband so she could use both hands to swim.

All right, she thought. *This is it.*

She took a deep breath, then another, and dived. Down into the shadows. Down under the boat. Down past the tear that was threatening to sink them all. It was deep, deeper than she anticipated. Panic threatened to overwhelm her and she thought, *I'm not going to be able to make it all the way.* But she was committed now, too deep to go back. She swam hard, kicking and stroking, dragging the tarp down into place. Her lungs were already straining. She moved under the centerline of the boat, the lines in her hand, and started coming up the other side. The lines caught—stuck somewhere—she felt herself held, trapped. She didn't want to let the lines loose and have to start all over again. She tugged on them, her lungs straining, panic rising. All at once the lines slipped free, and she swam and swam, up to where the light sparkled, so far away still, up and up, her lungs so tight she was about to burst—

She surfaced, sucking air in with a huge shuddering sound.

Pod was staring down at her, his face fearful. "You okay?" he yelled.

"Fine!" Annalie shouted back.

She held the lines up to him, and he grabbed them with a boathook and secured them, hauling on each one until the plastic was pulled tight. When all the lines were in place, Annalie swam back around to the holed side and ducked under once again to see what she could see. The tarp was wrapped tight around the hull. The hole was covered.

Pod helped her back on board and for a moment Annalie just sat there, gasping, the adrenalin rattling through her system.

"We should go and see if the water's still coming in," she said once she had her breath back.

Pod gave her his hand and hauled her to her feet.

Essie turned to them as they came into the water-logged cabin. "You did it!" she said. "The water's stopped!"

Annalie and Pod came and crouched down next to Essie so that they could examine the hole. The plastic was stretched tight across the gap in the hull and it did indeed look like the water had stopped coming in.

"It's not a permanent solution," Annalie said, "especially once we get underway again. But at least now we can try and use the repair kit, and that should hopefully be enough to get us to Uncle Art's place."

Pod turned to her. "You saved us," he said, his voice formal.

"I haven't saved us yet," Annalie said, touched, but also slightly embarrassed.

"I couldn't have done what you did," Essie said. "Neither of us could. That was amazing."

Annalie felt unexpected tears prickle in her eyes. But all she said was, "We'd better try and get this boat dry."

Fever

With the hole repaired, at least temporarily, they sailed on, putting plenty of distance between themselves, the reef, the channel, and any more boats the destroyer might have sent after them. Spinner's self-steering mechanism kept them on course, freeing Pod, Essie and Annalie to clear up the mess. They had plenty to do: there was more than a foot of water in the bottom of the boat, and everything was sodden. It took them the rest of the day to get the boat pumped and baled out. Graham sat up high, well clear of the water, squawking, "Hate wet!"

"You want to swim?" Pod said, playfully threatening the bird with a bucket full of water.

Annalie used the repair kit they had on board to patch the inside of the hull, and hoped that would fix the problem. Then they dragged all the wet things up and spread them out on the deck, hoping they'd dry out.

"Where to next?" Pod asked, when the work was done.

"I still have to work that out," Annalie said.

In their flight from the destroyer, they had abandoned their old route. When they planned the journey originally they had intended to take the route everyone took, and which the destroyer would still have to take: up the normal shipping lanes, around the top end of the reef, then south-east again to the Lang Langs. By taking the tiny channel through the middle of the reef they had managed to lop at least a week's sailing from the journey; now, instead of sailing up the reef, crossing it where everyone else crossed, and then sailing back down in a south-easterly direction, they would have to travel more or less due east to reach the Lang Langs. Their goal was now much closer than it had been at the start of the day, and that had to be good news.

When night fell they were all exhausted. Will slept where he'd spent the day, on the bench seat in the saloon. The girls retired to their cabin, while Pod slept up on deck. He claimed not to mind—he wasn't used to beds anyway. Annalie set the autopilot before she went to bed, intending to get just a few hours sleep before she went back up on deck. But in fact she slept deeply until dawn.

When she emerged from her cabin the next morning she found Will already awake.

"How are you doing?" she asked.

"My leg hurts," he said. There was blood soaking through his dressing.

"We should change that," she said. She got the first-aid kit and found that Essie had already used up a lot of the dressings. She unwrapped the bandage carefully and eased the sodden dressings off the wounds. They didn't look too good, although she wasn't sure what a good gunshot wound was supposed to look like. His skin felt hot.

"Do you have a fever?" she asked. "You feel hot."

"I'm not hot," he said fretfully. "I'm cold."

"Let me put new dressings on," Annalie said, "and I'll get you something to warm you up."

She cleaned the blood away, put a little more disinfectant on the wounds, and wrapped them up again carefully. Then she went to find something warm to wrap him in.

The blankets were still wet, and Will had not brought any warm clothes of his own. Annalie couldn't think what she'd be able to find to wrap him in— perhaps a forgotten beach towel?—but then she opened a locker in the boy's cabin and saw something hanging there. It was a wool sweater, Spinner's sweater, knitted with huge chunky stitches, warm and dry. Annalie took it out and snuggled it against her, thinking about Spinner. He used to put this on for cold days in the unheated workshop, or nights on the boat when the wind was howling and you could feel the cold of the ocean pressing in on you from every side. It smelled of salt and sweat and Spinner, and Annalie felt a wave of sadness and longing sweep over her. How she missed him. How she hoped they'd guessed right when they chose this destination. She had no next step, no Plan B. If they were wrong, they would be truly lost.

She went back into the saloon and helped Will put the sweater on. He put it on without a struggle, perhaps not even noticing what it was as he huddled into it.

"Are you hungry?" she asked.

290

"No," said Will.

Soon the others appeared and began to make breakfast. Pod looked at Will, frowning, then said to Annalie, "He don't look good."

It was true; Will didn't look well at all. "I think he needs a doctor," Annalie said.

"Where do we find one out here?"

Annalie could only shrug.

It was Essie who made the next unwelcome discovery. "Something's wrong with the tap," she said, turning the tap that supplied water from the main water tank.

Annalie turned to look, not yet alarmed. "We should have plenty of water," she said. She went to check the levels in the tank, Pod and Essie following.

The tank should have been full. But it wasn't. When they pulled it out for closer examination, they discovered two bullet holes in it. One of the other smaller tanks had a hole in it too, about halfway down. The last was intact.

"We've lost most of our water," Annalie said in dismay.

"That must have happened when the marines were shooting at us," Essie said.

Pod looked a little guilty. It was him the marines had been shooting at.

"This is still enough though, isn't it?" Essie said.

"No," Pod said. "Not enough."

"Not if something goes wrong, or we get becalmed, or lost," Annalie said. "We're going to have to get more water before we move on."

Once again she checked the charts, and saw that there was another pair of islands not too far out of their way—it would add perhaps another day or two's sailing to their journey. But with their water supplies so depleted, they had little choice.

"D'you know anything about this place?" Pod asked.

"Nope," Annalie said.

"Let's just hope they have water," Essie said.

Annalie adjusted their course, but the winds were slight, and they sailed all that day and the next without seeing land.

Will's condition did not improve. He swung unhappily between burning heat and shivering chills, ridden by fever. They ran out of dressings and had to start making them from spare clothes.

On the morning of the following day, the rising sun revealed the bumpy edges of an island emerging on the horizon. They sailed toward it, eager but trepidatious. Would there be water? What else might they find there?

When they got closer they could see the small island was topped with long-dead trees.

"Any point going ashore?" Annalie asked, although she'd mostly made her mind up already.

"Nothing there," Pod said. "Only salt."

They sailed on.

They came to another island that looked much more promising. It was larger, and covered with greenery. Growing things meant the island had water. But would they be able to access it?

They sailed closer, and saw a smudge of something above the trees: smoke. "There might be people on the island," Annalie said. "If there are people, there has to be water."

"We don't know who they are," Pod said. "Could be pirates. Could be anybody."

"But maybe they're just ordinary people who'd be happy to sell us some water," Essie suggested, trying to look on the bright side.

"It's not like we've got a choice," Annalie said.

Pod and Annalie had made repairs to the two damaged water tanks as they traveled. Now, they headed for the green island, looking for somewhere to land.

Graham was not at all happy about this plan. "Bad island," he said, watching it loom from the safety of Pod's shoulder. "Lots of cats."

"I hope it's just cats," Pod said, stroking Graham's plumage.

As they sailed into a likely-looking bay, people began to appear on the shore.

"They've seen us," Pod warned.

Graham flew up to a perch high in the rigging.

The people began to drag out an assortment of boats—old-world tinnies and sea-kayaks, canoes made from island materials—and came paddling out to meet them.

"See any weapons?" Annalie asked.

"Not yet," Pod said.

The boats drew closer. The people in them were open-faced, smiling. They all wore white.

"Hello there!" a man called.

"Welcome, travelers!" called a woman from a second boat.

Annalie and Pod exchanged a look. This wasn't quite the welcome they'd been anticipating.

"Hi," Annalie called back. "We don't want any trouble. We were hoping you could help us with some water."

"You won't find trouble here," the woman said, paddling closer. She was in an old kayak labeled with the name of a long-defunct adventure travel company. "We welcome all travelers to our island, if you come in peace."

"We definitely come in peace," Annalie said.

The little flotilla of boats was now arriving around the *Sunfish*. Smiling faces turned up toward them, like a field of daisies.

"How can we help you, young woman?" the first man asked.

"We need water," Annalie said.

"Water is a gift," the man said. "We share this gift with you."

"Share?" asked Pod, checking the terms of the deal.

"In return, you may share a gift with us," the man said.

"Um, okay," Annalie said. "We have some money—only a little money. Or we can trade with you, if you'd prefer.'

"Your gift is your choice," the man said.

"I don't suppose you have a doctor on your island, do you?" Annalie continued. "Or some antibiotics?"

294

The people in the boats looked at each other, murmuring. "No doctor," the woman said. "But perhaps we have antibiotics. If we do, we will share this gift with you too."

Annalie looked at Pod and Essie. "What do you reckon?" she whispered.

"They seem so *nice*," Essie said.

"Too nice," Pod said darkly.

Annalie turned back to the woman and said, "Forgive me for asking this—I don't want to insult you. But we haven't met many people out this way who are as friendly and welcoming as you."

"We are the Welcoming Friends," the woman said. "We believe that we celebrate our god by offering our gifts and hospitality to all. We welcome others to our domain as one day our god will welcome us to hers."

Annalie looked at the others.

"They're religious," Essie said. "I'm sure it'll be all right."

Pod scowled, but said, "Not much choice."

"Okay then," Annalie said. "We accept your kind gifts. Thank you."

The Welcoming Friends

It was decided that Essie would stay on the boat with Will, while Pod and Annalie loaded the water tanks onto the dinghy and took them ashore. Since they still weren't quite sure how the gift economy worked, Annalie took some money, one of Spinner's old books, a tin of peaches, and some spare parts. Surely there would be something in there the islanders could use.

Pod rowed, miserable and hunched.

"At the first sign that there's anything wrong with all this," Annalie reassured him, "we run. Even if we haven't got what we want."

Pod nodded, still not looking happy.

They pulled up on the tiny strip of sand with all the other little boats. The islanders clustered around to help them lift the water tanks out of the dinghy. They led Annalie and Pod to a huge water tank and filled their tanks for them, then carried them back to the dinghy.

"The gift of water," said the woman who'd spoken to them first.

Annalie recognized a prompt for payment. "Here is my gift in return," she said, offering them some money.

The woman smiled politely, but it didn't quite seem enough, so she gave her the peaches as well. This seemed more satisfactory. The woman took the peaches with a broad smile. "Now," she said, "you seek antibiotics?"

"If you can spare them," Annalie said.

"Come to our village," the woman said. "And we will see."

The woman began to lead the way. Annalie followed. Pod didn't look keen, but he didn't resist either.

"Are you hungry?" the woman asked. "We love to share a meal with our guests and let them experience our way of life. We could prepare a banquet for you."

"That sounds really nice," Annalie said nervously, "but I don't think we can stay. We'd love to know more about your way of life but we have people waiting for us, and we're already running late."

Was this the moment when the smiling, kindly people switched from welcoming to wrathful?

But the woman kept smiling. "What a pity. I hope you'll reconsider. Our banquets are very special."

They were now on the outskirts of a village. Once, it had been something much grander, perhaps a resort. Now, the tropical foliage was trying to tear it down, and it looked like it was going to succeed.

"Come," the woman said, arriving at the steps of what had once been a grand lobby, "I will take you to our stores and you can look for the thing you seek."

"No," Pod said, before Annalie could answer. "We'll wait here."

Pod could not shake the suspicion that something was not right about this place. On his own, he would never have gone to their village, and he would certainly not step inside one of the buildings, and he wasn't going to let Annalie step inside one either. The crumbling resort looked like the kind of place he'd grown up in: a slave-hole you couldn't escape from. He wouldn't willingly step inside one ever again.

Annalie looked at him, surprised, but then nodded.

The woman looked only mildly disappointed, then disappeared inside the building.

Pod and Annalie waited. The sun blazed down. There were white-clad people all around them, more of them all the time. They all seemed very interested in Pod and Annalie and were eager to talk to them.

"Will you join us for the feast?"

"You must come for the feast!"

"You have never experienced anything so delicious!"

"I'm sorry," Annalie said, politely but firmly. "We can't stay for the feast."

"You will be the guests of honor!"

"You must stay!"

"You must!"

They were bringing ingredients and cooking utensils. Some of them began trying to move them along to a different part of the resort. The children wanted to stay where they were but the crowd pressed in closer, jostling them. Unwillingly, they found themselves moving deeper into the compound.

"This way!"

"Come!"

"You'll enjoy it!"

"Look, I don't think—" Annalie tried to say.

They were jostled through an open archway into a courtyard that opened onto jungle. The people were all moving toward what seemed to be a communal kitchen—probably the source of the smoke they'd seen earlier. Pod's eye was caught by something on the far side of the courtyard. There, where the jungle encroached, was a great midden, a heaped pile of rubbish, the detritus from their kitchen and their banquets. There were the shells of many shellfish there, but there were other things as well, things that were too big to have come from anything that swam in the sea.

Bones.

Long bones. Human bones.

"Run!" Pod hissed at Annalie.

He grabbed her arm. She looked at him, startled, for just a moment. Then they rammed through the crowd that was surrounding them and broke into a run.

The crowd moaned and cried and came rushing after them.

"Stop!"

"The gift!"

"We need you!"

"Don't go!"

Pod and Annalie ran, ducking and dodging. Finding the archway they'd just come through blocked by more people in white, they turned and slipped through a different doorway and came out into what had once been a swimming pool area. Rising up out of the pool was a colossal figure, built out of chrome towel rails and old TV sets, broken chairs, pool recliners and tennis rackets. It had a huge, dreadful painted face with an enormous mouth, smiling and red, the pointed teeth made out of shards of broken crockery. In each upraised hand she held a human figure. Scattered at the foot of the figure were skulls and leg bones, carefully carved.

This was their god. A cannibal god.

Pod ran toward the statue and grabbed up one of the huge carved leg bones. A few people behind them gasped.

"We're not your gift," Pod shouted. "We're not your banquet."

Then they began to run again. The white-clad people gave chase. Somehow they found their way back to the main path to the beach and Annalie ran down it, fleet-footed, Pod following behind. Whenever anyone tried to grab him, he swung his bone-club, not caring how much damage he did.

At last they reached the beach. The dinghy was still there, heavy with its weight of water. Annalie put her back into it and shoved it down toward the water while Pod turned and faced the white-clad cannibals.

"You must give us your gift!" they cried. "Your gift is a blessing!"

"We already paid!" Pod shouted.

"Come on Pod!" Annalie called.

Pod tossed the club at them, ran down the beach and leaped into the dinghy. They roared away from another island, back to the safety of the *Sunfish*.

"Cannibals," Pod said in disgust. "I hate cannibals."

Little Lang Lang

With the water safely on board they sailed east without stopping, toward Little Lang Lang. They didn't want to risk any more encounters with the strange and dangerous people of the Islands, and they knew now that their best hope of finding help was to get to Uncle Art's house.

The weather turned bad, and rain and strong winds made life a misery for a day or two. Essie did her best to look after Will, but his condition did not improve. He was weak, pale, plagued by fever, drifting in and out of consciousness. But at last they sailed up the strait toward Little Lang Lang, with Annalie at the wheel. After all the trials and dangers they'd been through, she could hardly believe their journey was almost over. Soon they would be safe at Uncle Art's house. Safe with Spinner.

Little Lang Lang Island was long and gently sloped, with a smallish mountain—really, more of a large hill—in the middle of it. There were scrubby, windswept trees on the island, but it was mostly open ground sloping toward pebbly bays, with a few caves scattered around. Annalie and Will had spent many summers here with Spinner, so the landscape was familiar, although the angle of their approach was different: before, they'd always arrived from the north and this time they approached from the south. But the mountain loomed up just as it always had, and soon they were sailing into the bay where Art had a jetty.

Art's house was old—it had been old before the Flood—a large, rambling, drafty place with wide verandas and lots of bedrooms, set up high on a ridge of hill well above the highest sea levels. It had had various uses over time: once it had been the lighthouse keeper's residence, although the lighthouse no longer stood; it had also been a trading post, a communications array, and a military outpost.

Now it was a weather station; Uncle Art maintained the instruments and made sure the readings were relayed properly. It wasn't a well-paid job, but the house was included, and Art had five children. There was a little town at the other end of the island, so they weren't completely isolated, although they seemed isolated enough.

The house had commanding views over everything that moved up or down the strait; by the time Annalie and Pod were tying up the *Sunfish* at the jetty, Art and his wife Rene had come down to meet them. Art was a small, smiley man with a roly-poly face, and Rene, who was slightly taller than her husband, had a freckled face and a very long fountain of frizzy hair.

"Annalie, welcome!" Art said, coming toward them, smiling, his hands out. "To what do we owe the pleasure?"

"Where's your dad?" asked Rene, her brow crinkling.

Annalie looked from Art to Rene in dismay, and then burst into tears.

Art and Rene exchanged a look. "You'd better come up to the house," he said.

Where's Spinner?

Will was carried up and a doctor sent for; Pod and Essie were introduced; Uncle Art's cat was locked outside so it couldn't try to catch Graham; sandwiches and fruit and drinks were provided and consumed; and then the children told their story.

Art listened while they described the wrecking of the workshop, Spinner's flight, the visit from Beckett, the theft of the *Sunfish*, and the story of their long and eventful journey to reach Little Lang Lang.

"I can't believe you managed it," Art said, when at last they were finished. "I don't know if I could have pulled off a journey like that."

"I wouldn't have let you try," Rene said.

"The main thing is, you're safe now," Art said, smiling at them kindly.

"First things first," Rene said, "we'll need to get Will's leg looked at. The doctor should be here soon. I'm sure she'll have you fixed up in no time."

Although still terribly pale, Will had refused to be put to bed. Rene had tucked him up on the sofa and dosed him with the strongest painkillers they had in the house while they waited for the doctor.

"We can look at getting the *Sunfish* mended properly too," Art said.

"But what about Spinner?" asked Annalie, still unable to believe that he wasn't actually here.

"I'm sorry, Annalie," Art said. "To think you came all this way...What made you think he'd come here?"

"When we heard he'd gone to the Moon Islands, we thought it must've been to stay with you," Annalie said, her chin beginning to wobble.

"You're his oldest friend," Will said. "Where else would he go?"

"I hate to say this," Art said, "but did it ever occur to you Spinner might have been trying to put people off the scent?"

"What do you mean?" asked Annalie.

"Maybe he put the word out that he was going somewhere really far away, because he was actually planning to stay right where he was," Art said.

Annalie and Will looked at Art in dismay. "You think he never left Lowtown?"

Art put his hands up. "I don't know where he went. If I did, I'd tell you. All I know is, he hasn't shown up here."

"That doesn't mean he *won't* show up here," Rene put in soothingly.

"That's right," Art said. "And you don't need to worry about a thing. You've got a home with us for as long as you need it. Your friends, too, if they want to stay."

"Or we can find out about sending you home," Rene added, smiling at Essie and Pod.

Essie smiled uncertainly back, then looked at Annalie for reassurance. But Annalie was staring down at her hands, overwhelmed.

Pod was scowling. "I got no home," he said.

"Then you're welcome to stay," Rene said.

A silence fell. Rene eventually broke it by getting to her feet and saying, "I'd better get out the spare bedding."

"I'll give you a hand," said Art.

"Feel free to help yourself to more sandwiches," Rene said. And then the two of them left the room, leaving the children alone.

"I thought he'd be here," Annalie said brokenly.

"Maybe he's been held up," Will suggested gamely.

"He could be anywhere," Annalie said, "which is just the same as being nowhere. We're never going to find him."

And she broke down and began to sob.

Essie put her arm around Annalie and made soothing noises, rather frightened by it all. She was used to Annalie being strong and in control; her certainty had helped carry them all this far, to what seemed like a simple and undoubted conclusion. Now, suddenly, everything was confusion. She had no idea what they were supposed to do next.

"It's okay," Will said, trying to sound commanding. "We'll stay here for a while and get the boat fixed, and if he doesn't come, well, we can just go on and keep looking for him."

"Where?" Annalie sobbed. "We don't know where to start."

"What about the list, the people from the desert? One of those addresses was here in the Islands."

Annalie shook her head hopelessly. "I'm sick of wild goose chases. I'm sick of danger. We can't just keep on sailing."

"Fine. Go back to your school, and I'll keep looking for Spinner. Pod's with me, aren't you, Pod?"

Annalie glared at Will. Pod looked uncomfortably from Will to Annalie.

"Let's not make any decisions now," Essie said soothingly. "We're all tired. Will's got a gammy leg. Let's wait until he's better and the *Sunfish* is fixed. No one's going anywhere until that happens, right?"

Later that afternoon, Art's children came rampaging home from school, and Art went off to town to make enquiries about getting the *Sunfish* repaired.

Art had five children: Jake, who was two years older than Annalie, Daisy, who was Annalie's age, then two more boys who looked like twins but weren't, and Alice, who was the youngest. Evidently Art had told the kids something about what Will, Annalie, and their friends were doing there, but it was nowhere near enough to satisfy their curiosity. They carried Annalie off to the garden to bombard her with questions, while Essie showed Pod what a trampoline was for.

"Is Spinner in trouble?" asked one of the younger boys.

"No," Annalie said, "it's just a mistake."

"Then why did he run away?"

"I don't know."

"Are you all going to stay with us?"

"I guess so. Just for a little while."

"*You* can stay in my room," said Daisy, who was already slightly jealous of Essie.

"Thanks," Annalie said. She'd always liked Daisy the best out of all her adopted cousins.

"What did Spinner do to get in trouble?" asked Jake.

"I don't know."

"Was it something really bad?"

"Is he a smuggler?"

"Is he a pirate?"

"Of course not!"

"Do you think he's been arrested?"

"Maybe they're going to take him to Rogue Island!"

"No!" Annalie protested.

"I don't want to go to Rogue Island," wailed the youngest girl, who was afraid of everything. Rogue Island was an Admiralty prison with a terrifying reputation.

"That's where all the worst people go," Jake said.

"I heard they keep people in dungeons there."

"And they keep them in the dark forever and ever."

"And once you go there, you never get out."

"He hasn't been arrested and he's not going to Rogue Island!" Annalie cried. "He hasn't done anything wrong!"

Rene looked out the back window and yelled, "Kids, leave your cousin alone!"

The kids backed off, although not before one of the younger boys said, "He must have done *something*."

The doctor arrived to see Will. She cleaned, stitched and redressed the wound and prescribed strong antibiotics and plenty of rest; she expected him to make a full recovery. Art returned and reported that the *Sunfish* was booked in for repairs. Annalie felt a little anxious about handing the boat over to someone else, but she knew she was being silly. They were in a safe place now. The boat would be fine.

The night closed in. Art and Rene made dinner.

Dinner in this house was always a scrum, because all the children had huge appetites and there never seemed to be quite enough food to go round. Jake had once stabbed Annalie's hand with a fork as they reached for the same potato—he'd claimed it was an accident but Annalie had known it wasn't, quite. That day, Annalie tried to eat the food Rene had served her, but worry had dissolved her appetite and soon her cousins were eyeing her leftovers.

"Are you going to eat that?" one of the younger boys asked, and when she said she wasn't, her plate was cleared in moments.

When dinner was over, Aunty Rene took the other kids away for some post-dinner clean-up, books, and bed. Art stayed at the table with Will, Annalie, Essie and Pod.

"I think it's time we talked about your father," he said.

The Collodius Process

A rt inclined his head toward Pod and Essie. "Is this something you'd rather do in private?"

"We don't have any secrets from them," Annalie said. "They came all this way, they might as well hear it too.

Art paused, then began. "How much do you know about Spinner's past?"

"Not much," Annalie said.

"That Beckett guy said Spinner used to work for the Admiralty, in the Science Department," Will said. "But Spinner's not a scientist."

"Admiralty Science was where they put all the smartest people," Art said. "Not just scientists, but engineers, mathematicians, all kinds of people. They put them into teams and gave them problems to solve. Food problems, water problems, energy, transport, communications...Lots of problems, all serious, all needing solutions. Your dad was on one of those teams, and so was your mom. That's how they met."

"So Beckett was telling the truth about that too," Annalie said.

"Their team was pretty good—one of the best. So the Admiralty decided to give them the biggest project of all." He paused. "Have you heard of the Collodius Process?"

Pod shook his head, while Will looked vague.

"It was something to do with the Flood," Essie suggested.

"It *caused* the Flood," Annalie said. "It's one of the great scientific disaster stories."

Art nodded. "That's right. Fifty years ago, we were suffering from rapidly rising temperatures and catastrophic climate change. We were transitioning to low-carbon energy, trying to adapt to the changing climate, but one thing was a real problem: we were running out of fresh water. Did they teach you about the droughts, the water riots?"

Annalie and Essie nodded. "There was one year where the crops failed and whole countries were starving."

"Even people in rich countries were hungry," Essie said.

"The North Dux Dustbowl," Annalie said.

"That's right," Art said. "It was terrible, truly terrible, and something urgently needed to be done. A lot of scientists were looking at large-scale geo-engineering solutions to try and fix some of the problems. There were plenty of wild ideas around, but no one wanted to put them into practice—for one thing, they were expensive, and there was no real agreement that they'd even work. They might even make things worse.

"A group of scientists had been working on a radical new technology that they believed could work

312

on the biosphere to release more fresh water back into the system. It was called the Collodius Process, and in lab tests and computer models it seemed to work. After the famine of '92, the government of Brundisi was desperate enough to give it a try. I guess you know what happened next."

"It went haywire and caused the Flood," Will said.

Art nodded. "The process started a chain reaction, which caused massive worldwide flooding and a permanent change in sea level."

"But what has any of that got to do with Spinner?" Will asked, a little impatiently.

"Under the global accords that were drawn up a few years later, all research into the Collodius Process was halted permanently. The device was destroyed, and everyone thought that all the research was destroyed too. But it wasn't." Art paused. "About fifteen years ago, the Admiralty heard a whisper that an outlaw group had uncovered some of the original research and were working on it."

"Why?" Annalie asked, astonished.

Art shrugged. "Maybe they were hoping to use it. Maybe they just wanted to hold the world to ransom. I don't know. But once the Admiralty thought someone else was working on the Collodius Process, they couldn't risk letting anyone get ahead of them. So they put together their own top-secret group of scientists to start working on it too."

"Spinner?"

"And your mother," Art said. "The Admiralty set up a secret research base out in the desert and sent them off to study the data, look at what went wrong, and find out what they could do to stop the process—or even reverse it."

"What, you mean put the sea back where it was?" Essie asked incredulously.

"It's a little more complicated than that," Art said. "But yes."

"Wait a minute," Will said. "If this was all so top secret, how come you know about it?"

"Spinner told me later. None of the classified stuff. Just the broad outlines."

"But why would they do something like that?" Annalie asked. "Why build it again? What if they made things even worse?"

Everything she'd ever learned about the Collodius Process made it clear that it was one of the worst ideas ever to be unleashed on the world. The Flood had drowned cities, changed coastlines, killed millions of people, and destroyed ecosystems. It had been one of the worst ecological disasters to hit the planet since the extinction of the dinosaurs. And the Admiralty—the Admiralty!—were considering unleashing it again?

"At first, Spinner thought they were trying to find ways to stop it. But gradually he realized the Admiralty actually wanted their own device. And that's when he started to get worried. The original device had been destroyed; did we really want to create another one? The scientists questioned the direction of the research and recommended the program be shut down."

"The Admiralty said no, right?" Will said dryly.

"You got it. Then the scientists heard a rumor the top brass were going to shut them down and replace them with a new team. That's what made Spinner decide to do it."

"Do what?" Annalie asked.

"What they said he did: steal the research."

Annalie's mouth fell open.

"Spinner believed the research they were doing was making the world a more dangerous place. He didn't trust the Admiralty to use that research responsibly. So he and his colleagues took the key elements of it and disappeared."

He paused. "I didn't know about any of this Collodius stuff at the time. All I knew was my mate Spinner worked at the Ministry of Science. Then one day I woke up and found out he'd gone away to work on a research project that was so secret he couldn't even tell me his address, and all his communications were censored. I didn't see him for a year. Then suddenly he popped up again. He was on the run and he needed my help to go off-grid. So I helped. It was only later that he told me about what had actually been going on."

The children sat there for a while, stunned.

"So he really is a thief," Annalie murmured.

"No he isn't," Will protested. "Not really."

"To use an old-fashioned term," Art said, "he's a conscientious objector. He did something that he believed was right, for the greater good of humanity. Only problem is, the Admiralty doesn't see it in quite the same light."

The children all fell silent, considering this.

"So Spinner really is in terrible trouble, isn't he?" Annalie said.

"Yes, he is," Art said gravely.

"Is there any way out of this?"

"For you, or for him?"

"Both."

Art sighed. "I wish I knew. All I can think is, maybe, just maybe, if Spinner gave up that research, they might be satisfied. After all, it's the research they really want."

"You reckon?" Will said skeptically. "You haven't met the guy who's after us. It seems pretty personal with him. I reckon he wants to hang Spinner out to dry for making them look like idiots."

"And why would Spinner change his mind and give them back the research, after all this time?" Annalie asked. "If it was a bad idea to let them have it then, surely it's still a bad idea now?"

Art shrugged. "Look, I don't know what's in Spinner's mind. Maybe it is a bad idea and it's better if the research stays hidden. But I'll tell you what I see. Your old life, that's gone. Your home's wrecked, Spinner's business is wrecked. He's been separated from the two of you. Annalie, you've run away from school, after everything he did to get you into that place. And you all could have been killed or kidnapped twenty times over just getting here."

"Or eaten," murmured Pod.

"And for what?" Art continued. "Some piece of research, which may not even mean anything without the rest of it. Is that research really worth all this trouble? Is it worth risking the lives of his kids for?"

Annalie was silent, troubled. She didn't like the light that this shone on her father.

Neither did Will. "He didn't *ask* us to come," he protested, in defense of Spinner. "It was our choice. And we didn't die, and we didn't get kidnapped. We made it here safe and sound."

"You were lucky," Art said flatly. He paused. "When you do see Spinner again, I reckon you should ask him. Is all this really worth it?"

Destinations

That night, the children gathered in the spare room, which had been set up for Pod and Will. (Annalie and Essie were to sleep in Daisy's room, and Daisy had been moved in with Alice.)

"I never really thought it might be true," Annalie said.

"It's not true, because he's not a thief. He's a hero," Will said.

"That does sort of depend on your point of view, though, doesn't it?" Essie said cautiously. "Whatever his reasons were, it *was* a top-secret project. And he did know what he was getting into."

"What should he have done then?" Will said fiercely. "Let them go on with research that could have destroyed the world for the second time?"

"For all we know, they found a different bunch of scientists and finished the research," Annalie sighed. "The real question now is what do *we* do?"

"We go on," Will said unhesitatingly. "We've got those addresses. And now we know what they are."

"What are they?" Essie asked.

"They're where the other scientists live, obviously,"

Will said. "Maybe one of them will know where Spinner is."

"No, wait," Annalie said. "We can't just keep sailing on around the world indefinitely. What about Pod and Essie?"

Will looked at her and frowned, then turned to look at Essie and Pod. "What about them?"

"We've dragged them far enough," Annalie said. "Uncle Art's right about one thing. We were lucky to get this far without anything too terrible happening. We can't keep pushing our luck."

"I got no home," Pod said, his face closing down into ferocity.

"You don't know that for sure. If we asked Flood Relief to start looking, they might be able to find your family again." Annalie turned to Essie. "And what about you? If you could go home now, would you?"

Essie didn't answer, but her silence had a conflicted look about it that made Annalie think she possibly *did* want to go home.

"You signed up to come this far," Annalie said to her, "and we made it. But maybe it's time to go back now."

"Would you come with me?" Essie asked.

All eyes were on Annalie now.

"I'd have to think about that," she said.

It was strange to spend a night sleeping on beds that didn't move with the swell. In the morning, Rene put everything they owned into the wash, while Annalie and Art sailed the *Sunfish* around to the marine repairer in the town.

"How soon do you think you can have her fixed?" she asked, when the man had finished looking at the damage.

"Day after tomorrow," he said. "Three days at the latest."

"Are you in a hurry?" Art said, not quite joking.

"Course not," Annalie said lightly.

They left the marine repair shop and walked back toward the slip where Art's dinghy was berthed. "Suppose Essie wanted to go back to school," Annalie said casually. "How would she go about it?"

Art raised his eyebrows at this, but all he said was, "There's a passenger service that leaves for Dux every Wednesday," he said. "It's not glamorous, and it's a bit slow, but it's usually safe. I think it stops in both Southaven and Port Fine, and she could take a train the rest of the way. You both could." He stopped walking, turning toward the town. "We could go and ask about tickets if you want."

"No," Annalie said. "I was just wondering. Thanks."

Back at the house, Will watched Pod sitting up a tree, talking grumpily to Graham and refusing to come down. He was clearly ill at ease in the house, and eventually Will decided he'd better find out why.

He limped out and stood at the foot of the tree. "Are you planning to come down any time soon?" he called.

Pod peered down at him through the leaves. "Why?"

"You've been lurking up there for ages," Will said.

"I'm not lurking," Pod said, scowling.

"Then come down here."

Will waited while Pod swung down from the tree, and said, "Is something the matter?"

Pod said nothing.

"Why are you being so weird?"

There was another long silence, then Pod said. "I don't want to go to no camp."

"Camping good!" Graham said. "Tent. Guitar. Trees." Graham had been on their family camping trips. Spinner used to bring a guitar with him and they'd sing old songs around the campfire, Graham squawking along.

"It's not that kind of camp," Will explained, for Graham's benefit. "Why do you think we're going to send you to a camp?"

"People with no papers get sent to a camp," Pod said stubbornly.

"No one's trying to get rid of you," Will said.

"Will not get rid of Pod!" Graham shouted.

"Isn't that what I just said?" Will said, frustrated. "I want you to stick around. Annalie probably does too, she just thinks we should give you an escape clause."

"A what?"

"A way out."

"Graham wants escape clause!"

Will ignored Graham. He looked over his shoulder to make sure no one was listening, then said, "Look, don't tell Art and Rene, but as soon as we get the boat back, I'm out of here. Annalie and Essie can stay or go, it's up to them, but I'm going on." He paused. "I really hope you'll come with me."

"We find Spinner?" Graham asked hopefully.

"Yes," Will said. "But Graham, not a word about this to anyone, okay? It's a big secret."

"Big secret," Graham repeated, bobbing up and down.

"You with me?" Will asked Pod.

A smile spread across Pod's face. He nodded.

Annalie and Essie sat on one of the wide verandas, swinging gently backwards and forwards on an old porch swing. "You could go back, you know," Annalie said. "There's a passenger ship that goes once a week. We could book you a passage under a false name and we could let your dad's lawyers know you were coming so they could make sure you get picked up safely at the other end."

Essie looked at her in surprise. "You've given this a lot of thought, haven't you?"

Annalie looked embarrassed. "I just feel bad about what I put you through. Anything could have happened to us. We've finally got a chance to send you home, and I think we should take it."

Essie was silent for a long moment, then said, in a slightly wobbly voice, "Don't you want me here any more?"

"Of course I want you!" Annalie said. "Haven't you been listening? You're my best friend, of course I want you around. But I don't want to put you in any more danger. You've got a family back home, you should go to them."

Essie ducked her head, full of troubles. "I don't even know what I'd be going back to," she mumbled. "Dad's out for now on bail, but what if he gets convicted? And there's no way I'm going to live with mom and her new boyfriend. Even if she wanted me, which I doubt."

"They're still your parents," Annalie said. "They'll work something out. They have to."

"Why don't you come with me?" Essie suggested.

"I can't," Annalie said.

"But if we ask the lawyers to help, maybe they can protect you—"

"I can't go back. I've got nowhere to go. Even if Triumph wanted me back, I wouldn't be safe there. As long as Beckett's hunting Dad, I'm always going to be a pawn in the game."

"So now what? What are you going to do next?"

"I don't know," Annalie sighed. "Wait. Hope that Spinner turns up. Because I don't know what I'll do if he doesn't."

Two days passed. Will was anxious to go into town and check on the *Sunfish*. "They said it might be ready today, right?"

"They did," Art said, "but I can't take you today. I've got to go and check my instruments. It'll probably take me most of the day."

"But—"

"This is my work, Will. I can't neglect it because you want to go to town."

"And besides," Rene said, more conciliatory, "what difference will a day make really?"

"There's nothing to worry about," Art said. "Like I said, you and your boat are perfectly safe here."

The four of them spent a restless day, waiting. Essie, in particular, had a lot to think about. She went back through all the messages she'd received from both her parents, reading between the lines, worrying about what she should do. On the one hand she knew her parents missed her—she missed them, too—and the only sensible thing to do was to jump on the very next boat and head straight for home. She thought about all the things she'd missed, like hair conditioner and hot showers, chocolate and new clothes.

But then she thought about everything she'd seen and done with Annalie and the others. Even though it had often been frightening and dangerous, it had also been exhilarating. She'd done things she'd never imagined she was capable of until she joined the crew of the *Sunfish*: had adventures, taken risks, experienced true, dizzying, terrifying freedom. *The next boat doesn't go until Wednesday*, she reminded herself,

324

torn. *I've still got time before I have to decide.*

After dinner that night, Annalie and Pod helped with the dishes, and when the work was done, they walked into the living room where Art was sitting with the younger children. Alice was playing with something; it took Annalie a moment to realize what it was.

"Where did you get that?" she said, her voice louder than she intended.

Alice looked up guiltily and burst into tears.

She was playing with Lolly. Annalie had brought the doll all the way from school, stuffed in the bottom of her backpack.

"Alice, give it back!" roared one of the brothers.

"No!" Alice shouted.

The boy tried to grab it from her, Alice resisted, there was a brief but intense tussle as they tried to drag it from each other, Art remonstrating unsuccessfully—and then Lolly separated.

Lolly's legs were in the boy's hand.

Lolly's head was in Alice's fist.

Lolly's torso, ripped open, dangled.

And something fell out.

For a moment they all stared at the object that had fallen to the floor. Annalie was the first to scoop it up.

It was a memory chip.

"What's that?" Art asked, trying to sound casual.

"It's mine," Annalie said.

"Are you sure?" Art said. "It looks old. They haven't looked like that for years. Since before you were born."

The noise had brought the others into the room: Rene, Will, Essie.

Will was the first to say it. "That's it, isn't it? It's what they've been looking for."

Art got up from the couch. "Annalie, give it to me."

"No!" Annalie said.

Instinctively, the other three drew closer to her, forming a protective pack around her.

"They're not interested in you. They only want the research," Art said.

"How do you know?" Annalie said.

"Because I already know everything. They warned me you were coming here. They've known for weeks this was where you'd come."

Will and Annalie looked at each other, eyes wide.

"It's going to be all right," Art said. "They only want the research. If they can get that, they're not interested in you."

"But they think we can lead them to Spinner!" Annalie said.

"They hoped you would, but you can't. You don't have any more idea of where he is than I do," Art said.

"We have to get out of here," Will said.

"There's no point," Art said. "They're coming for you. They're already on their way."

"You sold us out?" Annalie cried, appalled.

Art looked wretched. "They already knew!" he said. "Don't you understand? I work for them!"

"You work for the Weather Bureau!" Annalie objected.

"And who do you think controls the Weather Bureau?" Art said. "If I didn't tell them you'd arrived I would have lost my job, the house—"

"I thought we could trust you," Annalie said.

"Forget him," Will said. "Get your stuff. We're leaving."

Annalie scooped up the pieces of Lolly, and she and Essie ran to their room to collect their things.

"You can't go," Art said. "It's too late."

"We've outrun them before, we can do it again," Will said. "Come on Pod."

Will and Pod hurried out the front door and went careering through the moonlit garden, down the path and out to the jetty where Art's little motorboat waited. Soon, Annalie and Essie followed, breathless, carrying bags and bundles. It was all they had in the world, and it wasn't much.

Art and Rene ran after them, in a last desperate attempt to talk them into staying. As the children climbed into the dinghy and began to maneuver away, Art and Rene called to them from the end of the jetty.

"We can protect you!" Rene called. "Please come back!"

"How could we ever trust you again?" Annalie cried.

"They're going to come after you," Art called. "They'll never stop looking for you. The Admiralty will find you wherever you go."

But their voices were blown away by the wind, drowned by the roar of the engine.

"Let them try!" Will shouted.

The four of them looked out at the silky dark water lit by a wide ribbon of moonlight, half-expecting to see an Admiralty ship come sliding toward them. But the sea was quiet and empty.

They roared up the coast and around the headland toward the town. They sailed directly into the marine repair slip. It was closed for the night, of course, but the moonlight was bright enough to see by.

"There!" Will said, and pointed.

The *Sunfish* was there, riding serenely at anchor. They pulled up alongside it and climbed on board, then Will and Annalie rushed below to check the starboard cabin. The internal joinery hadn't been tidied up yet, but they could see that the hole had been repaired.

They hurried back up on deck.

"We going?" asked Pod.

"Yep," said Will.

They jumped to their posts—Annalie casting off, Pod hoisting the sail, Will at the wheel—and soon they were sailing out of the marine repairers and into the dark waters of the night.

"Which way?" asked Will.

"Let's keep going east," Annalie said.

"Aye aye," said Will, and turned the wheel.

The *Sunfish's* sails filled, and the little boat went gliding out into the Moon Islands once more.

The trilogy will set sail again in summer 2019. Get set for more thrilling adventure in *The Castle in the Sea*.

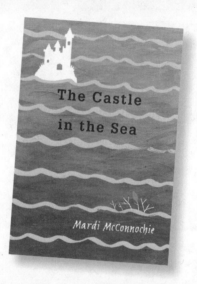

Annalie, Will, Essie, Pod, and Graham's new plan to visit the four scientists from Spinner's coded list is thrown into chaos when a terrible storm wrenches two of their company overboard. How will they ever find Spinner if they can't even find each other?